Swindled

by

Ginny Frost

Oakwood Tavern, Book 2

Swindled

Cover Art by *Rae Monet, Inc. Design*

The Wild Rose Press, Inc.
PO Box 708
Adams Basin, NY 14410-0708
Visit us at www.thewildrosepress.com

Publishing History
First Champagne Rose Edition, 2019
Print ISBN 978-1-5092-2723-5
Digital ISBN 978-1-5092-2724-2

Oakwood Tavern, Book 2
Published in the United States of America

His brow furrowed, but he didn't seem angry. "I bet you snag credit cards too." He set his cup down, smacking his lips slightly, sending lightning bolts up and down her skin.

She answered his question honestly. "We don't go for credit cards. Only cash. It's untraceable. Cash from bills, tips, and open purses. So much more lucrative than pinning your hopes on one lonely guy at the bar."

His eyebrows shot up. "You think I'm lonely?"

She stared into those arctic eyes, emptiness emanating from within. "Yeah." As she said the single syllable, she expected to see hurt and shame in his eyes. Instead, a spark shone, melting the glacier a tiny bit.

He laughed—pure music to her drunken soul. She wiggled closer to him, putting her hand on his arm. Everything inside her screamed. *Ask him* and she did. "There's always plan B."

Still chuckling, he asked, "And that is?"

"Go back to your place and screw our brains out." She grinned.

Alan raised an eyebrow, piercing her with his penetrating gaze again. He held up a hand to the waitress. "Check please."

Dedication

To Jen and Vampire Stories on the beach

Acknowledgments

Thank you to my kindhearted ogre and our two amazing kiddos. I love that you let me do this crazy writing thing.

Thank you to my critique partners, Autumn Jones Lake, Cara Connelly, and Kari Cole, for all your help, especially Cara for fixing my saggy middle.

Another huge thank you to my beta readers—Ben, Jen, and Grace. Your input was invaluable.

Thank you to my editor, Judi Mobley, for all her hard work on this project.

And of course, hugs and kisses and thanks to my writing community—Capital Region RWA, and the Albany NaNoWriMo group. Your support helped make this happen.

Part One

Ginny Frost

Chapter One

Marley observed the lone man at the end of the Oakwood Tavern's bar carefully. He nursed a tumbler of whiskey, only speaking to the bartender. His demeanor suggested he was a leftover from Happy Hour, unwilling to leave the sanctuary of the tavern. His suit indicated money, but his hunched posture said closed-for-business. Not interested in a hook up or buying a girl a drink. Glancing at Becca, Marley brushed her hand down her arm, an old con game sign for *abort*.

Becca snarled, showing her perfect, white teeth. Rather than flashing two fingers back, the sign to agree, she pointed fiercely at the end stool. Sighing, Marley rolled her eyes. She wasn't getting out easy tonight. If she followed through with dragging the unsuspecting mark out back to roll him, she might earn another night of safe slumber. At least Becca's place was bug-free with heat, food, and a tolerable bed. Better than the shelter. Safer than Troy's.

Marley paused, shooting withering glances at Becca. If the bitch backed off, Marley might have a chance at a normal life, free from con games and street hustles. Owing Becca compared to having terminal cancer. Marley barely kept ahead of the spreading reach.

If she bailed on the suit, Becca might choose another mark. A dozen drunk college boys floated around the tavern. Not a huge score, but most frat guys fell for her dipsy-tipsy act.

Marley scanned the room again, her attention flicking from person to person, never staying for more than a micro-second. Even though constant eye movement was a tell, she continued. With their pick of marks and con games, choosing the sad sack was clearly punishment. Marley's gaze roved. Until she lit on the bartender.

Crap. She'd been in Oakwood Tavern a dozen times. The barkeep, Eric, recognized her face but not her game. When her eyes met his, the edge of his lip popped up in a weary smile.

Looking away, Marley quickly calculated. Flirting or watching? Probably both. Eric was no slouch. His reputation as a good mixologist and better listener preceded him. No doubt an excellent judge of character too. She'd need to avoid him.

The weight of Becca's glare burned into Marley's back. Glancing one last time at her mark, she folded to the pressure. First, she had to shift her game from drunken hottie to damsel in distress. Every guy played sucker for a poor helpless girl, even a seasoned bartender. Second, she devised a great story to pull at the heartstrings of any man. A better plan might be to ditch Becca, avoid larceny, and leave Iverton permanently. But even if Marley paid her debt, Becca still owned her.

Game time.

Pulling out her phone, she frowned, hemmed, and hawed at the screen. Catching her lip in her teeth, she twisted her expression into pure anxiety. She tapped furiously at the screen.

Twitching as if the phone pinged, she typed another message, her focus returning to the screen. She morphed her expression from annoyance to fear as she pretended to read texts. Biting her lip, she willed tears to form in her eyes.

Phone pressed against her ear, she played out a one-sided argument while weaving through the crowd to the bar. The spot next to the mark sat open, but she didn't take it. Instead, she slid between the seats, right up to the counter, pulling the phone away from her ear.

Raising a slightly shaking hand, she caught the bartender's attention. "Johnnie Walker, please," she said. Eric, brow furrowed, mouth pursed, placed a glass before her. He stepped away to grab a bottle as Marley continued her phony argument.

"Yes, I absolutely ordered a whiskey," she hissed into the phone, loud enough for both Eric and her mark to hear. "I can drink whatever I want." She paused. "Don't tell me what to do. I don't care…" She stuck her bottom lip out, fingers twisting a lock of hair. "Duh. I'm at a bar." Pause. Tension filled her words. "Yes, I'm picking up men right and left. Dragging them to the ladies' room for some fun."

She tore the phone away from her ear and pressed it against her chest, a sob rocking her. False tears flowed down her cheeks. After a cleansing breath, she resumed her "call."

"No, I won't tell you where I am. It's none of your business." Her voice rose an octave with her next line. "You dumped me. I don't have to tell you anything. You…"

She growled, slamming the phone on the counter. Eric poured her a generous portion, and she downed a gulp. Coughing, she grabbed the edge of the bar, the liquor leaving a trail of fired down her throat.

"If I may ask, why would you put up with that crap?" A voiced sounded next to her. The mark.

Perfect. She'd piqued his interest. Not the response she'd expected from him, but she played along. "I'm not..." she stammered, partly to keep in character, partly because the whiskey charred her vocal cords. "He keeps calling and..."

Turning her head, she finally met his gaze. His icy blue eyes bore down on her, snagging her full attention like a deer in the headlights. She swore those eyes, weighed down with dark circles, saw through her bullshit. Blinking, she shook her head, trying to focus, but the drink stymied her. She sucked in a breath, waiting for him to call her on the con.

The phone lay screen up, with the call app open. She'd actually been arguing with Becca's voice mail. He didn't know that though. Or did he? Something in his expression said he knew the truth. A red flag flapped over her game. What would Becca do if Marley lost?

"There's a simple solution," he said and hit the End Call button on her phone. The device sounded a pathetic beep as the call cut off.

Marley stared shocked, not anticipating the play. Touching a stranger's phone—so taboo. An act of bravery or social *faux pas*?

"You don't have to listen to nonsense," he continued unfazed, taking a long slow sip of his drink. He held up the mostly empty glass, gazing at the amber liquid before setting it back on the bar. "You're worth more than that." After a pause, he swiveled in slow motion to face her. Marley's mouth dropped open in surprise.

She finally got a good look at her pigeon. Alan Reid, the damn owner of the Oakwood Tavern, sat next to her in a tailored gray suit with a miniscule pinstripe. Sharp.

Words failed. She stared at him wide-eyed, willing her mouth to work but no luck. Alan Reid, for God's sake. He and his partner played a key role in the revitalization of downtown, running a dozen or more bars ranging from stuffy smoking lounges to the hottest dance clubs. Until recently.

Now he held the title of local celebrity and not for good reasons. The press trashed his name in every paper, on every news program, and all over social media. According to the most recent reports, Reid's business partner, Conrad Bennett, embezzled millions of dollars from their entertainment conglomerate. The IRS essentially shut down the entire enterprise and pursued a criminal investigation. Meanwhile, bars around town closed right and left. Marley's brain formed one thought: *The man's been through enough.*

She followed the story relentlessly, homing in on any source of information available. Normally, she wasn't a news junkie, but something about the situation smelled fishy. Reid took the brunt of the abuse while Bennett skated off scot-free. Her experience on the con circuit told her someone rigged the game.

A good con artist would never be so sloppy, leaving such an obvious blame trail. Alan's head ended up on the chopping block first, then Bennett emerged as the villain—flamboyant, brilliant in his financial deals. Too simple, too obvious. There had to be more. Someone like Alan wouldn't sit by and let his business partner—his best friend—do this to him.

And then Bennett disappeared. How convenient. According to the media, he'd left on an extended vacation weeks ago. But getting lost in the modern world was hard to do.

Reid stood there, holding the bag. He might be the mastermind behind it, playing innocent while Bennett laundered the money or lay dead in a ditch somewhere. But Reid didn't fit the bill for embezzler/murder. He epitomized the strong silent type. To Marley, the whole thing reeked of an amateur grifter setting up a pigeon.

Also, the fact Alan Reid was drop-dead gorgeous kept her riveted to the story. Not your typical businessman, he held a quiet sense of power that bled right through the smear campaign. He spoke minimally to the press and never once blasted Bennett.

Snapping back to the present, she drank Reid in, from his sandy blond hair to his square jawline, the superior cut of his suit to the stony expression. His mouth was a smooth line with his bottom lip more rounded and plumper than the top. But his eyes stole her breath. The impossible blue of an Adirondack snowstorm—icy, dark, and so very sexy.

His lips quirked up in a smile before returning to a flat expression. "You can always walk away." Pausing with his glass to his mouth, he continued, "Trust me, sometimes it's for the best." He grimaced as he swallowed the drink.

Maybe the game could be saved if she'd stop fangirling. "I try, but he keeps harassing me." She squirmed in her seat, her chin dropping to her chest. The phone buzzed, probably Becca playing her part. Marley reached for it, but Alan's hand closed over the top.

"You can walk away," he repeated, keeping eye contact. A wobbly sensation rode over her body. The same flash of desire that zapped her whenever they did a close up of him on the news.

Feigning a reach for the phone, she skimmed her hand over his. "But if I don't answer, keep him talking, he might show up." She shrugged, playing the lost little girl.

"Old boyfriend?" he asked. She nodded. "But not very 'old'?" She shook her head. "Still love him?"

"God, no. He's mean, has a rotten temper." She paused, biting her lip. "Always yelling at me, trying to keep me in line." She never meant to use her history with Troy, her "not-so-old" ex. She tried not to talk about him to anyone. Besides who'd listen? Becca? Hardly. "It's over."

"Then why give him any of your attention?" he asked, head cocked to the side, the stony expression slowly disappearing.

Eric walked over to stand across them. "You good?" he asked, his gaze darting back and forth between the two. Marley pouted, trying to seem pathetic.

"Leave us a bottle, Eric," Reid said. The bartender's eyebrows rose, but he placed the Johnnie Walker in front of Reid. "And thank you." The bartender, duly dismissed, headed down the bar to less discerning customers.

Alan held up the bottle. "Refresh, Miss…?" Ah,

good, buying her drinks and asking her name. She had him exactly where…Their eyes met, and the gears in her brain locked up.

News stories and photos flashed through her mind. Hungry reporters searching for the big story, hunting Alan down, at his home, at his office, here at the Tavern. The witch hunt played on the news every hour. They tore the man's life apart on camera, hounding questions about the business deals, missing money, secret bank accounts. Then they'd discovered the partner, Conrad Bennett, portrayed a better villain. Alan's expression when they asked about his business partner touched her deeply. His haunted eyes and the glum expression said losing his best friend devastated him. On camera, he showed a brave front. But Marley saw the face of loss. Her heart ached for him.

She didn't want to steal from him, hurt him, after everything he'd been through. The feeling of being tossed to the lions was all too familiar. Damned if she'd turn him into a victim again.

"Uh." What did he ask? Oh, her name. She paused, making her choice and steeling herself for the consequences. Becca might destroy her, rip her apart, and toss her ass out on the street. But she saw only one choice. "Marley. I'm Marley."

"Well, Miss Marley," he said, the bottle poised in his hand.

"It's just Marley," she said, reaching for the glass. Her fingers brushed his, and a thrill danced up her skin.

He nodded, pouring her an inch of the amber liquid. His grace and style were foreign to her. Men in her world didn't pour drinks. Instead, they slapped her ass and demanded she make them a sandwich.

Alan's soulful eyes reflected rock bottom, the same look she saw in the mirror when she finally ran away, and again when she left Troy for good. No fucking way she'd be the one to kick the man when he was down.

Taking a deep breath, she sat on the stool next to him and mentally committed. Might as well go for the whole enchilada here. No more cons. The boss would demand retributions beyond what Marley already owed her. But Becca be damned.

"You're Alan Reid."

His lips quirked up again, not quite a smile as his head dipped down. The two sat for a moment in silence, and Marley wondered if she'd blown it by saying his name. Glancing side-eyed, she noticed the change. She no longer saw his body language as vulnerable and easily manipulated. The man next to her had been through hell and drowned his sorrows one whiskey at a time.

He straightened. "I never expect it," he said with a slight tone of bewilderment. "For gorgeous women to know my name." He glanced at her sideways and sipped his drink.

Her grifter instinct nudged her to play along, follow his lead. Eat up the compliments and bat her eyelashes until she tangled him in her web. But the game ended tonight, maybe forever once Becca got a hold of her. A sense of relief washed over her. She'd deal with the fallout later. For now, she set her glass down with a clunk and wiped away her crocodile tears.

"That kinda celebrity sucks. Sorry." She cocked her head, a vague smile on her lips. "I don't envy you one bit."

He blinked, eyes sparkling. "Really? You don't

want gorgeous women to know your name?"

"I prefer to hide in the shadows," she said, wiggling her eyebrows at the melodrama in her voice.

"Me too, but I own the place. I have to show up occasionally."

Marley scanned the room. A small door toward the back hallway read Office. "That looks like a good hiding spot," she said pointing.

Alan sipped his whiskey then shook his head. "Too many bad memories there." Marley automatically grinned. Such a statement begged for her to offer better experiences.

Instead, she said, "The end of the bar is kinda conspicuous. You need a better plan."

He chuckled. "Yeah, me and plans don't work out so well." He emptied his glass.

Trying to keep the mood light, she picked up her phone. "Me either. I had a great plan, but now it's shot to shit and I'm winging it." She smacked the phone back on the bar, shaking her head.

"You weren't really going to hook up with that ass?" He raised an eyebrow.

Decision time. Come clean about the call or wiggle around it until another idea popped into existence. Scrutiny under his baby blues caused her to sweat, and she decided to go with full truth, God help her.

"Actually, my roommate is holding some things over my head. She'll make my life a living hell if I don't do exactly what she asks." She paused.

Narrowing his eyes, Alan examined her. "Is she who you were on the phone with? She's your ex?" he asked delicately.

"No." Marley swiveled back and forth on her bar

stool. "She's the one forcing me to run a con on you. She wants me to play Damsel in Distress and flirt relentlessly until you offer to either give me money or give me a ride."

He blinked at her, wide-eyed. Sitting up straighter, he stammered, "Now wait a minute…"

Marley patted his arm, loving the texture of the fabric and the man underneath it. "Oh, it gets better. I need you drunk—falling-down, ugly drunk."

"Really?" he asked, his gaze sliding over to Eric.

She waved the bartender off. "Don't call him yet. Let me tell you the rest of the plan. I get you liquored up, hot, and horny. Then take you outside, preferably through the back door. Once there, Becca will help me roll you in the back alley. Leave you drunk in the gutter, penniless, and probably half naked." She sipped the whiskey. The smoky liquid flowed down her throat, warming as it went. Confession was good for the soul, nearly as good as Johnnie Walker.

"Is that still your plan?" His eyes burned like ice, his jaw tight, as if he were ready to spring into action. Another thrill swirled up her spine. "You still intend to rob me and leave me in an alley?"

She giggled behind her glass, the whiskey kicking in. Settling her hand on his arm, she slowly turned it into a caress. "Weren't you listening? I told you my plan fell through. No way I'm going to try a junior high school 'Come save me, big boy' routine on you. You'd never fall for it for a second."

He cocked his head, studying her again. She lifted one shoulder in a half shrug. He'd either toss her out or play along. The ball was in his court.

****

Alan studied the young woman next to him—huge green eyes, winter pale skin with long dark hair surrounding her delicate face. Petite, beautiful in a street-wise sort of way. And apparently about to mug him, though he sensed nothing hostile about her. Then again, his radar erred to the left lately. He'd trusted Conrad and look what happened. Conrad lost, the business lost, he, himself…lost.

He scrutinized the woman. Something about her tingled his senses. He should send her packing, but his gut balked, telling him no.

"You're aware my wallet's empty, right?" he said. "I get free drinks here because I still own the bar."

Marley, head cocked, furrowed her brow. "You didn't lose the Oakwood Tavern in the IRS seizures?"

For a mugger, she spoke rather intelligently. He rewound their conversation. Her style of speech and vocabulary sounded college-educated, but she'd confessed to planning a tag-team encounter in the back alley—and not the good kind. She'd consumed two drinks. Maybe the drunker she became, the less danger she posed. An easy theory to test.

He filled her glass again. "My family has owned the Tavern since the founding of the town," he said. "I'd sell it only as a last resort." Leaning in, he whispered conspiratorially, "You might want to consider another target."

He caught a whiff of her perfume—simple vanilla—and his heart double-timed. He pulled back and stuck his nose in his glass, breathing in the aroma of the whiskey to mask her scent. Vanilla on a woman's skin always drove him crazy. No explanation for it, other than it got him hot. Very hot.

"Nah, I've changed plans already." She shrugged. "Becca can bite me. I'm tired of playing her games. If she wants to lift wallets, she can run down her own marks."

This Marley, if that was her real name, certainly sounded like a grifter. Exactly what he didn't need. After Conrad disappearing, then the IRS making his life a living hell, he really didn't want any more complications in his life. He opened his mouth to ask her to leave. But she continued.

"You are a good guy, Alan Reid. I watch the news, really watch. They've persecuted you from day one. The fuckers never leave you alone for a second. There's no way I'd add to your misery, mister. I've been at the bottom of the crap pile. It ain't fun."

Alan closed his mouth with a snap, staring at the woman in disbelief. His few friends waxed sympathetic, but then distanced themselves almost immediately. With no family for backup, he'd felt isolated. It didn't help the press had barbecued him until he became the town pariah.

No one ever offered him much sympathy. The media hounded him day and night. Many of the businesses lost money and customers. Some closed. A crowd of drunken college kids, assuming he'd cheated them, completely trashed one bar. They'd spray-painted the walls. The spelling questionable but the message clear.

He'd stayed away from the Tavern for fear of driving away customers. But his long-time manager, Terese Brock, moved on to greener pastures when the financial crisis hit. He couldn't blame her for leaving. The combo of a dream job and new boyfriend were everything she needed. Alan was happy for her. Eric chose not to pick up the ball when Terese quit which left Alan in charge.

Every time he'd fulfilled the obligation, he sat far from the crowd in the end seat. Occasionally, someone sat next to him, but he never engaged. He sipped his whiskey, hoping for a quiet shift. Tonight, Marley's phone conversation tugged at his heartstrings. No woman should have to put up with such bullshit.

After hearing her confession, he assumed the ugly conversation never happened. Probably no boyfriend, or Becca either. Only Marley trying to…what? Squeeze money out of him? The joke was on her. He had nothing, even his name was soiled.

He faced her head on, putting one hand on the bar near hers either to bounce her out or stall her until he or Eric called the cops. No decision yet. A third option arose in his head. Lead her to the back office and take advantage of her empathy. Heat crawled over his skin, desire coiling in his belly.

Geez, Terese must've rubbed off on him, taking young things home for a quickie. Of course, her affair turned into a real relationship based on mutual respect and true affection. Marley with her long dark lashes, blood-red mouth, and skimpy outfit which clung to her every curve didn't appear to be a woman interested in long-term anything.

He shook his head, banishing thoughts of bending the cutie over the desk. *Be an adult, Alan.* Straightening his shoulders, he said, "And I'm supposed to take you seriously? You announce criminal intentions then immediately rescind them. I don't know what to think."

Marley twisted back and forth on her stool, an

endearing gesture. He'd loved to do it too, but he didn't want to appear childish. She bit her lip, her eyes on the ceiling as if the answer were written in the oak rafters.

Finally, she said, "I hate how the media mistreats you. Honest." She swung her legs like a child. Her gaze met his, and her body stilled. "I thought I'd come clean. Maybe to show you not everyone on the planet is an asshole. It pissed me off they portrayed you as some pathetic, lonely man whose best friend cheated him and left him to rot."

She stopped playing with the chair and placed her hand over his. Electricity sparked on his skin. Alan started to draw back, but staring into her green eyes, he stopped and waited for her to speak.

Squeezing his hand, she said, "Your life, your business. I'd love to give those fuckers a piece of my mind." Her words poured out with such passion, he wondered again about her tolerance to the whiskey.

"Oh really?" he asked, swallowing a laugh.

"Fuck, yeah." Definitely drunk. "If anyone put a camera in my face when Troy trashed my clothes and tossed me on the street, I woulda knocked them on their asses."

His brain churned, processing the statement. "The call from the ex-boyfriend?"

She pulled her hand away, and his body tilted toward her expectantly. He didn't want to lose contact with her. His throat dried up as if he were going through withdrawal. His brain assumed she was conning him, but neither his libido nor his heart believed it.

Oblivious to the war going on inside his body, Marley lazily spun her phone on the counter. "Yeah, okay. Fake call, but it's a close re-creation of one from a while ago." She glanced up at him through thick lashes. "Troy is my latest shit story. Or second latest, if you count Becca."

Alan smirked. "Not a good judge of character then?"

With a bark of laughter, she said, "Not a bit. Not with my upbringing. My parents are…well, anyway…" She shook her head, pocketing her phone. "Thanks for the drinks, Mr. Reid. I'll see you around." She stood, wobbly on her heels.

Better judgment said to let her go. Nothing good could come of it, but Alan wasn't ready to end this, not yet. Something in his caveman brain roared, taking him aback. The old beast had remained quiet since college. He wanted her to stay, if only for one more drink.

He wrapped his hand around her upper arm. "Stay. Let Becca believe you're making progress. We'll wait her out. She'll hate it. Besides I'm not letting you get behind the wheel."

Marley cocked an eyebrow. "You know Becca, huh?"

"I know Becca's type. She won't confront you while you're sitting with me. She'll stay until you're alone." He leaned in, whispering conspiratorially, "Let 'er stew for a bit."

She stifled a giggle, shifting closer to him. The vanilla scent filled the space between them. A groan boiled at the back of his throat, begging to come out. But Alan didn't want to be an ass. She hadn't taken advantage of him yet, nor he, her.

He guided her back over to her stool, her body brushing against his. "You're a real gentleman, Alan

Reid."

"Yeah, well, we're in public," he said, sitting back down and emptying his glass.

Chapter Two

Counting to ten, Marley pummeled her brain to focus. Why did he have to pick whiskey? It beelined to her head, making her chatty. God, the things she'd told Alan already. But his offer to keep Becca away made any embarrassing comments worth it. If he was the gentleman she thought, he'd call her drunk ass a cab. Of course, Becca would be right behind her.

Marley envisioned following the sexy Mr. Reid home. No attachments, no bullshit. Just lots of monkey sex with tall and handsome. She plopped her elbow on the bar, holding her chin up with the back of her hand.

"Mr. Reid…" Her words sounded a little mushy. Time to lay off the whiskey. "Do you know what sitting here in this bar night after night says about you?"

He chuckled. "It says I have nothing else to do."

"It says"—She drew the words out slowly—"you're a good person and innocent of the crap they put in the paper." She waved her hand, washing away the bad press. Unfortunately, she forgot her head rested on her hand, and she slipped.

Alan caught her before she hit the floor, tucking her against his side. Her every nerve tingled at the closeness of his body. She snickered, leaning against him, her hormones dancing.

"Too much whiskey?" he asked. She blushed.

"I don't drink much." She bit back the rest of the thought–*I'm into party pills, or I used to be*. He'd probably let her hit the floor if she shared that. "I'm trying to stay"—clean—"sober. Keep my wits about me. Fail, I guess."

His lips pressed into a line, but his gaze flicked up. The bartender had wandered over after she slipped. Shame pulsed over her for some odd reason. She didn't want Eric to witness her clumsiness. Alan saved the day, again.

"Why don't we find a nice table or a booth?"

"I'm fine, Mr. Reid. Really." She tittered, feeling boneless. She placed her head against his chest. "Pour me into a cab. No worries."

"Hmm," he said, steadying her. "Will Becca be at home?"

Her fingers snagged one of her dark locks and twisted it in tight circles. "Yeah, probably."

"Then some coffee's in order." He glanced at Eric before walking her to a quiet booth in the back. Once she slumped into the seat, head resting on the wall, he continued, "And if I'm going to have to watch over you, you can call me Alan."

"You sure?" she asked. He nodded. "I'm sorry. I've really fucked this up." Her shoulders dropped, and she closed her eyes. "I'm so stupid."

"Marley, you're either a great con artist or a woman in over her head."

A perfect assessment of her essential self. She opened one eye to examine him, a decent fellow, charming, and kind to a stupid drunk girl who'd trashed her game before she'd started. And she liked him. A lot. More than reason dictated. More than the influence

21

booze usually provided. She wiggled her body into the corner, one arm on the back of the booth one on the table.

"I like you, Alan. I'm glad I didn't go through with Becca's stupid plan. Totally short-sighted."

"Oh?" he said, taking a couple mugs of coffee from the waitress. He placed one in front of her and sipped his own. "You'd do things differently."

"Duh," she said, spinning her mug on the table. "Why put all your money on one guy? Let's say you aren't you."

"I'm not me."

"You're funny."

"I know."

She snickered into the back of her hand. "Let me explain. See, your place is a nice bar, filled with upper-class people who don't consider getting mugged or having their wallet stolen. So, the bar's prime picking."

"I'm glad you think my family business is ripe for evildoers."

His comment stabbed at her heart. She gasped a short breath, tears prickling in her eyes. Stupid whiskey. "You think I'm evil?"

"No," he said flatly. "Continue."

She studied his face, searching for truth or sympathy or even hatred. Nothing but a quiet confidence in his expression. "It's kinda weird to reveal our secrets." She tugged at a stray lock.

"Consider instead you're helping me with security." He flashed a smile. "Does that help?"

She narrowed an eye. "Security?"

"I have a bouncer and a good lead bartender, but my manager recently left for greener pastures. She probably would've spotted you early and shown you the door."

"Yeah, Terese. She was sharp. We only came here on her days off. Now on a night like tonight, you have lots of millennials, middle-classers, and college kids. Easy marks."

They drank their coffee in silence for a few minutes. Idle conversation didn't seem necessary. An old and comfortable silence wrapped around them. Her head cleared as the coffee worked its way through her system.

After about fifteen minutes, he asked, "How would you work the room?"

She curled around her coffee, suddenly self-conscious. "I guess take from a few open purses. Women can be damn naïve about leaving their bags. Then these college kids with their baggy pants. Easy wallets."

"That it?" he asked, his cup at his lips. She stared at his mouth for a second imagining he held something else in his hand. Something intimate of hers. Heat rolled up her skin, and her cheeks burned. The whiskey claimed only half the blame.

His lips curled up, as if he read her mind, but he stayed on topic. "Any other easy money?" he asked, setting her back on task.

Embarrassment flushed through her. Studying him across the table, she hated to admit the things she'd done. Might as well spill the lot. She pressed her hands to her cheeks burning with heat and embarrassment. If she planned to "help with security," she better tell him.

"Bills and tips left on the table are an easy grab." She ducked her head, afraid of his reaction. Emotions warred inside her. She wanted him, wanted him to want her, but the desire for his approval overwhelmed her sexual cravings. Reluctantly, she peeked at his expression.

His brow furrowed, but he didn't seem angry. "I bet you snag credit cards too." He set his cup down, smacking his lips slightly, sending lightning bolts up and down her skin.

She answered his question honestly. "We don't go for credit cards. Only cash. It's untraceable. Cash from bills, tips, and open purses. So much more lucrative than pinning your hopes on one lonely guy at the bar."

His eyebrows shot up. "You think I'm lonely?"

She stared into those arctic eyes, emptiness emanating from within. "Yeah." As she said the single syllable, she expected to see hurt and shame in his eyes. Instead, a spark shone, melting the glacier a tiny bit.

He laughed—pure music to her drunken soul. She wiggled closer to him, putting her hand on his arm. Everything inside her screamed. *Ask him* and she did. "There's always plan B."

Still chuckling, he asked, "And that is?"

"Go back to your place and screw our brains out." She grinned.

Alan raised an eyebrow, piercing her with his penetrating gaze again. He held up a hand to the waitress. "Check please."

****

He said yes to casual sex after the garbage she'd dumped on him? Whoa. His good manners must've worn out. A gentleman like him would never really take her home. Not after what he'd been through. Not after her giant confession. Every cell inside her thrilled to go home with him. Just the idea of his hands on her body…

"Becca still here?" he whispered.

She tilted her head, nodding slightly, eyes flicking toward Becca. "Hot blonde at the corner table. She's watching us but trying not to be conspicuous."

"Understood." He pulled out his cell and tapped a quick message. Like clockwork, the bouncer grabbed Becca and showed her the door. A neat trick, but one Marley would pay for later. Right now, she didn't care. Alan Reid erased her problem with one text.

Mind-boggling.

"Give her ten minutes to vacate the area. Then we can be off," he said.

Ten minutes? No. He'd have time to reconsider. She wanted him, beyond the whiskey's whispers. His smooth composed nature left her breathless, needy. And she needed a take-charge kinda guy in her life. And in her bed.

Immediately.

Of course, she couldn't take him home, not after she betrayed Becca. She had no home.

"Since the bouncer tossed her, she'll probably back off now. Let's go." She slid out from the booth. "As long as we stay away from dark alleys, we'll be fine." She winked.

"Okay then." He stood, holding his arm out toward the exit, allowing her to lead the way.

She tottered on her heels, happily buzzing and randy as hell. She sashayed across the bar, flaunting her ass. Indulgent fantasies on an oak and steel king bed raced through her mind. She hit the door and burst outside, thrilled with the turn of events. She and Alan connected somehow. In all the crazy, they saw something in each other. And now on to the hot sex. Grinning, she spun to put her arms around him and froze.

No Alan. Only a closed oak door.

Panic crept up her spine. Had he played her? Did he know the game from the start, gotten her drunk, and then dumped her outside? Her shoulders sagged as she faced the empty street. Her purse tumbled to the ground. Not a white knight after all. A wave of self-pity rushed through her. Nothing changed. She'd have to crawl back to Becca again.

She stood there, pain seeping into her chest. A feeling of complete loss swelled inside her. Risk a cab to the apartment? Beg Becca for forgiveness? God, no. Women's shelter? Ugh, not again. The place left her feeling useless and low.

She wrapped her arms around herself, wishing she'd grabbed a jacket. Her warm winter clothes would be history, either tossed in the garbage or incorporated into Becca's wardrobe.

Fuck. She was too stupid to live. He'd played her and blinded her with whiskey. And…

"Careful there." A voice sounded next to her. "Don't wanna lose that." Alan placed her purse on her shoulder. "Sorry. Eric stopped me. What a nosy parker."

Relief washed over her in a wave, rocking her on her heels. Swallowing hard, she feigned being casual. "Wow. You sound British."

Alan laughed. "Too much BBC, I guess." One side of his mouth quirked up. "Shall we?" He crooked his elbow, letting her curl into his arm. Such an old-fashioned thing to do. It thrilled her to her bones. She pictured dragging him to the back alley and having her way with him, up against the wall.

Alan burst through her thoughts. "A cab might be better. I don't want to end up in in the papers for drunk driving. Yeah, not good." He smiled, and Marley leaned in.

He caught her cue and pressed a kiss to her lips, featherlight and all authority. She broke the kiss after a few seconds with a little gasp. She'd never been kissed that way—gently, sweetly. Her whole body quivered. Alan licked his lips, watching her carefully.

Wrapping his arms tighter around her waist, he kissed her harder, demandingly Neanderthal but somehow still classy. She draped her arms around his neck, drowning in his kiss. Something clicked inside her. Emotions, desires she'd never truly experienced before, flooded her mind and body. She wanted him. All of him, from head to toe, for better or worse. She gave herself over.

****

Alan kissed Marley back, ignoring the voice of reason in his head. The whole situation stank to high heaven of bad decisions and ugly consequences.

Eh, fuck it. He no longer cared.

The sexy brunette hung all over him—a little slip of a thing, with a narrow waist and exceptional cleavage. A non-zero chance? Didn't he deserve it? His name already equated with mud. And her threats of mugging him, merely hot air. Still, the way her gaze darted up and down the sidewalk. Maybe…

He stared down at her, desire battling trepidation in his heart. "Tell me the truth, Marley. Did you drag me out here for my wallet or my cock?" Tequila usually made him horny as hell, not whiskey. But it felt like tequila, in spades. He wanted her bad, but damned if he'd be a victim again, even for a beautiful girl.

"Jesus, Alan." Her words slid out in short pants, steamy, hot. "You're sexy when you're mad." She reached up to kiss him, but he turned his head away.

"Tell me," he demanded, their faces inches apart. Marley squirmed in his grip, not trying to flee, but actually moving closer. God, he'd never been so turned on in his life. He wanted her now. If she wanted his wallet, he'd gladly give it to her after they finished. "Tell me the truth," he said, his voice strained.

"Alan," she said, gazing up at him through her thick eyelashes. Her eyes sparkled, glowing with lust. "Take me home." She tugged at his hair emphasizing her last word.

Her words broke the spell which held him back. Alan kissed her harder, his hands running over her body. She moaned and writhed beneath him.

An odd feeling hit Alan's gut. Not exactly anger, not totally frustration. Whatever the emotion, it coiled in a ball in his stomach, absorbing the whiskey. Twitchy and hostile, he dragged her along by the hand toward the curb.

Stopping short, he pulled her against his chest. Other emotions boiled up. This little thing, with those haunted eyes, captivated him. The black harsh lines of her eye makeup and the trashy skimpy outfit didn't hide a thing. He read her easily through the green and gold of her pupils. He saw his own depression, fear, and loneliness in her eyes. Once he understood, he dismissed her joke about mugging him. She wouldn't.

She was his, if only for tonight. Exactly what he needed.

Holding tight to her elbow, he ran his other hand through her hair. She gazed up at him, her eyes swimming with lust and whiskey. He liked it just fine. Wrapping his arm around her, still holding her hand so it pressed against her back, he asked, "You sure?"

She nodded as he hailed a cab. Not an inch between them. He leaned down to examine her, her face a hair's breadth from his. He didn't think, just placed his hands on either side of her face and kissed her, relentless and hard, leaving them both breathless.

A car honk spoiled the moment, and Alan reluctantly released her. A yellow cab idled by the curb, the driver leaning out, leering at them. "You wanna ride or what?" he asked.

Alan snapped to and helped her into the cab, climbing in beside her. He rattled his address off to the driver and returned his attention to the sexpot sitting next to him. She lounged across the seat, her eyes radiant.

Practically climbing on top of her, he pressed his lips to hers, pushing her back against the seat. With one hand, he grabbed the headrest. With the other, he stroked her body from shoulder to ankle. She purred. Pressing in, he kissed her again, letting his hand wander, listening to her moans and coos to direct him. He wanted her, right here in the cab. If the media still chose to splash his face everywhere, maybe he'd give them something good to print.

****

Marley bit her lip as she leaned back, tempting Alan. Holy fuck, he had her begging for it. She couldn't wait to get him alone. He crawled over her, pressing her into the seat. Wrapping her legs around his waist, she tweaked his nose.

"Come here often, sailor?" she asked. He answered with a grunt as his mouth met hers again, revving her motor further. Mentally, she calculated the distance to the address Alan told the cabbie. Five minutes, maybe less, depending on traffic. Not enough time to really get anywhere serious in the cab. Carnal knowledge would have to wait.

Instead, she ran her hands over his shoulders and back. Reaching his tight ass, she squeezed him, causing a rumble to come from his throat. One hand meandered up to the back of his head, directing his lips to her neck. He shifted, his body pressed against her, his erection throbbing against her stomach. A sharp pang of lust ripped through her. She didn't want him to stop, but the cabbie watched the rearview mirror more than the road.

She raised her lips to his ear as he kissed and sucked at her neck. "Do you have any idea what I want to do to you, Alan?" she whispered. He groaned, twitching his hips in slow circles, driving her mad. "God." She gasped as the heat rushed through her. "Nothing good, honey, nothing good."

The cab stopped with a jerk, practically tossing them to the floor. Marley glanced up at the driver. He stared back, hungrily. She bit her lip, turning away.

Alan took exception to the cabbie's interest in them. He urged her out the door, his gaze never leaving the driver's. "Hope you enjoyed the show," he snarled, tossing money into the front seat. He exited the cab, slamming the door.

But she didn't care about the driver or showing her

goods to the world in the back of a car. Leaping into his arms, she wiggled against him, lust pouring off her in waves. "If you don't bring me inside soon, we're doing it right here on the sidewalk."

To emphasize her point, she thrust her tongue down his throat while grinding her hips against his pronounced erection.

"Well, then…" he said in a strained voice when she finally let him up for air. "What are we waiting for?" He carried her up the steps.

At the door, still holding her, he leaned her against the frame. Sliding his hand up and under her leg, he tickled her. She moaned and squirmed, squeezing her legs tighter.

He tsked at her, breathing hotly in her ear. "The keys, woman." Marley relented, releasing him.

"I've got it," she cooed. Plunging her hand into his pocket, she stroked the inside of his pant leg, playing at grabbing for them, but conveniently missing.

"You need some help there," he asked, his lips on her neck again, drawing her flesh into his mouth, sending tingles down her spine.

Plucking out the keys, she fluttered her eyelashes, her mouth in a pout. "What do I get if I give you these?"

Chapter Three

Marley's brain fogged from the whiskey and the heat generated between her and Alan. She never had such a reaction to a man before. All rational thoughts evaporated the minute they hit the cab. She wanted him. Now.

Pressing tightly against him, she ran her hands over his arms, his chest, fishing lower and lower while he fumbled with his keys.

"The faster we get inside..." he chided. Marley responded by running her tongue down his neck. She heard him snort and then strong hands pinned her arms, holding her against the door.

He pressed his knee between her legs, pushing them apart. He leaned his long, trim body against hers and kissed her hard, ferociously. Marley sucked in a breath, hardly able to withstand his assault. He grabbed her chin as he deepened the kiss. As she melted, his touch softened. He dragged a finger across her cheek as he pulled away from the breathless kiss.

"Patience," he said. Marley stood pressed against the door where he left her. He unlocked the bolt in a swift, deft motion. He twisted the knob, and the door slipped opened behind her. Marley, boneless from the kiss, almost collapsed to the floor.

He regarded her, for a second before raising an

eyebrow and gesturing her inside.

Marley quickly glanced inside the house. The dimly-lit entrance opened to a small foyer with a long staircase a few yards away. She met his gaze for a second then she took off like a shot for the stairs.

Alan let out a startled cry as she flew by him. "Hey!" he called. Fingers brushed her back as she dashed by. But of course, whiskey and overly-high heels worked against her. Even with pausing to type in the code to the security system, Alan caught up with her easily, grabbing her from behind as she hit the stairs. She collapsed on her stomach, roaring with laughter.

"What do you think you are doing, young lady?" he asked, his mouth tight against her ear. She lay flat out on the stairs with Alan on top of her, his body pressed against every inch of her. His erection dug into her backside. Heat flashed through her, and, instead of answering him, she wriggled her ass against the bulge pressing into her, tempting him, teasing him.

"Oh, that's how it is, huh?" His breath tickled her ear. He'd pinned her to the stairs, but she squirmed and wiggled against him, pretending to try and get free. Then he relented, easing back, freeing her to scramble up the steps.

She climbed a step or three when she heard him speak. "I don't think so." A hand clamped down around her ankle and tugged. Breathless, she glanced over her shoulder. He loomed over her, his eyes flashing with heat and power. Marley licked her lips, eyeing his sexy form. A smug smile crawled over his lips. He climbed to her, his gaze piercing her soul.

Take me now.

Releasing her ankle, he knelt on the step right

behind her, pushing her legs apart with a rough shove. He grabbed her hips and propped her on the stair, her legs around him, her ass in the air, her elbows two steps above. A secret thrill ran through her. She'd never thought from those press conferences that quiet and mild Alan Reid could be such a forceful, dominant lover.

He ran his hands over her legs, up to her ass, and along her back. A low hum of his approval sounded as his fingers roamed to her thighs. Tossing her hair, she watched his every move. A dark smirk crossed his lips. He flipped her mini skirt and paused. Their eyes locked, but his hands worked, rubbing caressing, touching her.

"Yes?" he asked, one eyebrow raised.

"Oh, yes, Alan. Yes."

Sliding the edge of her panties aside, he pressed a finger deep inside her. She spasmed, her eyes clamping shut, her legs squeezing together, but Alan tapped a hand on her ass.

"None of that now," he said, and she almost came again. His fingers moved like lightning, pushing her toward a second orgasm with spectacular speed. He chuckled low and sexy as she wiggled and squirmed against his relentless demands.

She buried her head in her hands, no longer able to resist him, letting him do as he wished and loving the attention. He pushed her thighs farther apart and paused. She heard the rustle of clothing and then the rip of a condom wrapper. She swayed, hurrying him along. In one swift plunge, he took her, fast and rough. She screamed, loving his commanding touch.

He rode her hard against the stairs and she met him stroke for stroke, losing track of how many times she came. She'd always been multi-orgasmic, but damn…She was heady with the onslaught of sensation.

He grabbed her hips hard, pulling her up against him. He thrust into her several times quickly, a string of expletives pouring from his lips as he came.

Marley leaned against him, panting. Her body weak, tired but exhilarated at the same time. Softly, he pressed his lips against her sweaty neck, and a shiver rushed down her spine.

"Want to see the bedroom?" he whispered. Marley could only nod.

****

Alan held a hand out for Marley. Gently, she placed her hand in his. As their eyes met, he read a thousand things. Smart, beautiful, adventurous. The corner of his mouth kicked up. She cocked her head to the side, questioning, challenging him.

Pulling in a deep breath, he wrapped an arm around her waist and hefted her onto his shoulder in a fireman's carry. She squealed, calling his name. The weight of her on his back, her vanilla scent enveloping him…If he hadn't been in caveman mode before, he certainly shifted into it now.

Inside the bedroom, he dropped her lightly onto the bed. She bounced once before grabbing the mattress to steady herself. Her eyes sparkled like the stars, her mouth drawn up in a wide smile. He wanted nothing more than to rip every inch of clothing from her body and take her in every way possible.

Slow down. He stared at Marley, sprawled on the bed and reeled himself back a bit. She was tiny, no more than five feet. And the fact he'd carried her up the stairs with ease attested to her small size. But those eyes, that body. A surge of heat wafted over him.

She trailed a finger over torso, thighs. Her eyes flashed back up to his. His body reacted, his cock like stone, but he waited. Tucking her legs underneath, her, she knelt on the bed. Gathering a lock of hair, she twirled it around her finger. The gesture hit him like a punch. He groaned.

Releasing the hair, she ran her hands down her chest, pausing at her breasts and finally resting on the hem of her shirt. His lips twitched again, his hands clenching to fists.

His desire overwhelmed him but drawing out the act made the end sweeter. Brakes engaged, he said, "Very slowly." His words straining through his teeth.

Marley's eyebrows popped up for a split second before her mouth turned back into a sexy pout. She peered up at him through thick lashes. Desire burned a hole in him. Gripping the edge of her shirt, she slowly raised the material millimeters at a time. They only broke eye contact for a second as she pulled the garment over her head, tossing it on the floor.

He licked his lips. "Now the skirt." Rising to her knees, she wiggled the tiny bit of material down over her hips. She sat back, dragging the skirt to her ankles. Looking at him intensely, she put a hand on her shoe to remove it.

"I said the skirt." The sentence spilled out in sharp reprimand. "Leave the shoes on." Not a word escaped her lips as she carefully pulled the skirt over her shoes. Alan jutted his chin toward her.

"And the rest."

She flipped her hair to one side, seeming to struggle with her bra clasp behind her back. The image of her arms pinned behind her stirred something primal inside him. He'd never been a dominant. Never played those games before but maybe Marley wanted to explore the dark side. He cleared his throat as she pulled the bra from her body and dangled it over the side of the bed. Her long hair fell over her bare breasts blocking his view.

Dropping the bra, she sat tall again. She hooked her fingers into either side of her minuscule panties. With painful slowness, she slid them down her thighs to her knees. Then she rolled onto her back, her legs up and tight together, giving him a show as she slid the thong over her calves and shoes.

No blood remained in his brain for rational thinking. The beautiful woman displayed before him turned his thoughts into staccato sentences. Somehow, he managed to form a word. "Stop," he choked out.

She ceased moving, one hand still gripping the tiny piece of fabric. Swallowing hard, he clawed at his tie and shirt, practically ripping the buttons off. As he stepped further into the room, he groped in his pocket. Absently, his fingers closed over his wallet, and he tossed it on the dresser.

Marley shifted on the bed, as she peeked around her legs to see him.

"Freeze," he ordered again. She blinked but stayed stock still, her legs in the air, wobbling from the effort. His pants hit the floor as he toed off his shoes. She didn't move, never wavered, never shrank from him, merely waited patiently. Slowly, he crawled over the mattress to her. He knelt before her, caressing her legs in long smooth strokes. Arching her back, she bit her lip.

"Do you like that?" he asked. She nodded. "Speak." A request, not a demand and she complied, voicing her pleasure at his touch in slow groans and breathy outbursts.

"Your legs are perfect," he intoned, his hands still busy mapping her calves. "And the shoes..." He brushed his fingers along the stiletto heel. "Very nice."

Gently, he slid his hands between her legs and pushed them apart a few inches. Her gaze burned with hunger. Without even touching her, she looked wanton, desperate. He loved it.

With one hand clamped on her ankle, he let the other drop down between her legs, his fingers grazing the soft patch of hair there. As her back arched, she looked at him pleading. "You're so ready," he said, exploring her folds delicately, trying to drive her mad.

She bucked. "Please..." Her voice was breathy and full of want.

Opening her legs a bit more, he grasped her other ankle. He raised an eyebrow, and she nodded. He unwrapped another condom supplied by Eric who'd forced several on Alan as he left the bar. Without missing a beat, he rolled it on and pushed inside her in one swift movement. Again, she bucked beneath him, her back bowed.

"Yes," she screamed as her hips turned in a tight circle. Alan followed her lead, letting her guide him to what she needed. They found a rhythm easy, able to read each other with little verbiage or gestures. She asked, he gave, over and over again.

When she finally screamed his name in a watery, desperate cry, Alan folded over her, pounding her into the mattress until he came. They collapsed together in a tight ball, neither saying a word but both holding on tight.

****

Marley nuzzled deeper in the lush fabric of the quilt. Her head throbbed, but she ignored it. Nothing compared to waking up warm and safe in her own bed. Wait…she wasn't in her bed. Her breath caught, and she sat up quickly, the covers pooling around her. She glanced around the room, taking in the rich decor. Alan's place. Biting her lip, she glanced at the pillow next to her.

Empty.

Spending the night with a classy guy like Alan Reid equated to insanity. Who did she think she was? Julia Roberts? Alan didn't plan to scoop her out of the gutter and transform her into a princess. Hell, his money problems left him in up to his neck in trouble.

Twirling a lock of hair, Marley examined the situation. She didn't want to leave but…How could she bow out of here gracefully? After the secrets she spilled last night, the cops probably waited for her by the curb. Her head ached as she navigated through the hangover. No ideas or coherent thoughts formed. Skirting out without making a bigger fool of herself seemed an impossibility.

And what must Alan think? The biggest slut on the planet or the easiest girl in Iverton, the way she'd offered herself up. She shook her head and bemoaned the pain. He was handsome, funny, and successful. And she was…the kind of woman to get a guy drunk and roll him in the back alley.

Releasing the hank of hair, she pulled back the covers and searched the floor for her clothes. The sound of footsteps on the stairs froze her in place.

Alan.

Warmth radiated over her skin at the thought of repeating last night's fun. And the idea of spending the morning in his arms curled her toes. Perhaps she put words in his mouth with her over-thinking. Grinning, she tucked herself back into the bed and pretended to be asleep.

****

Donned in his bathrobe, Alan leaned against the door frame, coffee mug in hand, staring at the queen-sized bed. He sipped, watching Marley sleep, knowing full well how creepy it seemed. But nothing about last night had been the norm. His mind raced through their evening together, wonderful at the time, but as the sun rose, a mix of emotions churned in his stomach.

He tilted his head, trying for a better look at her. Her face cuddled in the pillow showed a picture of youth and innocence. In the light of morning, she looked ten years younger than him. Fear flashed in his chest. What if the press found out about it? Robbing the cradle, scandalous affairs. Not that he'd ever done either of those things. One-night stands weren't his preference. He wasn't Conrad.

Dammit.

He never should've taken her home. The wagging tongues. The mocking. The taunts. His brainless actions would subject her to the ugly side of the media, making Marley the latest victim in the train wreck of his life.

He could hear the name-calling now—whore. He flinched, his fist clenched at his sides. Marley needed to be out the door before some reporter nosed around and witnessed her walk of shame. Her scant clothes and smudged makeup didn't tell the media about a nice girl down on her luck. Alan would not have her trashed by the press.

Queasiness hit his stomach, and he lowered the cup from his lips, wondering how to handle the situation. Marley let out a sleepy sigh and turned in the bed. His breath caught in his throat. Sexy, beautiful, and energetic, she'd gone along with every crazy order he'd given, with a grin on her face. His lips twitched into a smile for a fraction of a second. She'd been what the doctor ordered, but he never considered the consequences of his actions He'd been thinking of his own needs.

But the other side of the coin, he couldn't be associated with her. She told the truth about the attempted mugging. She probably lived on the party scene, an easy thing to do in a college town like Iverton. Between the clubs, the drugs, and the nightlife here, con games were easy money. And she was so young. He shook his head. Further involvement with her constituted an impossibility, no matter how good the sex, no matter how well they'd connected. Not with everything on his plate.

She had to go.

After putting his mug down on the dresser, next to his wallet, he stepped closer to the bed, stopping at the footboard. Folding his hands in front of him, he opened his mouth to speak, to rouse her, but again, he fell in her wake.

She turned and stretched her lithe body, blinking at him. Her eyes widened for a second then closed as her mouth formed a huge smile. She licked her lips and, in a husky, morning voice, she said, "Hi there."

His body reacted. Blood drained from his brain to his cock in a rush. Dizzy with lust, he grabbed the bed's finial to steady himself. He cleared his throat, unable to act, much less throw her out of his bed.

Marley decided for him. In one agile move, she rolled over and crawled toward him, naked. The breath left his body. His hands fell numbly to his sides. Grinning, she climbed cat-like up to him, pressing her naked body against him. She tugged on the belt of his bathrobe.

"Good morning, Alan. Plans for today?" she purred.

"I…" The word squeaked out. He closed his eyes, licked his lips, and tried again. "Well, I…" He ran his hand down her arm, her skin like butter, so soft, so…*Focus, idiot. Don't make the problem worse.* He snapped his head up, eyes open. "I have to go to work." His words dropped like stones from his lips.

She pouted, cocking her head to the side. "Right now, or can it wait?" Releasing of the belt, her hand wandered down to his crotch, cupping him, squeezing him gently.

He sucked in a breath. Picturing news headlines and fresh headaches, he bravely stepped back. "I have to go," he said, his words flat even though fire roared in his veins.

She dropped her hands, slumping as he backpedaled. "Well…I guess I understand." She climbed off the bed, gathering her things. "If you have to go…"

He nodded, fidgeting, wanting to say more, to explain things. But the less said, the better. "I need to be at the office, and I can't leave you here." There.

He'd said it, dropping the bomb like a complete asshole. She flinched when he uttered the words. Her eyes said the implication cut her to the bone; he didn't trust her, and she knew it.

Throwing her top over her head, she didn't meet his gaze. Trepidation rising in his chest, he backed away to the door, putting more space between them. He was handling the whole thing badly, but what could he do? What would Conrad do? Alan put on a stoic mask and pretended he didn't care.

He didn't offer her coffee, though a fresh pot sat in the kitchen. He didn't offer her cab money, though she probably needed it. He didn't grab her arm and force her out the door. It was the last thing he wanted to do.

Another part of his brain screamed to go to her, to wrap her in his arms, to let her stay indefinitely. To feed, clothe her, take care of her for as long as she'd let him. He swallowed hard, forcing the emotions down into his gut.

Finally dressed, she glanced at him. Her weary look caused the guilt to bite harder. "Well, then," she said. The lightness in her voice didn't reflect in her body language. "Nice to meet you, Alan. Take care."

He nodded, afraid of what he might say if he opened his mouth. Marley flashed him a half smile as she exited the room.

Following her down the stairs to the front door, he tried desperately to find the words to make it less ugly, less awkward, but nothing came to him. He held the door for her until she descended the steps. His gut screamed at him to stop making a terrible mistake.

Going against his instincts, he closed the door, falling against it with guilt and relief ripping his insides apart. Why her? Why now? Wasn't he in enough trouble already?

Chapter Four

Marley cursed the bright, sunny day. Rain, sleet, and ten degrees below zero fit her mood better. She hung her head as she slumped down the road. Why did he throw her out? She'd been alluring and accommodating and the sex, fantastic. And she didn't go near his wallet, not once. A real gentleman might call her a cab or at least give her bus fare.

A black mood settled over her as she remembered his silence and his stiff attitude. He'd definitely been hot for her when she crawled across the bed. Hell, she'd not only seen it in his eyes but felt it in her hand.

She halted short of the bus stop, glancing back toward his house. He'd only wanted a fun night. He didn't connect with her after all. Probably thought her some sleazy skank out for his money and his time. Well, she kinda played that role at first, but then they talked, bonded, and she committed to the idea of being perfectly awesome for him.

Her eyes stung, surprising her. She blinked rapidly, turning back toward the bus stop. Walking slowly, she twisted her hair. Maybe she was too low class for Alan Reid. And he had every right to throw her out. A sob escaped her lips, and her hand flew over her mouth.

What the fuck was wrong with her? Where did the "I'm not worthy" crap come from? Taking a breath, she straightened her shoulders and wiped her eyes. She was good enough for Alan Fucking Reid. Too good, in fact. The kind of woman who understood when asshole friends treated you like shit. Understood a world which saw you through a skewed lens and never revealed your true self.

She didn't need him. She didn't need anyone. In fact, she'd go home and tell Becca to fuck off, then find a new place with a roommate who wasn't pond scum.

Pond scum like me.

Plunking down inside the Plexiglas bus stop shelter, she shook her head. She'd come a long way since she crashed into Iverton at the tender age of sixteen, homeless, jobless, friendless. She'd escaped her parents' world to build a new life. Who was Alan Reid to say she wasn't amazing?

She was a fierce, sexy woman, not some slut looking for a quick roll and a payout. Standing, she lifted her chin as the bus arrived. She sashayed past the driver with a flip of her hair. The man merely shook his head.

Marley took a seat, a look of grim determination on her reflection in the window. Then she saw the faint blush of a love bite on her neck. Her eyes stung with tears again. If she didn't need Alan, then why did leaving him hurt so much?

****

Alan pressed his head against the closed front door, decidedly not watching Marley walk away. The war between his head, his heart, and his cock raged onward, his head slightly in the lead. The shit storm from Conrad's disappearance and embezzlement claim left him buried to his neck. A woman like Marley by his

46

side, a confessed criminal, a con artist, would put his head under the gray water.

With a sigh, he headed up the stairs to the bathroom. A long, hot shower might help him forget those green eyes, the compact body, her mouth...He closed his eyes as he stepped into the spray, hoping to erase her from his memory. It never happened. A night of indulgence for them both, now over.

The steam hit him, practically searing his skin, the pain of the hot water a good punishment for last night. He knew better, but she'd appeared so...lonely, vulnerable. His life roller-coastered out of control, but last night he hoped he'd helped Marley. But in the end, he'd thrown her out without even offering a ride home. He leaned against the shower wall, feeling like a heel.

He'd never be able to make it up to her. And how could he ever find her again? Chewing his lip, he wondered if she might live up on Maple or down by Third Street.

No.

He couldn't afford to think about her. The IRS placed more pressure on him every day. News agencies called all the time. She'd never want the publicity of being around him.

He froze as he toweled off. Why hadn't he said that to her? Instead of treating her like a two-bit whore, he should've explained how she'd hate the spotlight as much as he did. Cursing his stupidity, he rushed through his morning routine, including stripping the sheets. Guilt tweaked him again. Growling, he tossed the bedding to the floor and headed downstairs for more coffee.

His answering machine blinked insistently. He

ignored it, but a small voice in the back of his head niggled Conrad might have called. Twitching his lip back and forth, he considered listening. He paused in front of the machine, dreading what those five flashes represented. But what if Conrad called...

Standing over the answering machine, an odd sensation of another presence swept over him. More than an aura reminding him Marley had been there, been with him. As images of last night flooded his brain, he gripped the table. *Not helping me forget her.* Pulling in a deep breath through his nose, he counted to ten, banishing the thoughts of Marley on the stairs, in his bed.

Icy fingers tickled the back of his neck as his unease intensified. Something felt off in the house. Slowly, he glanced around, the sensation of being watched lingering. His gaze fell on the front door. A sliver of light showed around the edges, indicating it wasn't closed.

Goddamn reporters. But something in his heart thunked. The alarm system never sounded. Thoughts of the answering machine evaporated as he hustled to the front door. He closed his eyes for a millisecond, letting a lightness enter his heart. *Maybe Marley came back.* He'd repair the damage he'd caused. Grasping the knob, he wrenched the door open, hoping for the best, expecting the worst.

Outside, nothing. Well, almost nothing. A few neighbors busily prepped for work, grabbing papers, starting cars, escorting kids to the bus stop. No press, no vultures. Nothing for his concern, except perhaps the ugly stare from his next-door neighbor, Mrs. Marconi. But then again, she always gave him the stink-eye.

Breathing a sigh of relief, he closed the door tightly, eyeing the bolt lock. Did he lock the door when Marley left? He didn't remember. No matter. Sliding the bolt, he still couldn't shake the idea of someone else in the house.

Slowly, he took a circuit through both upstairs and down. Nothing looked out of place, but the air still felt electrified. Worry bled into his stomach, and he grimaced. *Please, not Marley.* An errant reporter slipping into his home was one thing or even a misinformed robber who didn't know Alan's financial situation. But Marley sneaking back to take something…

Shaking off the paranoia, he headed back upstairs to finish dressing. He dug through his clothes from yesterday still strewn on the floor. Checking his pants pockets, he fished out his keys and change. But his wallet came up missing.

Silently, he cursed, tamping down the panic. The whole night passed in a rush. His wallet might be anywhere. Taking a slow breath, he started the search.

Twenty minutes later, Alan sat on the stairs with his head in his hands. His house looked as if a tornado partied with a hurricane. No wallet. He'd found a few items he'd lost in the past—an autographed baseball, an old set of keys to the garage, and eight umbrellas.

But no wallet.

The yard didn't turn up anything either. He tried to be discreet as he combed the lawn for his billfold. Of course, Mrs. Marconi came out and questioned him. Her nosiness held no limit.

"I didn't think you'd be home," she said, her arms crossed over her skinny chest. "I didn't see your car drive in. I usually do. Your headlights—"

Alan cut her off. "Yes, yes. They always shine in your window. We've talked about this, Mrs. Marconi. It's the curve of the driveway. Even when I back in, I seem to still flash you." He slapped his forehead at the double *entendre*. She wasn't a woman he wanted to wander down that road with. She blinked at him, pulling the collar of her sweater tighter around her neck. "The headlights flash you," he corrected lamely, wanting the conversation to end four sentences ago.

"Yes, well, perhaps if you changed the driveway? The lights are annoying." Her mouth pressed in an ugly frown. Alan sighed. *Yes, move the driveway. A much easier solution than closing curtains.* But he held his tongue.

"I'll consider it, Mrs. Marconi. Excuse me." He thought about asking her about the wallet. Hell, Mrs. Nosy probably found it but would wait until he walked halfway to the door before telling him. The desire to find a new place to live burned inside him again. But with his assets gone, he had no choice but to stay. "Have you seen a wallet on my driveway or lawn?" His voice sounded old and tired.

Mrs. Marconi perked up. "Lost your wallet?" She harrumphed. "Not surprising. All the people you have in and out of your place. The reporters, the women." She glared down her nose at him. "Hard to keep track of your money, isn't it?"

Alan had enough. "Mrs. Marconi," he said, an edge in his voice, "innocent until proven guilty. I didn't embezzle the money, and neither did Conrad." He never defended himself this way. And one glance at Mrs. Marconi reminded him why. Her mouth stretched in a tight line, her brow furrowed.

"Sorry. Bad morning. Lost wallet and everything," he continued, holding his hands up in contrition.

Tightening the stranglehold on the neck of her sweater, she spewed her own venom. "Probably the tart who left your place earlier. Be careful of the company you keep. Especially when you're in such hot water already." She spun on her heel and marched back into her house.

Alan trudged back inside, plunked down on the steps up and hung his head. Marley must've taken his wallet. The soul-crushing reality of it hit him like a brick. All the "I don't want to hurt you. You've been through enough" was entirely bullshit. She'd been out for a buck after all. Even if she stole the wallet out of spite when she left, pissed because he tossed her out, she still…

She displayed the most sympathy he'd seen since the IRS disaster hit. The constant ache in his chest over Conrad's disappearance deepened. The whole world seemed to be swirling into a black hole. He couldn't trust anyone. Everyone left him, or he pushed them away. Leaving him alone and useless.

After a moment, he scrubbed his face. A call to the police didn't seem worth the trouble. Making a bigger target of himself by having flashing lights in his driveway held no appeal. He'd call the bank and the credit card companies. The accounts were empty anyway. His little thief would get nothing.

Chapter Five

Marley laid low at a diner near the apartment. Sipping coffee, she watched for Becca. Not wanting a confrontation, she somehow had to avoid the woman and retrieve her stuff. Becca would skin her alive for the betrayal last night.

But Marley felt ready to square up, done stealing and tricking people. She'd gone from a bad situation to a worse one. Her parents used her for money and for access to the right social circles. When she ran from their abuse and neglect, she'd landed right in the arms of another user.

Becca seemed awesome at first, taking her in off the streets, feeding and clothing her, teaching her things like an older sister. Until Marley realized Becca was training an apprentice. Her initial charity needed to be repaid in blood and money. Once Becca saw Marley's skill with numbers, the woman used every trick in the book to exploit her.

Last night illustrated another bad example in a long line of bad examples. The most recent refinance con tricked an older woman into payments on a fake debt consolidation. It had eaten away at Marley. They were bilking the woman of her life savings, of her means to a comfortable retirement. Marley couldn't take it anymore. Her heart bled at the thought of stealing another dollar from the sweet woman. She'd balked, and Becca punished her for it.

The three hundred dollars loss was now Marley's responsibility. If she didn't pony up, the cash would come out of her hide. Becca never hit her, not like Troy, but she'd threaten horrible things if Marley failed to lift the money at the bar. And Marley didn't deliver.

Stirring her fourth cup of coffee, she considered sneaking up to the apartment and grabbing her things when someone sat in the booth across from her. Marley startled, almost knocking over her drink. The smirk, those too-pink lips, and the blonde hair. Becca had found her.

"Where's my money, chick?" she asked, casual, playful. Becca didn't need to raise her voice a decibel or sound angry to put the fear of God into Marley. She only need hint at some unsavory character they both knew. Marley wanted to keep clear of the pimps and drug dealers. Crossing Becca led down a path to the cesspool.

"Uh." Marley's mouth dried up like sandpaper. Her brain stuttered, images of working corners or needles being shoved into her arm danced before her. She'd seen it before. Young girls fed on heroin so they'd comply with anything. "I can get it," she stammered.

Becca sucked her teeth. "Yeah, that's not going to work for me." She tapped her elaborately manicured nails on the table. "I gave you a job to do last night, and you bailed."

"It was more complicated than we first thought," Marley scrambled. "He doesn't have any money. He's broke." Hands shaking, she managed to lift the mug to her lips and soothe her throat.

"Didn't seem broke to me. Not one bit." Becca wagged one of her talons at Marley. "Three hundred, Marley, and three hundred more. Every day we aren't pushing those old fogies for cash, I'm losing."

Marley hedged, struggling to keep the tremor from her voice. "I picked a bad mark is all. I can fix it. I swear." A promise she didn't intend to keep. She was finished with Becca but too scared to tell her.

If she made it out of the booth, she'd have to hide, clear out of town, start over. Mentally, she calculated her resources to get out of Dodge. Her shoulders dropped as she realized she owned nothing but the items in Becca's apartment. Nothing. Like when she'd ended up in Iverton, and Becca took her in. Biting back tears, she slid down in the booth, trying to leave.

"Hold up there, girlie." Becca reached out, running her fingers along Marley's arm. Good cop time. "A bad mark? Well, then. Let's stroll tonight, find a good one. Forget the guy." She fiddled with her purse, her gaze never leaving Marley's. "Or hit him again." She threw a twist of coy into the words, and Marley's stomach turned.

"Nah," she said, withdrawing her hand but halting her retreat. "He's really broke. You know him?" Most of the fear left her. Becca stayed in nice mode—a good sign. No threats yet. If Marley played along, she could still hop a train, hide in the bathroom until the ticket guy passed by. When they discovered her, they'd at least have to wait for the next stop to kick her out.

"Yeah, he did seem familiar." Becca tapped a finger on her lip. "What's his name?" She reached into her purse and pulled out a man's billfold. Dread hit Marley like a punch, and she melted against the back of the booth.

She recognized it as Alan's. He'd placed it on the dresser when they'd entered his bedroom. Probably more subconscious than anything, he'd kept his wallet away from her. At the time, she hadn't cared. She'd only wanted a serious tumble with a man who not only gave her a chance but was interested in their mutual pleasure. The wallet on the dresser—a non-issue. Until now.

Now it sat in Becca's palm. She hefted it as if it contained riches. Pausing to glance at Marley, Becca made a show of opening it and examining the contents. "Let's see. His name is…oh, look. He's Alan Reid. Isn't he the guy you watch on TV? The one who got conned by his business partner. The pathetic sad sack who lost his money?" She snorted with laughter as she checked the money slot.

Pulling out two twenties, she grimaced. "Well, there's forty off your tab." She fanned herself with the bills. "You still owe me five sixty." She stood, adjusting her shirt to accentuate her cleavage and straightening a stray hair.

After Becca finished posing, she glared down at Marley. "The cards are probably shot." She flung the wallet at Marley who gulped, her coffee threatening a repeat appearance. "Call your boy, force him to front you. Or you're getting a visitor. Very soon." She flipped her hair and marched out the diner door, leaving Marley a sack of bones in the booth.

****

Dragging herself to her feet, Marley stood over the diner's table, her mouth dry, her heart aching. She stared down at the billfold in her hand.

Guilt swept over her in a rush. Damn Becca. She'd never escape the bitch. Head hanging low, Marley started for the exit.

As she pushed the door, a hand grasped her arm. Instantly, she flew into flight mode, instinct telling her to run far and wide. She tugged her arm out the grip, shouting, "Get off me." Her heels hampered a quick exit. Her feet tangled, and she grabbed the door before she fell in a heap.

"You gonna pay for the coffee?" the waitress asked, nostrils flaring. "It comes out of my pay." She snapped a pink wad of gum as if to emphasize the point.

"I'm sorry," Marley stammered, her bravado gone. "I forgot." She fumbled with Alan's wallet, praying Becca left her at least a dollar.

"Yeah, sure." The waitress held out her hand.

As Marley searched the wallet, an old picture fell to the floor. The waitress issued a rude noise, probably figuring Marley was creating a diversion to finish her dine and dash. All for a stupid cup of coffee. Grumbling, she snatched the picture off the floor, not wanting to lose Alan's property.

Glancing at the photo, she saw a faded image of a younger Alan standing next to a tall man a few years older. Arms around each other shoulders, both laughed heartily at the photographer. Marley's posture sagged as she gazed at Alan with his best friend during better times. No wonder the man walked around looking broken and lost. The picture illustrated their genuine friendship frozen in time forever, the perfect memento. Marley owned nothing like it. Not now, not before. Tears burned in her eyes.

The waitress cleared her throat, snapping Marley

back to the diner where she held a stolen wallet from a man she swore she'd never hurt. Glaring at the waitress, she resumed hunting for money. The credit cards were off limits, no good adding identity theft to petty larceny. She found a crumpled five-dollar bill tucked behind a credit card. Relief blossomed in her chest.

Placing the five in the out-turned palm of the waitress, Marley snarked, "Keep the change," and hustled out the door, the wallet heavy in her hand.

She must return it, no question. But how without disappointing him? The idea of seeing him again sent tingles over her skin. She closed her eyes, imagining another night in his bed. A smile crept over her lips.

A shoulder smashed into hers, and she blinked with surprise. "Get the fuck out of the doorway, bitch," a skinny, pock-marked teen snarled.

Marley's street instincts kicked in. Fight overruled flight. She might've been a foot shorter than this douche, but damned if he'd talk to her like that. "Big man knocking into a woman. Think it makes up for your tiny cock?" She flipped her hair.

Turning toward her apartment down the block, she lifted her chin, showing no fear, though an icy coldness built in her chest as she cruised passed him. One punch and she'd be flat out on the pavement. Moving as quickly as possible on her ridiculous shoes, she bee-lined for home.

Entering the building's broken door, she swept up the three flights to the apartment where she and Becca spent the better part of six years. Sometimes Becca took off for a while, sometimes Marley stayed with someone else. But lately, they both stayed here, too often, thinking up schemes to bilk innocent people out of their life savings. Marley stared at the tarnished gold numbers of 21B, knowing it was her last day here.

Ever.

Twisting the key, the door opened easily. She stuck her head inside, glancing from the small living room to the galley kitchen. No one. Becca most likely wouldn't have come back here after their meeting. She considered herself as a sharp businesswoman, but honestly, she was only another bully, afraid of a real challenge to her authority.

Stepping into the apartment, she called out, just in case. "Becca?" Her pulse raced. More confrontation would suck, but perhaps she could convince the bitch to back off, at least enough to slip through her fingers. No one answered. Marley's shoulders dropped. None of Becca's "friends" were crashing in the living room or bedrooms. Still, Marley tiptoed down to her tiny room, terrified she'd guessed wrong.

Closing the door, she sank down, her back pressed against its wood. Pulling in deep breaths, she willed her anxiety to tamp down. She'd been jumping from ecstasy to fear to anger and back again the entire morning. As she dropped her head to her knees, a single sob escaped her lips.

A mix of relief and sorrow filled her, not to mention, a hint of trepidation. The end of an era was never easy. The same waterfall of emotions hit her when she'd left her parents' place.

Centering herself, she tipped her head back against the door, her mind whirling. The wallet in her hand weighed a thousand pounds. Returning it was priority one, but she had to vacate the apartment. Pack, then go back to Alan's place. If she left it in his mailbox, she might avoid facing him. Then again, if she saw him, she could explain Becky's misdeed. Hopefully, he'd believed her.

No. He must know the wallet vanished by now, and she the only person around to have taken it. He must hate her. Staring at the leather, she traced a finger along the edge. On one hand, she could toss it. But something inside her demanded she explain everything to Alan, even though he'd dismissed her earlier.

Standing, she kicked off the heels, steeling her resolve. *Do the right thing. Even if he throws you out again. Be honest and maybe...*

She'd bring the wallet back, then go...anywhere but here.

****

Alan surrendered at lunchtime. He'd focused on the IRS emails and the piles of paperwork. But the empty office preyed on his nerves. No accountant, no Conrad to help him. Cursing, he called his partner's phone again. Right to voice mail, the same as it had been for weeks. Grabbing his jacket, he closed and locked the office and headed home.

His mind blanked as he drove through the streets of Iverton. It was the only way to drive in the city lately. Every corner, every street held something to remind him of his failures. No matter what route he took home, he passed something closed down because of him. Keeping his gaze forward saved him the heartache.

He pulled into his driveway, automatically reaching for the headlight switch even though it was broad daylight. Mrs. Marconi was really in his head. He sighed. A figure stood at his door, a short woman with a mass of dark hair. Alan recognized her in an instant.

Marley.

He hit the brakes hard, the tires squealing. *Back for more, huh?* But more what? Sex or money? She spun, her hair flying, her arms crossed over her chest.

Rage flooded over him. And honestly—lust too, which only made him angrier. The woman stole his wallet, and he still wanted her on the kitchen table. Grinding his teeth, he threw the gear shift into Park and launched himself out of the car.

She flinched but didn't run. Perhaps she wasn't about to rob the place. He marched to the door, anger heating his skin, his brain. He pointed an accusing finger at her, his mouth working to hold back the wrath battling inside. But, nosy neighbors had wagging tongues. Pressing his lips tight together, he stood over her, breathing hard.

"Inside," he snarled. Invite the criminal home for cocktails? Was he as terrible a judge of character as the newspapers stated? Maybe. "Now."

Staring at him with wide eyes, she said nothing, merely held out the object she'd pressed against her chest.

His wallet.

Chapter Six

Marley stepped back, while a glowering Alan unlocked the door. Anger wafted off him in tight waves as he marched down the hall. Clutching the wallet tighter, she followed in his wake, nerves jangling. He stopped at the first doorway and pointed into the room.

As she snaked past him, her gaze lingered on the stairs for a half-second. He caught her glance, his scowl deepening.

Inside, the room appeared enormous, with a vaulted ceiling and six-foot windows. The furniture and walls glowed white and gold. Marley wrinkled her nose as she perched on the edge of a linen couch. It looked like a catalog photo, totally wrong for Alan. She couldn't imagine him ever choosing the design scheme. Ever. Briefly, she wondered if he had a girlfriend somewhere.

He stood in the doorway, his gaze locked on hers. His mouth worked, but no words came out. Pointing a finger at her, he tried again. Marley twisted her hair, her palms slick with nervous sweat. As he struggled to speak, probably to reprimand or scream at her, she shoved the fear into the backseat. Pulling in a deep breath, she put the wallet on the white lacquered coffee table.

A peace offering.

Glancing down at the wallet, he threw his hands up and stalked away from her. After a heartbeat, he paced the room in tight loops. The silence deepened. A weight hung over them like a storm front. Marley found it harder and harder to breathe. The large clock on the mantel ticked off the pace of his laps, his face fiery red with the effort or the anger. Anxiety squeezed her chest, but the thought of leaving without explaining, without his understanding, kept her in her seat.

Filling her aching lungs, she spit out, "I didn't take it," hoping the shock of her words might stop his infernal pacing. Alan threw his hands up again, moving faster if anything. "Becca did," she added. He jerked to a halt.

His glare burned a hole in her chest. The frustration in his blue eyes broke her heart. Part of her said fall on her knees and beg for forgiveness. The other half wanted to chuck the wallet at him with a reprimand for having taken her home in the first place. He'd been right to classify her as a criminal from the start. He didn't want any more trouble.

"How?" He fired the word like a bullet, and she flinched. The backing of the couch supporting her against his ire.

"She didn't tell me how she got it. She must've broken into the house this morning, nabbed it, and then delivered it to me."

"Delivered?" he asked. *Damn, wrong word.* Marley sank down an inch. "Oh, she *delivered* it to you, huh? You two worked it out. Wouldn't it have been easier to roll me in the alley like you initially planned?" He threw himself in a regal leather chair, head in his hands. His shoulders sagged, illustrating his exhaustion.

Everything in her desired to go to him, rub his back, make it better. Regretfully, she dismissed the image of comforting him.

"She must've followed us or something. But she implied..." Becca made no threats yet, but Alan might not understand her subtlety.

"Implied what?" he asked, his head not lifting as fatigue colored his words.

Marley collected herself, scooching closer to the edge of the couch cushion. "She wanted money or she's going to send some bad people after me."

Alan's head popped up. A secret thrill electrified her skin. He cared. Slowing her breathing, she checked herself. He was probably reacting to his anger, her fear, and her wild story. Taking a gamble, she decided to share her chaotic lifestyle.

"Becca is my mentor in all things illegal. Not partner." A tremor hit her voice as she said the two words. Confession soothed the soul, and she spilled. "She took me in when I was young, on the streets alone. She taught me many ways to separate people from their money. And I'm indebted to her. After abandoning her plan last night, I owe her double."

Marley swallowed hard, disappointed she couldn't tell the tale well. Judging by Alan's level of patience, she didn't have time for details. She struggled for a way to easily explain Becca owned her without it sounding sleazy. Becca never forced her down that ugly road yet, but, with the latest failing, she might.

Marley felt a deep need to explain it to him before taking off. She'd never connected with anyone the way she had with Alan last night. No one else. In her entire life. He understood what it was like to be pushed around, to be alone. If she could make him understand, maybe she might end up on her feet.

"So," Alan said, raising his gaze to hers. "She's your Fagin?"

"Fagin?" A slimy sensation rolled over her, the word tasting foul in her throat. Tears burned as she shook her head vehemently. He thought she was a prostitute. Her brain shut down. *His good opinion once lost...*A sniffle escaped her.

Eyes widening, Alan held out a hand. "No, not...From Dickens, *Oliver Twist*. Fagin is the man who made Oliver steal."

She slid from embarrassment to mortification. Swiping at her tears, she said, "Oh, yeah. She taught me the business, and obligated me to work for her." Turning her head away, she reeled in her horror and terminated the tears. She did not want a pity party.

"Becca taught you how to run a con, and now you have to work for her. Why?" The question sounded simple and the answer seemed obvious. Heat brushed her cheeks as she gave him the only answer she could.

"Because Becca knows bad people." She shrugged. His gaze scanned her slowly, deliberately, and when their eyes met, his jaw fell. He understood with one glance. Relief filled her as she released a breath.

Pushing the wallet toward him, she hoped he'd take the olive branch. "Becca took the cash. But the rest is in there."

Alan glanced down at the wallet, his mouth pursed. "You're saying she broke in here, took it"—He pointed to the billfold—"and disappeared without my knowing?"

Marley nodded. "She's great with locks and a ghost

when she wants to be. B & E isn't her thing anymore. Hates the physical stuff, but she started off breaking into people's houses for fun."

Absently, he picked up the billfold and thumbed through it. "And no plan for her to commit burglary? Say, if the alley thing didn't work out?" Raising an eyebrow, he stared at her.

Marley shook her head. "No. God, no. I told you last night. I'm done with her. I packed my stuff and moved out. I thought I should give it back before I left."

Thumping the wallet on his leg, he considered her for a long moment. "Why?"

Marley raised her eyebrows. "Why? Because I'll always be under her thumb if I don't leave."

"No, I get it. Why bring it back? I mean, you knew the credit cards are useless. So, why bother risking a confrontation with me? I could've called the police or worse." Alan rose from his chair, like some giant unfolding, displaying his considerable height. He stepped in front of the door, blocking the sole exit. A cold fear rose in her throat.

I've made a terrible mistake.

Chapter Seven

Anger and hatred boiled in Alan's stomach. Who the fuck did this Becca character think she was? Dangling bodily harm in front of Marley, keeping the poor girl in a state of fear? And for how long? An image of crushing the bitch's head under his foot rose in his mind. Blowing out a heated breath through his nose, he struggled to keep his temper.

Marley hadn't betrayed him. She was everything today she'd been last night. Hope grew in his chest. He believed her. No one faked emotion that well. Not to mention, bringing the wallet back benefited no one. He'd done a bit of research about con games at work earlier. Unless she planned a long con for him—which he, honestly, did not believe. She was a victim here. Like him.

But Becca invaded his home, threatened Marley, and attempted to keep her prisoner. His Marley. Red filled his vision. He fisted his hands. The desire to hit something burned in his chest, and snarling, he searched the room for something to smash.

Marley stood hurriedly. "I'm sorry. I didn't mean to take up your time. I'll go." Her gaze darted wildly. Mentally, he smacked himself. His grizzly bear act terrified her.

"Marley." His voice velvet, his anger buried. Her

gaze stayed fixed on the floor. The desire to touch her, soothe her pushed at him. Struggling to catch her attention, he tried again. "Marley, please." Finally, she met his gaze. Her shoulders dropped, and the fear in her eyes muted.

"Thank you," he said, carefully, keeping his voice calm so as not to scare her. "You put yourself at serious personal risk to bring me this." He held up the hated piece of leather. He'd toss it immediately, use a money clip or a canvas billfold from the drug store rather than carry the tainted object again.

Unsteady on her feet, Marley staggered, and he reached out a hand to assist her. She flinched, shying away from his touch, a gesture which froze his heart. His frightening her earlier squashed any connection between them.

She said nothing, and he pressed on. "Why, Marley? If Becca threatened you, why did you come back here?"

Shaking her head, she turned away from him. When it finally dawned on him that he blocked the only exit. He stepped to the side. Chin ducked, she skittered around him, toward the hallway, the brazenness from last night gone. He hated the meek Marley.

"Have you eaten?" The question burst from his lip. He still felt guilty for not feeding her this morning. "I have sandwich stuff—cold cuts, bread—or we could order in." He hiked a thumb toward the kitchen, feeling stupid. The woman didn't need a sandwich. She needed a caseworker.

"No, I'm fine." She held up her hands as if he were assaulting her with the lunch invitation. "I've gotta go." As she stepped toward the hall again, Alan's instincts demanded he act. He grasped her hand, holding lightly.

"Where you gonna go, Marley?" he asked, worry coloring his words in purples and blues.

She glanced down at their entwined hands, a ghost of a smile crossing her lips. "Nowhere, Alan. I'm going nowhere."

****

Sitting at the tiny kitchen table, Marley chowed down on brand-named chips. Eating without thinking about the cost of each morsel felt new and decadent. Becca kept a tight account of the grocery money, buying generic unless she wanted something special for herself. Marley lived like an inmate with the jailhouse meals of canned meat and frozen entrees while Becca dined like a queen.

Alan raised an eyebrow as she pieced together a third turkey sandwich. Catching his eye, she laughed self-consciously and pushed the food away, guilt transforming her into a pig and a thief.

Sliding the plate back to her, he added more chips and another pickle. "Please eat. I'm enjoying the show," he said with a grin.

Gluttony abated, Marley rolled her eyes. "As if I didn't feel weird enough about eating your food…" The thought drifted off. The meal had been quiet, comfortable, and filling. Something she'd love to repeat. The memory of her bags waiting in a bus depot locker stopped a chip midway to her lips. Oh, yeah, she was leaving.

She snuck a peek at Alan who pushed crumbs around his plate, his eyes downcast, his lips slightly upturned. He looked the epitome of domestic bliss, and her heart ached for the quiet life Alan represented. No worrying about cops or dangerous characters on the street. And money...Her blood froze, the dismissive tone in her thoughts making her cringe.

Money problems, the IRS...And here she sat, adding to his troubles.

Finishing the sandwich, she gathered up her dishes and placed them in the sink. Alan didn't move. Collecting the extra lunch bits, she returned everything to their places in the tidy kitchen, enjoying cleaning up after a real meal, even a simple one.

"Well," she said, hedging. The dishes needed washing as did the table. But it only delayed the inevitable. She sighed. "I guess I'll go."

"How long?" Alan asked, still not glancing up.

She froze, hovering over the sink. "I'm sorry?"

"How long have been under her thumb?" His gaze slowly rose to meet hers. Emotion boiled in his blue eyes—anger, regret, concern. Her breath caught as her own emotions overwhelmed her. When had anyone ever looked at her like that?

Dropping her arms to her side, she stood still as straight as possible. Fear thrummed in her chest. She'd never spoken to anyone about this before. Shame and terror warred in her head, but she answered him. "Almost seven years now." Alan's head snapped back as if she'd hit him.

"Seven years?" His mouth dropped open. "My God. And you couldn't escape?"

Managing a half shrug, she glanced away. "I wasn't exactly a prisoner. Roof over my head, food on the table, well, kinda." She twisted her hair. "Grifting is easy once you get the hang of it. I liked working with the numbers."

Alan raised his eyebrows, and shame drifted over her like a shroud. Admitting she enjoyed the work would damn her for sure. Scrambling, she explained. "She led me into this party-filled lifestyle and funded it with other people's money. All fun and rainbows unless it wasn't." Like the thievery, mental abuse, and restrictions.

He nodded solemnly. "And now that you have a little perspective, it's not what you want."

She hesitated. "Becca loves how I can keep track of her scams. Spreadsheets are a foreign language to her. But when she realized how great I am with numbers, she moved up her game, running more complicated cons." She stopped talking, afraid of saying too much.

"And your family?" He raised an eyebrow. She shook her head. He paused, the air thick with anticipation. Bracing herself for a reprimand, she glanced at the exit. Instead of blasting her, he said, "Math genius, huh? I could use one of those right about now."

Marley laughed self-consciously. She'd always thought his troubles stemmed from bad accounting— one of the reasons she'd followed the story closely. Part of her yearned to find out what the IRS discovered and who pulled the con. Alan never appeared to be some clueless man, blissfully ignorant as his partner robbed him blind. There must be more to his story.

Curling a lock of hair around her finger, she swayed back and forth. "I'd love to see your books sometimes." Her words dripped with both sensuality and humor.

Alan chuckled. "That's the sexiest thing I've heard

since the whole mess started." Rising to his feet, he slapped the table. "The IRS guys do not flirt." Half a grin cracked his face.

"You aren't dealing with the right ones then." She winked, causing Alan to laugh again—a wonderfully sweet sound. "File with the department and get new agents. There has to be a seductive accountant in there somewhere."

He sighed. "Probably my problem from the beginning."

A sliver of ice fell down her back. "What?" Marley asked, taken off guard. She floundered, thinking of the overly-decorated living room. "I'm sorry I..." The papers never mentioned a woman, a girlfriend, a lover. Maybe some sexy bookkeeper distracted him and took the money. "I tried to..." She didn't know where to go with this.

Alan waved her off. "Don't worry, Marley. The IRS is screwing me nicely." He shrugged. "The question is what will *you* do now?" Knitting his brows for a second, he stared at her, his eyes flashing through several emotions.

She looked at him, really looked at him—from his sandy blond hair, his blue eyes, the sagging shoulders to his hands folded on the table, the nails chewed to the quick. Her heart skipped when meeting his gaze again. He'd fed her when he should've called the police. He talked to her when he should've thrown her into the street.

All her instincts were right about him. He was a good person in a sea of selfish, self-absorbed thieves. He'd been betrayed, and she brought more trouble to his door. But he didn't balk at taking her in again. He listened, believed, and…

Marley stepped toward him, closing the distance quickly before he brushed her off. She wrapped her arms around his neck, pulling him down into a kiss. Their lips met, and a flood of desire filled her.

She dropped her hand between them, skimming her fingers over the front of his pants. "What will I do now? Alan, you know the answer."

She'd make him forget his problems for a few hours. Make him unbearably happy. Then do the best thing for both—leave, taking her troubles with her.

Chapter Eight

Alan froze. Marley stood in his arms again, soft, sweet, and damn sexy. Images of last night flashed in his mind. Lust pulsed in his blood. So wrong, but her lips on his neck said otherwise. He *was not* the long con.

He was not.

She had no interest in his money or adding to his IRS problems. Marley wanted him.

Wrapping her in his arms, he kissed her as if his life depended on it. She melted against him with a low moan. His blood burned just like last night, as if his desire erased rational brain function and left him an animal. She was his at this moment, the future irrelevant.

Her hands tangled in his hair. But he couldn't give up her mouth. Not yet. Holding her tighter, he deepened the kiss, throwing everything he had into it. Marley, limp in his arms, let her head fall back, away from him. He mourned the loss of her lips.

Her neck, exposed, curved swan-like and delicate. Her pulse beat beneath alabaster skin. Something deep inside him woke, like a sleeping animal. It rose as a wolf—biting, sucking, and nipping down to her collarbone. Happy noises escaped her lips urging him to continue.

Pressing her against the table, he swept a hand behind her scattering the few remaining lunch items. A dark lust boiled up from his gut, compelling him to take her now, hot and fast. He ran his hands down her back, cupping her ass. She gasped as he lifted her onto the table, sliding her legs apart.

"Alan." She breathed but refused to give him back her mouth.

Fine. He skimmed his hands under her shirt, caressing her breasts delicately as he raised the cloth over her head. Kissing along her collarbone again, he blindly searched for the bra clasp. The damn thing thwarted his efforts. Frustrated, he cursed aloud. Marley chuckled softly, pushing him back.

She cocked her head to the side, her dark hair falling over one shoulder. Lust burned in him anew. *Take her on the table now.* He bit his lip, swallowing back the urge to have the woman without preamble. She seemed to sense his want and reacted accordingly...by teasing him.

With legs still hooked around his thighs, she stretched her arms behind her, taking her sweet time unhooking her bra. She appeared to struggle herself, but the glint in her eye said differently. Alan growled in the back of his throat, urging her to hurry up.

She arched her back. He couldn't wait any longer. As she finally released the catch, he caught the fabric in his teeth and snatched the bra away. His mouth found her breast, devouring it. She laughed as her legs squeezed tighter around him, pressing his crotch into hers.

Cupping her ass again, he lifted her off the table. Digging into the waistband of her leggings, he tugged, taking her panties down too. She wiggled, and her clothes disappeared in a heartbeat. They folded back together. In his ear, she whispered for him, her voice yearning.

His lust threatened to overtake his senses. No, he wanted more. For her. For him.

He continued kissing down her body, tasting each delicate inch of her flesh. She writhed beneath him, demanding more without saying a single word. Gently, he pushed her backward onto the table. A lock of her hair caught in her teeth and she nodded. Ready without question.

He shook his head.

Carefully, he lowered to his knees. The table stood at the perfect height. Greedily, he devoured the feast before him, taking Marley to the height of ecstasy before pulling her back. He teased and taunted her, loving every taste, every touch. He could have stayed there for hours, savoring her most intimate places.

With a touch as light as a feather, he brushed his fingers over her folds, sliding down inside her. Marley bucked and screamed as he tormented her with his mouth while his fingers explored.

She grabbed his shoulders, panting, "Now."

Alan stood, his hands trembling, loving how Marley ordered him. Taking his time unbuckling his belt, he glanced up at her. She stared at him, her eyes hot, her mouth molten red.

She locked her legs around him, digging her heels hard into his ass. "Now," she challenged, playfulness absent in her voice.

Donning a condom, Alan obliged.

****

Marley's head swam in the aftermath of several orgasms. Alan's tongue was as talented as his cock. He took her places she'd never been. Tears threatened to burst from her eyes. She struggled for oxygen, still flat on her back. The kitchen table. *Check it off the "I've never" list.* Her lips rounded in a smile.

Alan stood at the end of the table, half bent over her. He panted, a fine sheen of sweat covering his face. His shirt stuck to his chest. His half-dressed state made her chuckle. Clasping her hands around his neck, she used his body to lever herself up to kiss him. A warm sweet smooch that curled her toes.

He straightened, pulling her up with him. Her feet dangled in the air for a split second before alighting on the floor, her arms still locked around his neck.

"You're amazing," she whispered, her voice husky. If only she could open his shirt and bury herself inside it. She pressed against him, loving the sensation of the cotton against her bare skin.

Putting his arms around her, he gazed down, his eyes glittery. He said nothing, didn't have to. He believed her, trusted her. He must, or he never would've slept with her again. He was a good soul, something she understood in her heart. She wanted more than anything else in her life to keep in his good graces. But first, she wanted her own taste.

Alan shuffled back, but the pants around his ankles hindered his progress. He wobbled, grabbing the table for support. She glanced down at his bunched-up pants and they both laughed.

"Here. Let me help you," Marley said, releasing his neck and sliding her hands down his chest. He opened his mouth but shut it again quickly. Smart move.

As she dragged her hands down, she slowly crouched at his feet, carefully removing his shoes, then his clothes. His gaze burned on the top of her head boring through her, sending her messages of what he desired. She already knew.

After taking off the last sock, she peered up at him from the floor, her gaze tracing his body. Swallowing hard, he cupped her cheek then ran his hand over the top of her head, playing with her hair. Something about him touching her hair thrilled her beyond measure. Her gaze slid from his eyes to his cock as he combed fingers through her hair.

His breath caught, and she allowed him no time to think or change his mind. Her mouth engulfed him in one smooth motion. His hand clenched in her hair, pulling it a little. Electricity ran down her arms and over her body. She pulled back to the tip and swallowed him again in the same quick motion. Again, he tugged her hair.

Perfect.

She played with him as he'd done her. Bringing him to the edge and then dialing it back. Every time, he reacted by doing something to her hair—a pull, a yank, a caress. The sensation caused dark pools of ecstasy to form in her chest. Alan understood what she needed.

His body tensed. He must be close. She teased, a little teeth, a little tongue, but not enough to push him over the edge. He groaned, fisting her hair and tugging upward. Marley stood, obediently.

Alan's eyes, hollow with lust, measured her. "You," he said, his voice syrupy thick with desire. He scooped her up as if she were a feather and carried her upstairs to his room. He kicked the door closed. It hit the jam with a crash of finality as the latch snapped shut.

****

Afternoon sun dappled across his bed. Alan blinked, eyes bleary with sleep. Mid-day naps not his usual cup of tea, but a soft female voice sounded next to him, a low, soft hum of satisfaction. Smiling, he curled on his side.

A beautiful, naked Marley lay there, drunk with sleep and sex. He traced the lines of her torso with his fingers, the sensation of her soft skin stirring something deep inside him. This woman in his bed—he could make it a steady habit. They'd find a way if they both really wanted it.

"Hungry?" he asked, wanting something clever to say but failing miserably. Marley rolled over, pressing against him, her body molding to his.

"Not anymore," she whispered, ticking the hair on his chest. "I'm pretty good now."

"Pretty good?" he snorted, feigning annoyance, though he was secretly pleased with her happiness. "What's a man have to do to satisfy you?" He stroked her hair, and she purred.

"That. Two hundred and eighty-two more times," she said without stutter.

"Huh." He considered it. His head screamed *Yes*, his cock shouted *Now*. He said, "Maybe not immediately."

She snickered. The soft sound filled the room. "You asked."

They lay there quietly, the only noise—the rhythm of their breathing. He didn't want to let her go. Let the media have a field day about the affair if they wanted.

He needed her in his life. A woman, who despite her previous occupation, showed kindness and sincerity. He'd find her a new job and new life. With him.

"Tell me about you." He wanted details, everything. Needed to know her inside and out, her future, her past.

Marley lay there silently, her fingers drawing tiny figures on his skin, a square, a circle. "Just an average girl in a college town…"

Alan smirked. "Yeah, right. Here, I'll start." Marley remained silent. "My family has lived in Iverton since New York became a state. The tavern is practically a family heirloom, my legacy." Heat flushed his cheeks as pride welled in his chest. "How 'bout you?"

He waited, his chin pressed to her forehead. She sighed, snuggling tighter against him. "I'm not from here. I…" She hesitated. He stroked her hair, letting his fingers tangle in her mane. She appeared to love the hair thing. "I ran away from home at sixteen," she confessed. Alan held himself still, wanting to both hold her tight and yell at her at the same time.

"My parents"—She pressed her face into his neck—"are kinda bad people. Becca helped me when I got here but…" She stopped talking. Alan didn't have to look at her to see the shame on her face. He changed the subject.

"I studied business in college. My father gifted me the tavern when I graduated. Best trial by fire ever." He paused hoping she'd take a turn.

After a long silence, Marley said, "I'm really good with numbers. It's why Becca kept me around. I'm a great return on investment because I help her manage the schemes. Keep it streamlined, get her more money."

He stroked her hair again. "It must've been hard for you. Living that way." He bit his lip, realizing his mistake. She was still living it. He hadn't swept her away…not yet. "No way to return home?" he asked. He never imagined growing up without stable, supportive, loving parents. Hell, he longed for his own even now.

"Where did you meet Conrad?" Cleverly, she turned the conversation, as if knowing he couldn't resist the topic. He indulged, not because he couldn't refrain, but because he wanted her to feel at ease.

"At the tavern. He used the place for business meetings all the time." Sarcasm tainted the last three words. "He convinced investors he owned or ran the place. We were in the black by the time Conrad started sniffing around. He tapped into my success to further himself." He chuckled. Conrad the sweet talker. He and Marley were two sides of the same coin. Both con artists in their own way.

"How did you become business partners?" she asked. "Sounds like he tried to pull a fast one. You let him?"

"No. We talked. I convinced him my business was not his office and asked him to move along. The conversation lasted over an hour. We connected, but I still booted him out. I impressed him, I guess. The next time he held a meeting at the tavern, it was with me. He presented a grand business proposal to buy up a few bars near the Oakwood. Corner the market on Birch Street."

"And?" Marley asked, sitting up on her elbow.

"And we did. His sound business plan carried us over the course of five years and beyond. We own most of the properties on the street now. Or we used to." Alan touched her cheek, needing the comfort of her skin.

"But you still own the tavern?" She wasn't the only one who'd asked the question. Even with his other bars and restaurants, the tavern still did good business. Many people grumbled over how it managed to survive the axe. But it was his birthright, a family heirloom.

"She's open for now. Unless I'm forced to liquidate to pay…" He let the sentence run off, not wanting to ruin the moment with the black hole of his problems.

"I hope it doesn't happen," Marley whispered, leaning back against him. The warmth of her body pressed against him soothed the ache of losing the tavern. Maybe if she stayed, he'd survive.

Kissing her forehead with a gentle touch, he said her name. "What will you do now?" He brushed a hand over her arm, hoping she'd changed her mind. "What will we do about Becca?"

"I have to leave, Alan. She's got connections, and I owe her money now." Marley's voice sounded quiet, resigned.

"Owe her for what? Not robbing me? How much to do you need?" Right now, he'd give her anything.

Marley pressed her hand flat against his chest, pulling away by inches. He hated it, hated her not pressed against him, her not in his arms. "It's better if I go, Alan. Becca will keep bugging both of us. I've got nothing to defend myself against her. If I leave, then she'll stop." She retreated further on the bed. Her absence sent a pain through his gut.

"We'll pay her off," he said matter-of-factly. "Give

her her due and tell her to fuck off. Well, nicely, in a way to force her to back down. Then you can stay." He held his hand out inviting her to stay, inviting her into his life.

Marley stared at him hard, tears forming. "No, I can't. Not now. Not ever."

****

Nothing she'd ever done in her life that hurt like rejecting Alan. The wrong time, the wrong place, the wrong everything. She wouldn't drag his name further in the mud. She couldn't take his money or cause him another minute of grief.

Swinging her feet over the edge of the bed, she braced herself for the pain. "Alan, you're an amazing man," she said to the floor. "But you were right yesterday. It'd never work between us. Not in a million years." She glanced over her shoulder. Pain registered in his eyes for a millisecond before he blanked his expression.

"Marley, we can find a way. Becca's not the issue..."

"No, she's not." Marley stood, dragging a sheet over her body. She needed some armor for the conversation. "I am. You are. We can't be." She turned to face him, ready for the ache, the sorrow.

"I can straighten out everything." He sat up on the bed, his gaze narrowed. "Give me some time." He held a hand out. "Stay for now. Talk to me." His eyes lit up as if an idea had struck him. "If I guaranteed she'd leave you alone, would you stay in town?"

"Alan," she said. "Even if you did, we still can't be. My past, your problems. I won't do that to you. It's bad enough I led Becca right to you. For both our sakes, we have to let this go."

She headed for the door. He jumped from the bed, catching her before she hit the stairs. "I can get rid of her." His jaw set, and his chin high said much for his determination. "And someday, my name won't be in the papers anymore. Someday, I'll be free of it."

He looked at her imploringly. Caving in to his request was tempting but Marley knew she'd never be good enough for him. She couldn't fix him nor could he fix her. She sighed.

"It won't work," she said softly.

"Give me a week, and I guarantee you'll be Becca free," he said, no begging, only solid confidence. No wonder Conrad struck up a partnership with him. "One week. And a copy of the spreadsheet."

****

Marley refused a ride to the bus depot to pick up her things. Alan didn't understand she was walking away. She'd emailed him the file plus Becca's number from her phone, and he seemed delighted. But really, if his own business partner took him for all he owned, what chance did he have against Becca?

Promising him not to fly away for a week, Marley swore in her heart she wouldn't let him down. Even though she had nowhere to go now. He didn't know and didn't need to. Pressing a wad of bills in her hand before she left, he kissed her chastely. The cash might keep Becca off her for a few days, but if the pressure became too much, a bus ticket to Boston or Maine or Florida was an easy solution. For now, she needed a roof over her head.

Glancing at her phone, she plunked down in the seat of the bus stop. Where to go? The idea of the women's shelter depressed her, and few other places were safe. Longingly, she glanced back at Alan's house, the perfect size for two. Her heart ached, but she couldn't go back.

Marley spun through her short list of contacts. Jex's name caught her attention. She'd shared a place with the woman a while back when she and Troy were dating. Jex and Troy couldn't still be tight after all this time, could they? Nah. And Jex just might have a place for her to crash.

She hit dial as she boarded the bus. One week. What could happen in one week?

Chapter Nine

Alan sat alone in a booth at Stanton Coffee. After checking his phone again, he waved off the waitress who offered him a third cup of coffee. Additional caffeine intake might not be helpful. Jittery hands didn't scream authority. Better to sit, nurse a second cup, and wait. Always waiting.

A half hour after the time designated, the trashy blonde walked in. She tossed her hair around, as if trying to appear important, trendy, more. Alan easily saw past the façade to her true self. This Becca deserved to be locked up, and the key thrown away. His eye twitched as she waltzed down the row of seating and stopped at his booth.

"You lookin' for me?" she asked, a fake southern accent and more arrogance than Alan usually tolerated. But Becca required a soft sell to coax her into believing his good intentions. Once he'd assuaged her reservations, he'd throw the hammer at her.

"Please, have a seat." He smiled politely and held out a hand to the empty seat across from him. Her gaze raked him over, and her mouth held a smug smile. She slid into the booth as if it were a sexual act, all legs and breasts. Alan repressed a gag, not enjoying mixing with criminal types and the lowlifes. But for Marley, he'd dip back in the pool, if necessary.

She stared at him, leeriness combined with pure ego in her gaze. The waitress arrived with more coffee. Alan didn't wave her off. He let Becca think they were in the same place, wanting the same things.

After the server wandered off, Alan asked Becca, "Would you like some lunch as well?" Non-confrontational and well-mannered gestures held the key today. An impulse to reach over the table and grab her by the throat flashed in his head. Absently, he dismissed it.

"Nah." She examined her nails. "I got other appointments later. Get to it, mister." She put both hands flat down on the table. "Spill."

"Direct. Fine." He preferred dispensing with the bullshit. It worked well with Conrad too. The man could spin anything to anyone. Talk for hours and get nothing done or talk for ten minutes and close a million-dollar deal. Conrad trained him well for the likes of Becca.

She tilted her head to the side, looking expectant. Alan pitched a low ball. "Marley is in your employ." A fact, not a question.

Becca pulled back, her eyes slits. "More like a sister to me really. We've worked on several projects, but we've been roommates a long time." She left the impression they were more than roommates—an abusive relationship, a slave/master situation. It ended today.

"Not anymore," he said simply, his hands resting on either side of his coffee. His gaze locked on hers.

Becca blinked, genuine shock crossing her face briefly then disappearing into her reptilian depths. "You're asking me to end our friendship, our relationship because you say so. Wow. That's rich. Who are you again?" She snorted.

He smiled flatly and reiterated, "Yes, over. Entirely. The whole thing, whatever your spin on it. She's done. You two are through. You'll stay away from her." He continued speaking in the same cool, calm voice, never adding any emotion to his words. The urge to scream boiled inside him. He should be calling her out on the abuse, get the cops to drag her off by her hair. Instead, he folded his hands on the table, coffee untouched.

Becca studied him as if planning her method of attack. His brief research on con artists and social engineers identified absolute confidence as a primary trait. Crushing her ego would force her to release Marley. He waited, resolute, the epitome of confidence as well, matching her conceit and intelligence.

"You got some balls, mister." She shifted slightly, her back against the seat as if keeping the space between them. "Tell me again why? Why abandon my friend for some stranger she just met? She's Russian but not some mail order bride you can claim."

"Let's stop the spin. I know who you are, what you are to Marley. I'm aware of your schemes and your threats. So, let's get down to business." He lowered his eyebrows. "Leave Marley alone." He pushed over the envelope he'd hidden under his hand. Easiest to start with the language she understood.

"What's this?" she asked, sounding curious and confused. Alan refrained from rolling his eyes at the Oscar-winning performance. She opened the envelope, and her mouth widened into a ridiculously large O. She snapped the envelope shut with a gasp. "What's that about?" Slapping it down on the table, she crossed her arms and glared.

"Beautiful performance, Becca." He fiddled with his tie for a second. "It's the money you demanded from Marley." An advance from his retirement accounts, one of the few he could still access. He'd pay the penalties and the taxes without a blink if meant an end to Becca's schemes.

"I have no idea what you're talking about," she said, her words coy and infuriating.

"Oh, my error." He reached across the table for the envelope, but Becca pressed her hand down on it. She eyed him coldly, the reptilian gaze peeking out again.

"Let's not be hasty there, mister...?" Raising an eyebrow, she asked the question as if she didn't know.

"Reid," he said with a tight smile. "So, does she owe you money or not? I'd like it back if she doesn't." He held his hand out palm up. He hated games.

She ran a finger over the envelope, rather seductively, her mouth turned down in a pout. "Marley...she's a difficult one. She's gotten herself into such messes." Spinning the envelope slowly, she tilted her head to one side, then the other. "I'm not sure I can get her out this time." She pressed the money flat, stopping the spin.

Alan hitched his shoulders. He'd opened the door, and she'd kicked it wide. Gave her an inch, and she took a mile. He'd expected it but thought she'd hang back a little negotiate over the course of the entire cup of coffee.

After a pregnant pause, he said, "Well, then—" and snagged the envelope, dragging it to his side of the table. Her gaping mouth said she hadn't anticipated it.

"If you can't let her go, there's no point in giving you this." He held up the money, then feigned putting it in his pocket. She stopped him. Of course, she did.

"Slow down there, Mr. Reid." Blinking innocently, she sipped her coffee, glancing over the top of the cup. "We could spend hours talking about Marley's situation and her debts." She sighed melodramatically, peering out the window, her brows furrowed, her mouth turned down in a deep frown. Alan refrained from laughing.

"Marley never mentioned any debt, except for owing you." He didn't add the emotional blackmail, her enslavement to the illegal schemes, and the life of fear under Becca's thumb. He couldn't think about it. If he did, he'd be over the table, smacking the woman's head into the window. He cleared his throat, cracked his neck, and crossed his legs to expend the energy from his building anger.

"She's conning you, Mr. Reid." Becca reached a hand toward him, her gaze full of sympathy. "And after what you've been through too. That girl…" She shook her head. What a pathetic attempt at intimacy. He shook with revulsion and refused her hand.

Wait, didn't she just ask his name? Ah, a slip in her game.

He settled back into his seat, sipping his coffee. "Regardless, miss…" He tapped the envelope still on the table. "This is what I have to offer you to assist with Marley's debt. If you are aware of my troubles, then you know I had difficulty getting that money." He frowned, his own attempt to be pathetic.

"Alan. Can I call you Alan?" The game was up. He nodded. "Marley's issues go way beyond the little bit of cash she owes me for rent and utilities. Not to mention some huge credit card debt. She goes through them like water. Not my problem, except I cosigned on a few. She is rather young, isn't she?"

Oh, well played, throwing out the age card. Becca must've planned the conversation. Of course, con men, uh—women—were usually good on the fly. He almost admired her.

"She is," he said with a shake of his head. "So young to be involved with such things. And if only you'd do as I asked, she'd be on a better path." He put on his contract negotiation face—stony, firm, and serious. "Take the money, Becca and get lost."

She studied him for a few minutes. He allowed her to scrutinize him as he drank his coffee, the eavesdropping waitress refilling both cups too quickly. He dabbed at the spilled coffee.

Finally, Becca sighed loudly. "You're almost playing it right, Reid. But if you keep pushing the same agenda, rather than bargaining with new information, I'll never agree to your first demand." She slowly stirred her coffee, a smirk on her lips.

"And what you don't seem to get, Becca, is I'm not playing your game. Not a bit." He smirked back. "Take the money and go. Stay away from Marley." He waited for her reaction, unsure if he pushed too hard. But damn if he'd let her lead him around the way she did Marley.

"Then we have nothing to discuss." She put her cup down with a clatter, shoving her bottom lip out. "See you around, Reid."

No begging, not with this chick. "You don't want the money?" he asked, trying to sound confused. "Huh, I thought you'd at least take that. You surprise me, Becca. Or does the negotiation happen after you leave?

You have my number. I assume you'll text me incessantly, trying for more money. For Marley. Always for Marley."

He mimicked her, sighing too loud and slapping his hand on the table. "This didn't go anything like I thought," he continued, shaking his head. "Guess Plan B if you are determined to leave." He pulled out his phone.

Becca paused, eyeing him coldly. "What the fuck are you talking about?" Her casual demeanor deteriorating, anger tainting her words. "Of course, I want the money. It's not enough. You didn't bother to find out how bad it is for her. You act as if you care about her, but honestly, you only want to buy her. You make me sick."

He laughed, loud and long. "That's rich, Becca, but I'll play along. Sit back down and weave me the story of Marley's woes. I'd love to hear it."

She sniffed, her chin in the air, but she didn't leave. "You can't believe a word she says. She's a pathological liar. It's why I took her in. She was out of control. A young thing caught in a downward spiral of her lies and atrocious activities." Becca wrapped her arms around her chest and shivered.

Thank God, he and Marley had talked at length before he confronted the woman. The she said/she said made his head spin. Though ninety-nine percent sure most of what came out of Becca's mouth was crap, he found a thread of truth in the lies.

Sitting back on the bench, she faced the aisle instead of toward him. Her gaze stared off in the direction of the kitchen, as she continued with her sad story.

"Marley ran away at such a young age. Left her abusive parents. She'd never tell me their names or what they did to her, but it sounded like a horror show. She was, and is still, messed up. Her moral compass skewed." She sighed. "Oh, and such a serious drug problem…" She paused, her gaze darting to him then away again. "It took everything in me to steer her forward to a better life, rather than sell herself on the street to anyone with a twenty."

She cocked her head, her gaze locked on his. "How much did she charge you for two nights?" Her words, soft and sappy, hid the ugly behind them. Try as she might, her stories fell short of riling him up. He let her lies drop without reaction.

"Quite a story, Becca. Write it up and sell it to Hollywood. You'll make a mint. Marley the lost child, Becca the sainted savior. Too bad none of it is true."

Her expression morphed into pure anger—brow furrowed, mouth a tight line. "You've known her two days? Three? I've spent years with that demon child. You're lucky she didn't slit your throat in your sleep."

Alan rubbed his chin. "That's your pitch?" he asked, finished playing.

"Excuse me?"

"Marley is beyond help. She's a drug-addicted prostitute with murder on her mind and only you can fix her. How much it will cost to set her right?" He rested an elbow on the table, chin on his palm as if engrossed in the story.

"It goes beyond money, Reid. She needs help. I know a place she can clean up. They'll take good care of her. It's a good program, but it costs five hundred a week. She needs this, Alan." Becca held out her hand again. He stared at it. "Together we can help her heal."

"I'm dizzy from all the spin, Becca. Marley has accrued a ton of credit card debts, and she needs rehab with something about abusive parents in there too. Damn. Poor Marley. She seemed fine when I last saw her. Not crazy, not drugged, not criminal. Huh." He smiled tightly, his chin still in his hand.

"She's amazing at hiding it. But she needs serious help." Since he never took her outstretched hand, it still lay in the middle of the table like a dead fish. She flipped her hand over, palm up. "I'll take the envelope and enroll her at the facility. Intake fees and everything." She crunched her fingers as if saying "Gimmie."

"How about no, Becca? Why don't we talk about what we both really came here to talk about?" He dropped his elbow and slid the money back in his pocket.

"I thought we were talking about Marley, about how to help her."

He shifted back, his arms crossed over his chest. "No, I'm here for Marley. You're here for a profit. You wanted more than you were given." He patted the pocket of his jacket. "You told her $300 to roll me the other night. She failed, and you upped it to six hundred. I offered you the money. Plus, some more to go away, but you never bothered to count it. You refused. Now you want monthly installments. Huh."

Becca's mouth twisted into a deep frown. "What are you saying, Reid? You don't want to help Marley. What kind of man are you?"

"A businessman," he said in a firm tone. "Now, let's go over it. You will take this money"—He patted his pocket—"to pay back Marley's debt." He made quotation marks around the word debt. "And then you will part ways with her. No more contact. No more con games. No more anything. Am I clear?" He leveled his gaze at her, the one he used on Conrad when the man spun out of control.

She rolled her eyes. "You have no idea what you're messing with here." Finally, the façade dropped, and the real Becca came forward. "You think six hundred will make me ditch my money-gal. Seriously? What are you smoking? We're partners. Marley'd be dead in a ditch if not for me. She owes me big time. I'm not letting her go for less than ten grand. And you don't have it." She huffed, her lips in a tight line.

"You're right, Becca. I'd hoped you'd see reason. Take the bribe and walk away. I see now you aren't able to recognize a good deal when presented with one." He cleared his throat, squared his shoulders, and leaned in.

Placing his folded hands on the table, he lowered his head, his gaze boring into hers. "You will," he continued, "cease all contact with Marley or I go to the police. I believe Breaking and Entering is still considered a criminal offense unless they decided to charge you with burglary. You did take my wallet." He sat back and watched her carefully.

Not surprisingly, she laughed at him, a loud, obnoxious belly laugh. The poor, clueless girl. "B & E? Burglary? Are you serious? Marley took your wallet when she left your place. She bragged about what a sucker you were the next day." She waved a hand at Alan as if challenging him to do better.

Sitting stock still, he added, "You've been in my

home, Becca. My wallet wasn't the only asset in the house easily smuggled out. I'm impressed you didn't take more. Marley didn't take the wallet. You did."

She sneered. "Prove it."

"Okay." Alan reached down and snagged the folder next to him on the seat. When he plunked it on the table, the corner of a few photos peeked out. "Now I heard B & E used to be your thing, but apparently security systems have developed a bit since you engaged in the crime."

"What do you mean?" she asked, her confidence slipping.

"You turned off the power to the system. And well done since you didn't knock the power out to the whole house. But my setup has a battery backup. The cameras still worked, the door alarms registered though nothing sounded. The system recorded your movement."

As he said each sentence, he removed an item from the folder—a copy of the list of door openings and a half-dozen pics of Becca in various places in his house, specifically the upstairs hallway and by the front door. He brought the stills showing her looking nefarious. He thought he'd captured the whole thing well with a few shots.

Becca sifted through the pictures. She wrinkled her nose here, frowned there. He saw the wheels working in her head. She wasn't expecting it. Good, he'd thrown her off. If he kept it up, she might see the logic of letting Marley go.

He waited, examining her expressions closely, searching for the sweat to break out on her forehead. Nothing. She regrouped easily as she perused the data cool as a cucumber.

"Note the time and date stamp, there," he said pointing to the corner of a discarded photo.

"Easily photoshopped," she said dismissively. She glanced up at him, shoving the pile back toward his side. "Actually, none of this means anything. I can explain it away easily." She shrugged.

He glared at her. "These documents show you entered in my home without my knowledge, without my permission. B & E. Simple." He gathered the photos in a nice stack, pissed she didn't flinch at the sight of them.

Becca gazed up at him, her face transforming into a portrait of innocence. Her eyes wide, her mouth soft and sweet like a child's. "But Officer, I was trying to find my friend. She called me extremely upset because a guy refused to let her leave his house. I rushed over as fast as possible. She sounded really desperate. So, of course, I'm on his security camera. I was on a rescue mission." She dropped the innocent act as she said the last word, giving him an ugly sneer.

"And you think they'll buy it?" he asked, unsure himself. One little spin, one little story his word against hers. Fuck. He kept his face a stone mask as his heart fell.

"You have your version. I have mine. Who are they going to believe? A young woman who works hard at her little retail job, making ends meet. And you…" She waved a hand at him. "You're under investigation. Your name's in the paper quite a bit. Everyone in town knows you're a bad guy." The smirk appeared again. He strained not to slap it off her face.

"You think because of the IRS investigation that the police won't believe me?" He sounded skeptical, but she made a good point. The vibe around town wasn't positive. Thankfully, he managed to avoid any kind of confrontation with the police recently, no tickets, no problems at the bars. It might go down differently now versus a few months ago.

"I know it, Alan Reid. The town hates you. I've got no name, no rep, and Marley looks like a lost puppy. I cry foul over her, and the cops will be all over you. Show your pictures and see what happens."

He adjusted, trying to clear his discomfort. "But Marley…"

"Again, you're not getting it, honey. I own her. Marley will say and do what I tell her to do." The last remnants of decency disappeared from the woman across from him. In an instant, she became a hardened criminal, versed in street language, a survivor. For one brief second, the water covered his head.

No.

This punk had nothing over him. Conrad taught him well, his reputation not complete dirt yet, and somewhere someone held a police file on this woman under some name.

She tossed her head back in triumph. "You're strapped for cash, but we can work something out, weekly, monthly, whatever is best. And don't worry, I'll take care of Marley for you."

Her words twisted like a knife in his chest. Anger boiled up, and he caught fire. Easing out a breath to contain the molten emotions bubbling inside him, Alan licked his lips. His fingers twitched to grip the woman's neck. Hurt his Marley? Take care of her? *Ah, no*.

Flexing his fingers to restore the blood flow, he said a simple, "Huh."

Becca studied him. "Got another card, big boy?" She laughed and stood, brushing the photo folder to the far end of the table.

"Actually, I do," he said, relieved his voice sounded calm and as hard as granite. He produced a second folder from below the table. "I found some information even more interesting than the security camera pictures." Making a production, he opened the thick folder and handed a single page up to Becca.

"What the hell is this?" she asked, glancing over the page of numbers.

"The printed file appears impressive by the sheer amount of paper it produces. But to see the real scope of it, Excel works best. The spreadsheet is enormous, hundreds of pages, each box filled with tons of information. A database might be better, but, for your purposes, the Excel file works."

She balled up the page and tossed it back at him. "Good for you, little man. A page of numbers." She put her hands on her hips, trying to look amused, but doubt flickered in her gaze.

"Yes, hundreds of them. I didn't print the whole thing." He rested a hand on the new folder. "Every bit of data about your operation. It's fascinating to see all the names, the money passing through your hands. I don't know why you aren't a millionaire by now. What did you do with the money?"

Becca's brow furrowed, her mouth turned down. "What?" He'd knocked back her again. *Good.* Repressing a grin, he pushed the folder over.

"Take a gander. It's all there. Your marks, your bank accounts, your various aliases." He flipped a few pages. "It's fascinating reading."

She narrowed her gaze, obviously not believing. Pulling the folder toward him, a new element entered her expression, almost like fear.

"Now I have the digital copy in several forms on several devices," he said taking his phone from his pocket. "It translates well." He turned the screen to show her. "And thankfully the file isn't large. I can email it if necessary."

She stared at him, her face ashen. "This isn't…" She collected herself and snapped back to her usual demeanor. "It must've taken you days to make that shit." She pushed the pages away as if they dripped with poison.

"Come on, Becca," he said, turning pages. "You can see the truth here. This is your operation on paper and"—he tapped his phone—"digital. The bunko squad'd love to have the file." He winked at her.

"Where the fuck did you…" Her words petered as the realization hit her. Scowling hard, she hunched over the table. "She gave it to you? That bitch. I'll…"

"Uh, ah, there, Becca. Let's rethink. I have asked you several times to end your relationship with Marley. I offered you money. You turned me down. I threatened you with the police, and you scoffed."

She tried to collect herself, "Yeah same deal with the police on this bullshit. They won't believe any better with papers and computer files. You still got nothing."

Her expression crumbled, fear peeking through her confident air. Now for the last nail in the coffin. "You may be right. The police might not believe me even if I use both sets of evidence against you. But"—he scrubbed his chin—"the press might love it."

A roaring silence engulfed them. Alan folded his hands, the folders on one side, the phone on the other. A parade of emotions ran across Becca's face. She said nothing for minutes. He waited. If she didn't understand the levels he'd sink to protect Marley, then he'd failed here. Perhaps even made things worse.

After two minutes of silence, he spoke quietly, softly, trying not to add insult to the injury. Blackmail was not his bag but for Marley, worth it. "So, I'll ask you again. Please leave Marley alone. Stay out of her life, cut ties with her. Your relationship is over. Am I clear?"

Becca stood, indignation coloring her cheeks. Her eyes appeared teary. "This isn't over." Her words shook slightly, and he wondered if she'd ever failed at a game before.

"Yes, it is," he said quietly. "We're done here." He slid out of the booth, gathering up his materials. He made a show of straightening his jacket and putting his phone away. "You can keep these, if you wish." He held out the files.

She smacked his hand, causing the pages and the photos to flutter to the floor. Alan observed the action, detached. Not caring. But she finally burst with anger. "You asshole, you can't touch me. You can't do a thing to me. And Marley…"

Alan stepped forward until only a hairsbreadth of space lay between them. "And Marley's no longer in the game. She's done." He pulled the phone out and flashed it at her. "If you can't accept it, I send the file. Touch one hair on her head and you're finished."

He walked to the counter and handed the cashier triple his bill. Coffee was cheap but leaving the mess impolite. But it *c'est la vie*. He wasn't going to bend and clean up after Becca. *Not now, not ever.*

Chapter Ten

Jex wasn't so bad. Being her personal assistant, housemaid, and stooge for the a week or two was doable. If Alan failed in his plan, she'd be on the next bus out of town anyway. Jex wasn't her first choice of roommate, but Becca blacklisted Marley all over town. And she'd never ask Alan to crash at his place.

She'd briefly considered calling or texting him. But they'd struck a deal and promised many impossible things. He'd never be able to deliver anyway.

The blame landed squarely on her shoulders. Once she recognized him, she should've walked. The press still hounded him, his partner unavailable, and his hands full holding the bag. He didn't want to be seen with some young trampy con artist in his own home. The press would murder him. Better it ended without further scandal.

Sitting at Jex's kitchen table, her new roomie laid out her rules.

"Look, Marley. I understand why you didn't come to me before. Troy and I are still tight and you're gonna have ta deal with it. If you can't, you gotta go. You feel me?" Hand on a cocked hip, Jex wagged her finger. "Don't break up my sitch because you can't handle."

Marley squirmed in her seat. She hated the submissive roll her so-called friends always put her in.

They always underestimated her, treated her like a child because of her short stature. Of course, she hadn't found any real friends since she left home, only a series of users and losers. Like Jex. A place to crash and nothing more. And if Troy came around, Marley'd make herself scarce.

"Becca's not gonna come 'round here, is she?" Jex continued. "I do not want that bitch in my house."

Marley swung her legs back and forth. Realizing it was a childish gesture, she stopped immediately. "No, Becca and I are done. I grabbed my stuff and moved out. Apparently, I failed her when I messed up this one game." She rolled her eyes to emphasize the ridiculousness.

"What'd you do?" Jex crossed her arms, probably regretting allowing Marley to stay.

Standing to increase her stature, she said, "I refused to rob an old man for her. He had zero cash. So not worth the trouble. Becca disagreed." She shrugged, mirroring Jex's previous pose, hand on cocked hip, attitude all over.

"Fine. But you're paying rent if you're staying here. It's due on the fifteenth. Put in your share or you are outta here. Got it?"

Marley nodded. Deep down, she'd known Jex'd never let her stay out of the goodness of her heart. And four days to come up with the cash? Maybe she'd hit the bars on Thursday night. Plenty of college kids out without a clue how to keep their money safe. An image of Alan rose in her mind. He'd be disappointed if she resumed her life of crime. Maybe an actual job might be best.

But without credentials, retail or waiting tables

were her only choices. ID was key. Maybe Jex had some docs she could borrow to create a new identity. Something smart and classy, like Alan.

Jex appeared satisfied with Marley's simple answer. "You wanna hit the clubs tonight? I can loan you something to wear, long as you take care of it. If we dress right, we won't have to buy a single drink. But if you're gonna run a game, I want in. Free money never hurts."

"Um, sure." Rubbing up against some club hotties might help her forget Alan. She pictured him in one of the downtown clubs. He'd be at a back private area, sitting on a couch, sexy and powerful, watching the dancers. She licked her lips at the image.

"We ain't gonna have that kinda roommate relationship, Marley," Jex said breaking into Marley's fantasy.

"Oh no, uh, no." Marley stuttered, embarrassed, her cheeks blazing. Some of the girls traded sexual favors for rooms, but she'd avoided the whole situation. "Just thinking of a hookup from this week. Hot guy." She shrugged

"Details!" Jex said, hopping onto the couch, her eyes wide with mischief. She'd forgotten Jex's burning desire for any gossip.

"No one special. A one nighter." She lied, shrugging her off. Jex didn't need to know about Alan. She searched ruthlessly for a sugar daddy. Probably why she allowed Marley, who attracted all sorts of men, to stay. Jex had always played it up. When they went clubbing together, Jex always ended up with some Romeo to take home.

Marley glanced around the apartment, sparsely

furnished without a single electronic device. With no roommate for rent help, Jex probably pawned stuff. No wonder she'd already suggested a night out. She needed a payday.

Changing the subject, Marley asked, "Where do you want to go tonight?" The answer—the same as always. Jex maintained one hunting ground.

"Steel, so don't look too much like a 'ho. My clothes'll be big on you so…" Jex twirled her fingers.

Marley shrugged, playing little girl again. "Why don't you pick out my outfit then we can plan our night." She smiled sweetly though a greasy sensation formed in her chest. Why did she continue to live her life this way? There had to be an exit door here somewhere. The ticket to Buffalo or Albany sounded better by the minute. Anywhere but here.

But Alan's promise…Grinding her teeth, she resigned to the deadline. If it worked, she'd be with Alan, right? Hope didn't spark in her chest. He stood no chance against Becca. Marley'd run rabbit in a few days. Bus ticket and rent money tonight. She sighed, knowing she'd have to dip into her criminal skills one last time.

****

They hit the club at about 11:30 when the school kids—high school and college alike—vacated, leaving only serious clubbers. Marley really hated the scene. The loud music, the bodies crushing against each other, the icky old men trying to pick up the girls. But she loved to dance. And even if she had to endure wandering fingers and the smell of sweat to do it, she planned to dance her ass off and work off some of the stress from her crappy week.

Glancing down at her outfit, a crop top with a shredded skirt, she wondered if she was too old for clubbing. She thought of sitting with Alan in the booth at the Tavern, drinking whiskey from heavy glasses. Classy and adult. Right now, she resembled a slutty Barbie.

The huge stone building which housed Steel loomed over her as she stepped out of Jex's beater. Music pounded in the air, the sidewalk full of drunks and players. She pulled in a deep breath. Maybe this wasn't such a good idea.

"Come on," Jex said, pulling at her coat. "I know the bouncer." She dragged Marley up the door, and the bouncer waved them in immediately. Inside the rhythm intensified, hitting Marley like a wall. Her doubts disappeared as her body automatically moved to the music.

"I want a drink," Jex shouted in her ear. Marley nodded and pointed to the dance floor. Jex rolled her eyes and waved her away.

Marley let the beat take over and dove into the frenzy of bodies gyrating on the tiny dance floor. All worries and cares fled from her head as she lost herself in the heavy beat.

****

Marley sagged on the bar, panting and laughing. Jex hip-checked her into a bar stool.

"Damn, you still got some moves," Jex said, waving down the bartender.

"You say that like I'm an old lady." Marley spun, putting her elbows on the bar behind her. The place was rocking, bodies wall to wall. The energy of the place poured into her, making her feel vital and young. Well, younger. Twenty-three was not old.

"You *are* an old lady," Jex teased as the bartender floated toward them. Jex raised her hand to order, but Marley nudged her.

"Thought we weren't paying for our drinks tonight." She narrowed her gaze at Jex and attempting a serious frown and failing. She was too high on the music and dancing.

"Oh, yeah." Jex's shoulders fell as she mimicked Marley's pose. "Well, then you find a hottie to buy for us, because I'm thirsty." She spit out the last words out like she'd been in the desert for forty days.

"I'd love to buy you two beautiful ladies a drink," a smooth baritone voice sounded next to them. The hair on the back of Marley's neck stood up straight. She closed her eyes as her heart started pounding.

No. No. *No.*

"Hey, Troy," Jex purred. "Long time." She spun in a smooth silky motion, pouring herself over a tall, handsome, dark-haired man, Marley's ex. The last man on Earth she wanted to see. Happiness drained out of her like a deflating balloon. She set her expression to dead and said nothing.

"Hello, sweet ladies." Troy pulled Marley in under his right arm while Jex curled into his left.

Bile rose in Marley's throat, but she kept her mouth shut. Teaming up with Jex didn't always mean running into Troy. She rolled the dice tonight and lost. She'd live with it. One night, one drink. Then she'd scuttle to Jex's place and hide in the bathroom until he left.

Jex whispered sweet, silly talk in his ear while Troy got the bartender's attention. Marley's stomach churned with trepidation, and she slowly pulled away. The sick feeling running down her throat demanded she leave, now. Being near him brought back too many ugly images. Most of the time she'd been with him—only a few weeks in total, she'd been high off her rocker, thanks to him. He always carried some "candy" for his girl. Out on the street, before he entered her life, she'd never tried drugs. Not once.

Troy, handsome and charming, swooped in and knocked an innocent girl off her feet. Scratch that, she wasn't innocent—living on the street, conning for money. But she never used. Troy came in like a superhero, saving the day. And if she did what he asked, she'd receive a treat. At first, she tried to keep her distance, but he'd worn her down in short order. The food, the shelter, the drugs too tempting.

After two weeks of constant partying, sex and getting high, she was like a different person. A person she hated. She'd worked hard to keep herself off the streets since she'd run away at sixteen. She'd been sober and never resorted to any gross ways of earning money. Panhandling and picking pockets worked for income. Live in the moment and stay safe had been her motto.

Until beautiful Troy walked into her life. She completely swooned over him like some junior high school girl. Charming to a fault, kind and caring, he seemed perfect. Marley swallowed hard remembering some of the things she'd done with and for Troy. Her chest tightened at the thought of falling down the black hole again.

She managed to slip out from under his arm without resorting to violence. He formed his classic sourpuss face. "Now, why you wanna go do that?" His arm snaked off Jex's shoulder as he turned his full attention to Marley. When he turned his back on Jex, she flashed the stink-eye at Marley. Jex and Troy had been on again, off again for years. Jex cursed Marley's name the few weeks she'd dated him.

With a bitter taste in her throat, Marley realized what a terrible mistake she'd made in going to Jex. Hell, the shelter with the screaming kids and sad sacks might have been better. Asking Alan, though she'd sworn off him, also a better choice. Time to leave.

"'Scuse me, guys. I'm gonna hit the ladies." Marley flashed a tight smile, stepping away from Troy. The crowded club thwarted her, making her retreat miniscule. Troy grabbed her arm before she moved more than a foot away.

"Don't leave on my account." Troy's silver-tongued words poured over her, and for a half a second, she wondered why she thought about leaving. He was hypnotic. "I came over to say hello to my two favorite girls." His thousand-watt smile beamed, and she blinked, clearing her mind.

An image of drinks with Alan rose in her mind, a real man. Alan understood how to treat a woman right, even if she didn't come from the same side of town. Favorite, yeah right. "Favorite? We haven't spoken in a long time, Troy. Let's keep it that way. Hang with Jex if you want, but I'm outta here."

He stepped closer to her, and, for a panicked moment, she feared he might put his hands on her, again. He'd never been one for a public display of violence, but a year can change anyone. Marley shrank in her tiny frame. His touch placed a steel band around her chest, squeezing the life out of her. She cursed her small stature. People assumed they could intimidate or boss her around like a child. Her gaze darted from side to side, searching for an escape route.

"Hey, it's okay," he said, but he didn't let go of her arm. "Just being friendly, trying to put the past behind us. But if you don't wanna hang, it's cool." Guilt, Troy's favorite weapon. But at least he finally released her arm.

Tucking her hands to her chest, Marley slouched, her hair falling over one eye. Jex simmered behind Troy, vying for his attention. He was all smiles and graciousness. Why did she always play the bumbling idiot around him? Why did she allow him to make her feel less than?

"No, it's cool. You and Jex hang." She nodded to her roommate. "I'll see you later."

Jex threw her hands up and rolled her eyes. "Why you gotta be a drama queen? Let him buy us a drink. It's no big deal."

Marley swallowed hard, feeling like an ungrateful bitch. Jex saw everything that happened between Troy and her, but she apparently didn't think it a big deal.

"Fine. One drink," she conceded. "But that's it."

"You still like sex on the beach?" He waggled his eyebrows at her, and the band across her chest tightened.

She grunted in disgust, but before she could leave, Troy grabbed her arm again. "Chill out, little Miss. I'll buy you both a drink and be off." He winked at Jex and bellied up to the bar.

Marley's nerves danced with trepidation. Changed or not, Troy was still a sweet-talker. Her concern stemmed from his ability to charm any woman into anything. She'd seen him make the most uninterested girl beg to go home with him. The games exhausted her. Plus, she feared she'd fall for it. Tension tightened her shoulders, and she wished she and Alan actually stood a chance.

Marley waited, a step or two away from the bar. The constant jostling of the crowd against her much more pleasant than sitting at the bar with Troy. Crossing her arms, she wondered if he'd notice if she bolted.

Taking a deep breath, she scoped out an escape plan. Being short helped her hide in the crowd and avoid the awkwardness. Then to Jex's place, she'd pack her things again and find another acquaintance to take her in. Look for a real job, her own apartment. Maybe…

"There you are, my sweet." Troy's voice brought her attention back to the bar. Two vodka drinks sat on the bar with little umbrellas sticking out. "Enjoy, ladies." He bowed deeply.

Marley rubbed the nape of her neck, heat in her cheeks. Evidently, he actually meant one drink. He walked away with a lightness in his step, not easy in the packed club. Marley's stupid meter hit eleven. She slogged her steps back to the bar.

"Why you gotta be like that, Mar? He's just being nice, not asking you out. Nothing. You overreact to everything." Jex grabbed a drink and took a healthy sip. "Troy's trying to heal old wounds. Maybe don't be a bitch." She huffed, raising her chin in the air. "You're such a snob for a street kid." She drank again, licking her lips.

"You two together again?" Marley asked, grabbing her glass.

Jex puffed air through her lips. "No. I've got better prospects, but I'm not refusing a free drink." She pursed her lips, staring pointedly at Marley.

"Sorry I'm a snob," she snarked, twirling the umbrella. She stared down at the drink as if it were some unknown substance.

"See? Look at you, turning your nose up at free because you and Troy are quits. Are you happy or pissed he don't want you anymore?" Jex smirked, then downed more of her drink, the tumbler half empty already. Marley hadn't touched hers.

"No," she said quietly into her glass. She took a taste, sighing as she watched the crowd. A free drink was a free drink. She sipped through the tiny straw. Not bad but a little bitter. She glanced down the bar, not recognizing any of the bartenders. Of course, she hadn't been here in months. These places usually turned over fast.

A stray thought wandered through her mind. Did Alan own this place before the IRS witch hunt? She swayed back and forth slowly, glancing around taking in everything, weight lifting from her shoulders.

Jex wandered off. Marley offered her a pageant wave as she left. Not that Jex saw her. Jex beelined for a solid eight, rubbing against him provocatively as they danced. Marley's head flopped to the side, a silly smile forming on her lips as she watched her friend dance. *Oh, fun.* She sipped her drink, feeling no pain.

Marley twirled, taking in the entire club. The atmosphere thrilled her. The glittery lights and music spun around her in voluminous circles. She put her half-empty glass on the barstool and dashed into the dancing crowd, light as a feather and carefree.

She gyrated in a wild frenzy, sliding from partner to partner. She didn't care who she danced with. Sweat poured down her in the tight pack of bodies. Everything seemed a bit fuzzy, but alcohol usually affected her that way. She was a lightweight drinker. Look at what happened with Alan.

Mmmm. Alan. She spun in place, dreaming about the tall handsome hunk. Those nice suits hid his body well. She could still call him. He still wanted her after all, but he fell in the forbidden fruit category.

She slammed into someone hard. Troy. She blinked.

"Hey there," he said, sounding slick over the loud music. "I forgot you were such a machine on the floor."

Marley giggled. "I'm a machine everywhere, Troy." She stumbled against him, swinging her hips, her feet flying.

Troy moved with her as they'd done a thousand times. Exactly how they met. A fast and furious dance. Then a quickie in his car. Maybe. Probably. Marley didn't remember clearly. Vodka always went right to her head. Some Russian she was. Grandma would be ashamed. She laughed aloud, imagining Babushka at the club.

"Having fun, my sweet?" he asked, suddenly close to her ear. His body pressed against her as they tangoed, heat radiating up and down.

Marley wavered on her heels. The heat in the club scorched her face and arms, the lights too bright. She slowed her pace, leaning on Troy. He floated with her, his body pressed against her and for some reason, it didn't bother her.

His mouth pressed against her ear. "How you doin', baby?" He wrapped his arms around her, swaying to his own rhythm.

The contrast between the music's beat and Troy's dance movement jarred Marley. Her stomach turned as an epiphany slowly dawned on her. She held her arms out on either side of Troy to see both. They appeared too long and slightly wavy. Glancing up at the lights rainbows radiated from spotlights. Her stomach heaved.

She was high.

Chapter Eleven

How did this happen? She'd been drug-free since dumping Troy. Withdrawal had sucked, but Becca swooped in and rescued her. Jex assured her a clean apartment as Jex herself was on the wagon. Marley drank occasionally but not much. A couple whiskeys with Alan and one sex on the beach tonight…

Her mind clicked. The drink. The drink Troy purchased.

Gasping, she glanced up to see his huge, predatory grin. His guilt colored his expression on tones of gold and red. Desperately, she searched for Jex. Had her friend's drink been spiked too? The band on her chest reappeared, squeezing the life out of her.

The room spun in slow circles, everything too bright and unfocused. Such a contrast to how she felt when she hit the dance floor. What was in the drink? Placing her hands on Troy's chest, she pushed back against his hold.

"What's the matter?" he asked, his hyena smile wide and toothy. "You wanna find a booth to sit?" One of his arms gripped her shoulders tight as he spun her toward the private booths.

Her heart beat out of her chest. She dug her heels into the dance floor. Being alone with him was the last thing she wanted. She blinked away blurry tears. Her head whipped right and left searching for an exit. Troy's hold on her shoulder tightened.

Her stomach lurched. Her mouth dried. Fight or flight kicked in through the drugged-haze. Marley screamed at the top of her lungs, stopping one or two dancers near her. Grasping his arm, she bit Troy, trying to get her teeth to meet. He hurled his arm away from her, with a curse and an unmanly scream.

Her drugged state helped her now. Her sweat covered body easy slipped from his grasp. She stumbled through the crowd, begging for assistance.

"I need some help, some air. Someone help me."

The Steel patrons regularly witnessed drug-induced paranoia, and many of them laughed as they helped her along to a rear exit. But no one walked out with her. No one stopped dancing, and they held her up as she blundered toward the door. Her short stature hid her well in the crowd, and she made a clean exit out the back of the club.

The door slammed with a thunderous boom behind her. Marley staggered a few feet down the alley, using the brick wall to guide her. Her head spun, her body weak. She had to escape from Troy as fast as possible. The end of the alley looked a thousand miles away. Drawing in a deep breath, she started down the dark stretch.

Another crash sounded behind her—the door hitting the brick wall—and her blood froze. She glanced behind her. A man stood silhouetted in the open club door. Facing the end of the alley again, she resumed slogging to the street, her feet like cement bricks.

Maybe it's not him, she rationalized. Maybe it's

some good Samaritan come to help me. Then he called her name, and her heart sank in her chest.

****

Exiting his house, Alan pulled his phone from his pocket and stared at it. The indicator light on his phone flashed, red. Text message? Every thought sludged through frozen mud today. His body dragged from too many hours at the tavern. Tension from all the meetings with accountants and lawyers bit into his shoulders. Not to mention the loneliness since a cute Russian girl left his life. And his bed.

With little enthusiasm, he clicked his phone on. Apparently, a red light meant a low battery, not a text as he'd hope. Clicking the phone, he closed his eyes, letting fresh pain wash over him. He trusted Conrad implicitly, never thought for one second his best friend of ten years would hurt him, burn their business to the ground. Blowing out a breath, he took a step toward his car.

He slumped into the car seat, phone still in hand. The whole situation was still a chaotic mess. Everyday things twisted into more complicated situations and scenarios. What was his responsibility in finding Conrad, other than being his best friend and worried sick about him? Cash for a private detective might empty the coffers completely.

The police weren't on their case, but the situation contained a big YET. His lawyer, Jason Demeck, warned him at the onset of possible criminal charges over the missing money. Conrad tended to be bold, sometimes flakey. He epitomized confidence, jumping into situations without a parachute a dozen times. And he always, always came up smelling like a rose. His brass ones must've weighed a ton. In his mind, he was never wrong, so he never hesitated, never second-guessed himself.

Occasionally, Conrad disappeared for a few days but never this long. Never without an email, text, or drunken phone call at three am. Alan had spent too many nights, since the shit hit the fan, waiting for a call or something. But Conrad remained in the wind. It'd been long enough, Alan considered calling hospitals and morgues.

For all his impulsive, arrogant actions, Conrad was never subtle nor secretive. Alan glanced at the red light blinking on his phone again. Conrad wouldn't text now. He'd call or show up. Alan started the car, heading back to the tavern to cover for a sick waiter.

****

Outside Steel, Troy caught Marley easily. Her perception of the length of the alley, the lighting, and timing was off. He snatched her arm and spun her around. The club door slowly closed yards away. She hadn't gotten far.

"Marley, you okay? Why'd you run off?" He wrapped his arms around her, pulling her close. "You worried me, my sweet. Let's take you home."

"No," Marley said, her voice no more than a croak. Whatever he'd given her was either wearing off, leaving her spent or she was having a super bad trip. She licked her lips, swallowing hard. Her second "no" came out stronger, but Troy ignored her, as usual, pissing her off more.

"Why you running from me, my sweet? We always had such a good time before." He pressed her against the brick wall, her thin skirt useless to protect her skin.

"I've missed you."

Squirming in his arms, she tried to free herself, to find an escape route. She cried in pain as his fingers pressed into her thin arms. The fight inside her died, her bones like glass, ready to shatter if he squeezed any harder.

She gasped for breath. Her legs faltering as her vision narrowed and spun. She squeezed her eyes shut to stop the rocking. "Let me go," she managed weakly, hoping to appeal to his sense of pity. She blinked up at him through her thickly mascaraed lashes. "And I'll go with you."

Troy narrowed his gaze. "Oh really? Why do I hear another filthy lie dropping from your lips? You're always lying to me. A man gets tired." He leaned in, his mouth close to her ear. "You do what I say, you lying bitch. Because I know the protesting is just another one of your con games."

Marley twisted her shoulders, hoping to pull away from him. She only succeeded in scraping her back up against the wall. She hissed in pain. Even with her head full of fuzz, talking remained the best way out of the situation.

"Me a liar? You spiked my drink." She glared at him, steel pouring into her spine. "How'd you know I'd take the drugged one?"

He laughed, a low chuckle sounding like every supervillain in the comic books. "What makes you think I only hit one drink? I needed payment from one of you two hoes tonight. You're easier to catch."

Marley's temper flared. She hated being the victim, hated the bullying she'd endured since she was four years old. She pulled in a deep breath and spit in Troy's face.

"Bitch," he growled and slammed her against the wall, his fingers like a vice on her arms. Her head connected with the brick and floating stars replaced the cotton in her head. She swooned.

"Who do you think you are? Coming back in my turf and flaunting your tight little ass to everyone in the club? They know you wronged me, and now you're putting on a show. Not in my club, girl." He slammed against the wall again. Marley turned her head, letting her ear take the brunt of the impact.

Moaning, she leaned to the side. The ear stung like a bastard, and her head throbbed. She needed to escape somehow. Troy was out for blood and maybe something more. She leaned in putting her weight on her right foot. Waiting for him to be distracted.

"If you're here, then you're mine." He readjusted his grip, one hand holding her wrist, the other wrapping his hand around her thigh. His fingers dug in tight.

"Let go of me," she screamed, trying to use her free hand to gouge his eyes. He smashed her back into the wall again. The motion threw her off balance, and she grabbed his arm to keep upright.

His fingers crept up her leg, and her blood solidified into ice. *He wouldn't.* A scary guy when mad, but Troy was no—His hand slid further up—or maybe he was. His fingers scraped along her thigh. A piercing shriek escaped her lips as she realized Troy was far more dangerous than she assumed.

Thrashing violently against him, she no longer cared about scratching up her back or her wrist still tight in his grip. She had to get free. She hadn't given him any kind of permission. And never would. She'd bite his nose off before she allowed him to violate her.

"What's the matter, little girl? Don't like playing grown-up games anymore?" His purr sounded threatening. She flailed. Disgust and anger consumed her. She kicked him with all her might. The heel of her shoe digging into his shin. His grip on her wrist loosened, but Troy's other hand stayed clasped to the top of her leg.

She glanced desperately to either end of the alley, hoping someone heard her cries. Terror filled her throat until she was drowning. But both sides of the alley stayed dark and empty.

"Oh, you got some spunk, little girl," he hissed. She'd hurt him. *Good.* "And I'm gonna make you pay." Panic layered inside her as she gazed around for anything weapon-like. Something, anything. But she only had her own hands.

His fingers on her leg dug in. She gasped from the pain, red-hot and excruciating. Tears threatening, she begged him to stop. He wasn't finished. With his free hand, he wrenched her trapped wrist, forcing a scream from her lips. Something inside her clicked.

She couldn't stop him. He was too powerful and now seriously pissed. Squashing down the blind panic, she tried to think. Her mind whirled. *Must escape.* The indignity, the insult of Troy's hands on her body lit a fire inside her. Through the red haze, she focused on one thought—payback.

With everything she had left, she grabbed the hand on her leg, forcing him to relent. He didn't budge. She sank her nails into his wrist, tearing and clawing. They scuffled, Marley screaming the entire time, pouring her fear out in every syllable. His fingers raked her thighs as they fought.

"Cunt," he growled, anger pouring out of him in palpable waves. He yanked her forward until they stood face to face. Her legs dangled inches from the ground. She gouged her nails into his arm. Warm wetness touched her fingertips, and she snapped her teeth on his earlobe.

Pain exploded in her head. The world darkened at the edges. Her body became a weighty sack. Her screams died to whimpers. And she crumpled against her attacker, helpless.

A shout sounded from far away as the ground rushed up to meet her. Pain exploded in her head and her left wrist. Slowly, she blinked, taking in the detritus of the alley floor. Her gaze focused on an empty soda can—dented and crushed.

That's how I feel.

Vaguely, she heard footsteps running then silence. She waited, gathering her wild thoughts, allowing her heartbeat to slow. But no one spoke. No one came to save her. No one picked her up off the ground.

Typical. Have to save myself.

She dragged her body into a sitting position. Everything screamed. Pausing, she stilled her breath, trying to find the source of the pain. But it was too much. Bleary-eyed, she glanced around. No Troy. No guy on a white horse. She needed to move before the bastard returned. How long had he been gone? Slowly, she gained her feet, her head spinning. Nauseated, she glanced down at her bare feet. *No shoes. Great.*

Anything else missing? She patted her lumpy bra. *Good.* The money and phone were there. She staggered to the end of the alley where a lone light shone on the street's opposite side. The night rolled around her indifferent to her injuries. Her stomach sank.

Bracing against the wall, she scanned the street. Club-goers still lined the building, waiting to enter Steel. Didn't they hear her scream? People milled back and forth between clubs. Taxis and cars whizzed down the street. Where was everyone a minute ago?

A sob rose on her lips as she spotted Troy in the crowd down the block. He headed toward her, fast. How had he gotten over there? No matter. She wasn't waiting around to find out. She dove into the first taxi she found by the club, shoving a couple out of her way. Begging the cabbie to drive away, she ignored the curses hurled from the posh couple.

"Where to, lady?" the driver asked lazily, not glancing at her. Marley's mind spun. Between the drug and the whacks on the head, thinking about anything but getting away from Troy didn't register. She spurted out Alan's address without processing what she'd said.

"Sure, sure." The cabbie pulled into the sparse traffic.

Marley slid down in the seat, exhaustion rolling over her. Her eyes closed, spilling tears down her cheeks. And she fell into darkness.

Chapter Twelve

"Hey, wake up, lady."

Someone shook her shoulders. With great pain, Marley raised her head, blinking. "What?" she asked.

"We're here. Boswell Street, like you said."

"What?" Her voice was a hoarse whisper. Sitting up, she examined her surroundings. The world spun in a slow lazy circle. Streetlights burned her retinas, and some man kept talking on and on.

"Look, lady. You seemed a little desperate so I gave you a lift. I coulda picked up some cherry fares at Steel. Pay me and get out or tell me where to really take you. Because you don't seem to belong here."

Steel—the club she and Jex planned to hit tonight. Did they go there already? She chewed her lip. Where was she? And what happened to Jex…and…Oh, shit.

Troy.

Her head throbbed as a loud hiccup burst from her lips.

"Don't you dare puke in my cab." Rough hands snatched at her. When she shrieked like a banshee, he backed off. "Okay, fine. But get out. Now."

Marley scrambled across the seat away from Mr. Grabby. She stumbled out the far door, landing on her ass in the middle of the street. A car zoomed past her, blaring the horn. Grasping the car door, she lifted herself up and leaned on the cab.

A small man stood on the side of the car, his hand out. What did he want? Her head spun, and she swallowed a noxious wad of saliva.

"The fare?" the man asked, shaking his hand.

"Oh," Marley said aloud, realizing he was the cab driver. Her left wrist screamed in pain when she tried to retrieve the money. Puzzlement filled her as she stared at the unmoving hand. *Why?* The cabbie cleared his throat impatiently. *Oh...yeah...* A mystery for later then.

She fished in her bra and found a crumpled twenty. She handed it to him with overly-long fingers. Were they hers? It was as if they belonged to someone else. They floated before her, depositing the money in the cabbie's outstretched palm.

He closed his fingers over the bill. "Uh." He frowned, smacking his lips. "You sure you don't want me to drop you off at the ER or something."

She tilted her head to the side. Her brain slid over with a squish. "No, why?" She turned away. Holding onto the side panel for support, she staggered around the car to the curb. A row of houses ran along the street, modest buildings all pretty in the city. She smiled up at the moon shining over the tops of the buildings.

"You sure, lady?" the taxi driver called.

She scanned the neighborhood again, impressed by its beauty. Tidy and classy. Her mouth rolled up in a grin as her gaze landed on a red door of a colonial in front of her. She knew the place. The best one on the block. Her house, right?

"Oh yeah," Marley called back. "See the one with the red door. I live there." She teetered toward it.

The cabbie grumbled something like "slumming"

under his breath, but she didn't care.

She was home.

Using the railing as a lifeline, she lurched up the steps. Her left wrist tingled and pulsed at the same time. She leaned against the door frame as a wave of dizziness drifted over her. Something felt off.

She searched for her keys, surprised to find no purse. She wasn't some soccer mom with a fabulous coach bag, but she usually carried…something. She patted her pockets Nothing, not even a pocket. A buzzing noise whispered in her ear. She swatted at it, trying to chase the bug away, but the sound droned on.

"Now what do I do?" she whispered to the buzz. She traced her fingers over the house numbers on the side of the door. Reality slowly dawned on her, and the strength drained from her legs. She sat hard on the stoop, clutching the doorframe with her good arm. The last puzzle piece clicked into place.

Alan's house.

The whole night came speeding back to her in a jumpy, tangled vision. Jex, the club, and Troy. Motherfucker. Her spiked drink and the assault in the alley. And now, she'd fled across town to Boswell Street. To Alan's home. A man she should stay away from.

Some part of her drug-addled mind had imprinted on him. Run to the safety a man like Alan promised.

"I'm such a fool," she sobbed as the tears finally fell. The buzzing in her head rose louder, and she swayed. Her muscles and joints slackened, like in the car. Her vision darkened at the edges again. Passing out on Alan's front steps was the worst thing she could do. He'd find her drunk and drugged, half-dressed and bleeding.

And then he'd know what a true mess she was. Against her better judgment, she shut her eyes and cried hard. Pain and regret rolled over her. Giving herself until the count of five, she sobbed, sitting there on her mark's steps, like a piece of trash.

After she ticked off five fingers, she pulled the fear and self-hatred back, swallowed her tears and sat up. She needed a way out of here. But cabs didn't frequent his neighborhood, and buses were in bed for the night.

Reaching for the railing, she wobbled to her feet to begin the long journey back downtown. With her first step, the world shifted, tilting sideways, and something hit her face. She stared at the horizontal streetlights, wondering how to fix it.

Then everything went black.

Chapter Thirteen

Going back to the tavern usually proved to be a great distraction. He'd helped host and bartend a couple of times. The work took him back to younger days when he'd just started out, not a thirty-something starting over.

But tonight, Alan cursed his rotten luck. He'd been forced to be bouncer then janitor. A dozen drunk college kids burst in near closing time. He'd tried to move them along, ringing for last call a little early to no avail. They nursed last drinks forever. Then three, yes, three of them puked all over the men's room and the entire hallway leading to the bathrooms.

As much as he wanted to vanish and let the other staff handle it, he'd never do that to his employees. They'd taken the pay cut and remained silent when checks came late. They'd stayed with him, nursed the tavern back to health and him as well.

He, Eric, and Angelina cleaned the mess. Toasted each other with a glass of the good stuff afterward, then separated, heading home. Alan waited for both to drive off before he got in his own car. He felt no desire to rush home to an empty house.

He drove the long way, avoiding downtown with the clubs and restaurants he no longer owned. Driving three miles out of his way, he passed Conrad's place.

Something caught his attention, and he swerved to the curb. A flash of light in the window? He sat across the street, staring at the house, waiting, watching. But there was nothing.

The house stood empty for too many weeks. He considered taking a quick walk around the place to ensure no one had broken in. But what would be the point? He sighed long and deep. And the neighbors would probably call the police. More attention he didn't want. Checking traffic, he pulled out again and wandered home.

As he neared the driveway, he cut his headlights to keep them from flashing in Mrs. Marconi's windows. No sense in getting anyone else pissed at him.

"With those crazy hours you keep now," she'd griped. "I never know if it's you coming home or if some maniac is about to slaughter me in my sleep."

Alan didn't point out if she saw the lights, she wasn't asleep. Anyway, he now turned off the lights before he swept into the driveway, a small concession to keep the peace.

He switched off the car, forgoing the garage due to the rattling door. She'd complained about the noise too, told him it sounded like a chainsaw murder coming after her. Alan stopped short of suggesting she refrain watching horror movies. He'd learned the hard way not to engage with her. She shared her opinions on everything.

Trudging up the walk to the front door, he stretched his neck side to side. A satisfying pop sounded as he turned his head to the left. Managing the tavern was a good fallback position, but he was never a man to sit idle. The IRS business was dragging on far too long. He needed Conrad home with an explanation, and he needed…

His foot pressed on something soft, and he jumped back a pace. The kids around the block had been playing ugly pranks on him, leaving dead animals on the steps or in the mailbox. Retrieving his phone, he clicked the flashlight icon. Nothing happened. He turned the phone over to examine the back and the light burst from the phone blinding him.

"Dammit," he cursed holding the phone out, light down. He blinked at the retinal images flashed in front of his eyes.

He rearranged the cellphone to illuminate a lump at the bottom of his steps. Directing the beam down to his feet he saw what he'd stepped on. A petite hand lay on the ground in the circle of light. He shifted the phone higher. The hand was attached to an arm and, in turn, to a compact female with a waterfall of black hair.

"Dammit," he cursed again. Marley was passed out on his lawn…How did she get here? They made a deal, her deal.

He knelt and gently nudged her shoulder. "Marley," he whispered, trying to rouse her and not everyone on the block. "Wake up, love." He should drive her back to her place if she even had a place to live. Dammit, he was tired. And a perfectly good bed waited upstairs.

He touched her again. No response. Sighing, he carefully turned her over. A gasp fell from his lips.

Marley, his Marley, lay sprawled on his steps, blood on her face, hands, and legs. Her left wrist looked dark and misshapen, and her blouse and tiny skirt were torn to shreds.

Dropping to his knees, he cupped her face in his hands. "Marley, honey"—Nothing—"answer me." Adrenaline surged inside him. He stopped himself from grabbing her up and crushing her in his arms. *Don't move her*. Head injury, crime scene, someone lurking in the dark. He flashed his phone around, ensuring her attacker didn't lurk in the shadows.

He checked her pulse. A steady rhythm of beats pressed against his fingers. Lowering his head to her mouth, he heard slow breaths puff from her lips. A sigh of relief escaped him. He juggled his phone, nine-one-one the next logical choice.

"I don't know if you can hear me, Marley, but help is on the way." His hands shook as he attempted to pull up the phone app. The flashlight clicked on and off, creating a strobe effect on Marley. The light caused her injuries to appear more gruesome.

"Enough!" He clenched the phone tight in his hand, causing the case to creak ominously. *She needs me*. Breathing slowly, he pushed a stray piece of hair from her forehead. The lock refused to move, cemented to her ear with blood.

He shut his eyes, willing away the worry building in his gut. "I've got you, Marley," he whispered and hit 911. "Yes, I need an ambulance at…"

Marley started. Her hand flailing for his, she managed to pull the phone from his ear. "No." The word, no more than a whisper, sounded like steel.

Chapter Fourteen

"No?" Alan sat back stunned. He cupped her chin. "I have too, love. You're in bad shape."

Tears spilled down her cheeks. "No," she sobbed. "No, you can't. Let me go home." She attempted to sit up, but he put a hand on her arm, keeping her down. With unexpected strength, she shoved his hand off her. In a low pained voice, she gasped. "Don't. Touch. Me."

Alan stared at her, unsure. "Okay," he said with caution, drawing his hand back. "You're hurt. Your head…there's blood." A lump rose in his throat and he choked it down. He stared at her, considering and dialed 911 again.

Marley swatted at him, trying to take the phone, but he slid back out of her reach. A dull ache pulsed in his head, watching her struggle, but he didn't relent. He spoke to the operator in short clipped tones, relating his address and the situation.

"Can you describe the nature of her injuries?" The operator's bored voice caused him to wince. The woman should be more concerned. Marley, the woman…a girl who…he searched for the right term. Someone he cared about was lying broken on his lawn.

"Look," he said, standing. The ache in his head continued to pulse. "There's blood, a lot, on her head. Her hand seems…wrong. Can you just send someone?"

He poured every ounce of authority in him into the question, transforming the sentence into a demand.

"Sir," the operator intoned. "An ambulance is on the way." He swore he heard a muffled yawn. "Any information I can relay to the EMTs is helpful." Alan grunted in understanding, but his temper didn't mellow a bit. "Who am I speaking with?"

"Alan Reid. You have my address. What more do you need?" He paced the lawn, never straying far from Marley.

"The Alan Reid?" she asked, her tone ugly.

"Yes." He gritted his teeth.

"Are you the reason the woman is injured?" It was the last straw.

"Someone I care about is lying on my lawn, hurt." He stopped pacing and peered down at Marley. She curled in a ball, weeping openly. His heart lurched in his chest as the ache in his head deepened. He sank down on his knees again, hovering over her, protecting her. "I don't know if a car hit her or she fell down the steps. I need someone to get their ass here now and help this girl."

He dropped the phone and gathered her in his arms. Weakly, she resisted, but the fight seemed to have left her. She whimpered, and he shushed her, whispering assurance as he lifted her into his lap. At first, her body felt stiff as if she were fighting him, but after a minute she relented, curling into his chest. She dozed off in his arms. A numbness stole over him as he watched her breath.

An ambulance and police car arrived a few minutes later. Alan had a hard time releasing her when the EMTs moved in to examine her. His brain screamed to protect her, his heart aching. Finally, he opened his arms and gently set her down on the ground. The harsh light from the police car and the ambulance lit his lawn like daylight, and he finally took a good look at her.

Blood matted her hair, and her wrist appeared swollen and bruised. Alan's gaze skimmed over her body, each injury causing his headache to magnify. Then he saw bruises forming on her arms and thighs. Dried blood ran from under her skirt in long lines down her legs. He gasped, staggering backward. The ambulance guys peered at her legs, at Alan then back to Marley.

"I found her on my steps," he said in a rushing gasp. "I would never. I…I love her. I'd never hurt her."

"Who would?" a voice asked behind him. Alan swiveled around to the police officer standing there, pen and paper in hand. The dark-skinned man was tall, bulky, and damned intimidating. "Alan Reid, right?" He said the name with such contempt, but Alan ignored him.

"I don't…I don't know," he stuttered, realizing how bad everything looked. He glanced around. His neighbors filed out of their houses in bathrobes and pajamas. Most crossed their arms, ugly expressions on their faces. For the first time since the whole IRS story broke, Alan didn't care what those fuckers thought.

He stood, glancing down at the man's nametag, Officer Smith, before staring him square in the eye. "I came home a short while ago, maybe five minutes." Only five? It seemed an eternity. "I found Marley on my walk, out cold."

"And, where were you?" The cop jotted something down in his notebook.

Alan stared at Smith for a moment, keeping his face as blank as possible. "I was at the Oakwood Tavern until after closing, cleaning up a mess. I'd be happy to give you the contact information for my employees who assisted me."

Smith narrowed his gaze. "Got your alibi set then."

Alan squared his shoulders. "I'll answer your questions. If you want to accuse me, then accuse me. I'll tell you flat out I did not harm Marley. I found her this way."

"Uh, huh." Smith wrote in his notebook again.

His partner washed his flashlight around the lawn near the steps. "Blood pool on the steps, Smith," he called. "Little puddle, as if she sat here or something. Smears on the door frame."

"We'll need to look inside the house," Smith said, slapping the notebook shut. Alan glared but didn't move. He had no desire to babysit the police as they searched his house for an imaginary crime scene. Marley wasn't going to the hospital without him.

"I'll be with her," Alan said, his words firm.

"Because you have such a tight alibi, huh? I should cuff you now," Smith sneered. The overwhelming hate in his gaze set Alan back. He'd faced judgmental people, tons of ugly remarks in the press and on social media. Hell, hadn't it been the reason he taken Marley home the first time, then sought her out again? Because she'd been one of the few people who'd seen him as a victim rather than a bad guy.

Peering into the blazing eyes of the officer, Alan reassessed his position. Smith found him holding a badly beaten young woman, who didn't belong in his neighborhood. *Okay, not good.* But for the first time, he saw outright hatred pointed at him. The level of hostility in Smith's voice flew off the chart.

Alan opened his mouth to speak, but words failed him. He tried to be a good person, a nice neighbor, a gentleman. How could the police officer think he would hurt a woman?

"Yeah, exactly what I thought," Smith said and spun Alan around, grabbing one arm behind his back. The cold metal of a handcuff burned Alan's skin as it slammed closed on his wrist. The pain in his head pulsed, and he winced.

"Officer!" a woman called. "Officer, what do you think you're doing?" His next-door neighbor, Mrs. Marconi, here to save the day. *Great*. Alan hung his head. Not what he needed right now. "You can't arrest, Mr. Reid. He wasn't here when the girl arrived."

Officer Smith paused, not snapping the second cuff in place. Alan's head perked up, and the pain pulses slowed. "Excuse me, ma'am," Smith said moving toward her, dragging Alan with him. "Did you witness something?" Skepticism rang in his voice, but Alan only heard hope. *Thank you, Mrs. Marconi. I promise to buy you black-out blinds when it's over.*

"Yes, Officer," she said, stepping toward him, pulling her pink bathrobe closer around her thin frame. "About 12:50 am, a cab pulled up in front of Mr. Reid's house. The girl"—The woman regarded Marley with a mix of disgust and concern—"fell right out of the car into the street. Then the cab left, and she walked up to the front door." Mrs. Marconi crossed her arms over her chest, giving the cop a sharp nod.

"And how do you know the exact time, ma'am?" More skepticism but Alan repressed a grin. Thank God for nosy neighbors.

She huffed. "Mr. Reid runs a bar. He's never home before 1 a.m. lately. Last call in Iverton is 12:45." Her nose jutted in the air

The cop huffed, tugging on Alan's cuffed hand. "I'm aware, Mrs.?"

"Mrs. Marconi," she said with another tight nod. "If you know who Mr. Reid is, then you're aware he's working to keep his family tavern afloat. He works long hours and comes home late."

"And you know this because?" The cop sounded bored now.

"Because I worry about him. I always knew when he arrived home safe because his headlights flash in my window. They are very bright. Now he turns his lights off before he pulls in his driveway. He's a courteous neighbor."

"Thank you, Mrs. Marconi," Alan said, and Smith tugged on the cuff again. "Ow." Alan let the word fall flat, glaring at Smith who returned his gaze with the same intensity.

"I'm telling you, Officer. Mr. Reid wasn't home when she showed up. She went to the door, and the cab drove off."

Officer Smith edged closer to his neighbor who shrunk in her bathrobe. "You saw the victim arrive." She nodded. "You saw Reid arrive." She nodded again. "But you didn't call an ambulance for the girl?"

Mrs. Marconi's hand fluttered at her neck. "I didn't know she was hurt. She acted odd. I thought she might be drunk. When she fell across the lawn, I assumed she passed out."

Smith focused on Alan. "You have witnesses who

put you at the tavern at 12:50?" Alan nodded, afraid to speak, because a song of praise for his annoying neighbor was ready to burst out of him. He caught her eye. A tight smile flashed on her lips.

"Fine," Smith said, removing the cuff from Alan's wrist. "But I want a full statement from you."

"Absolutely," Alan said, his head swiveling back to Marley, who lay on a backboard with a giant neck brace holding her down. She resembled a tiny doll, a tiny broken doll drowning in medical equipment. He rushed to her, waving a hand at the techs.

"She's only five feet, maybe a hundred plus pounds. You need a smaller…"

"We know what we're doing, Reid," one of them scoffed then muttered something under his breath to his partner, a young blonde woman.

"She is kinda tiny, Joe." The woman examined Marley. "Let's switch out for the kid board. Joe grumbled, disappearing into the back of the ambulance.

"Hey," Smith said, snapping Alan's attention back to him. "We aren't done here."

Alan said nothing as they loaded Marley into the back, the new backboard secured. "You can interview me at the hospital," he said flatly and jogged over to the ambulance. The tech, Joe, blocked him from entering.

"Family only, man."

Alan pointed to Marley. "My girlfriend…and if you think I'm not going…" He let his words trail off, the threat hanging in the air like a hot air balloon. Joe swallowed and slid aside.

Alan hopped in, settling next to Marley. He gathered her hand in his, gently kissing the back. "I'm going to take care of you. I promise."

She slowly blinked huge green eyes. "Hi, Alan," she said. Her voice thick and distorted.

"Hi, love."

"What's going on?"

Quietly, he kissed her hand again. "Road trip."

Chapter Fifteen

Marley's eyes snapped open. A bright white light seared her retinas, and she cringed away from it. Pain erupted from her head, her wrist, her legs. She moaned, bile running up her throat. She'd endured bad hangovers before, but this took the cake.

Blinking hard, she tried to put the room in focus. Her addled mind attempted to place the odd furniture and machinery. Where the fuck was she? She scratched her head, but a cloth covered her ear. She sat up and her vision dimmed as a bomb exploded in her head. She twisted to the side, losing everything left in her stomach.

The door clicked, and the beat of rushing feet sped toward her. "Oh, Mar. Let me call a nurse." A male voice, sweet and sympathetic and sounding like Alan Reid.

Through one cracked lid, she examined the man fussing over her, cleaning up her mess, straightening her covers. "What the fuck?" she asked.

"You're at Iverton General, Mar. You've been out for four hours." He placed her hand in his. The gesture felt oddly reassuring. She blinked blearily as the outline of Alan formed. "You have a couple of bumps on your head." He pushed her hair to the side, gently, but she pulled back, afraid it might hurt.

She focused on his face. Bags sagged under his eyes, his hair rumpled. His usual suit jacket graced his shoulders, sans tie. *Weird.* What was he doing here? Did they hook up last night? She searched her memory but found only a black hole. She remembered dancing, and pain, lots of pain. She withdrew her hand from his.

The door snicked closed again, and a dark-skinned woman in white appeared behind him. "Time to go," she said. "Nurses, doctors, cops got work to do."

He sighed, stood, and squeezed her hand one last time. "I'll be right outside the door if you need anything." And then he disappeared.

"Well there, Miss Marley," the woman with blue-black skin dressed in white said. "Tell me your last name. Your boyfriend there didn't know it." She frowned.

Marley searched her face. She couldn't place the nice woman. *Do I know her?* She licked her lips and asked, "Hamilton?"

"Are you asking me or telling me?"

"Telling?" The pain jumbled her thoughts and feelings into a huge mass, muddling everything. Damn, one drink shouldn't do this. One drink. One Sex on the Beach with Jex. One drink from…Marley's mouth went numb, and she hunched over despite the pain. She retched and gagged until her back hurt.

The woman whispered quiet words of reassurance, while she held a plastic tub under Marley's mouth. After an ugly dry-wretch, she flopped back on the bed, her back aching, her head on fire. The room was blurry, the woman, a white blob moving to and fro, speaking over an intercom, and cleaning up Marley's mess.

Closing her eyes helped. The pain remained but

dulled a bit if she didn't have to focus. Something cold slapped into her hand. Fear touched down her spine, and she refused to open them.

"It's water. Open your mouth for the straw," the woman soothed. Marley blindly opened her mouth, closing it over something plastic. It might be another spiked drink, a thermometer, or the end of a gun. A gun would be a good choice at this point. Between the pain, Alan, and the memories she cobbled together from last night, well…not much to live for now.

Another blob joined the first one, and the two pulled and tugged the bedding around her. Marley didn't move. She shut her eyes and rode out the storm of swaying and turning. Finally, a cool hand swiped her forehead.

Marley's eyelids cracked open, and the white blob reformed into the woman again. She leaned over Marley, dapping a towel around Marley's neck and chin. The tag of the white uniform swung before Marley's gaze. It read Lana Nichols. Marley stared hard at it trying to understand its meaning.

"There you are," she said, her voice like smooth silk. "The police need to take a statement but don't worry. It'll be a woman with training in social services. I'll stay here with you if you want."

A nurse, she's a nurse, and I'm in a hospital. Marley grasped the nurse's hand with the little strength she had. "I want to leave. Help me."

"Marley," Nichols said softly, "you need help, and it's right here all around you. We got you." She squeezed Marley's hand gently and turned to exit. "I'll check with the doctor. Be back in two shakes." And she vanished out the door.

The second blob transformed into an orderly, following on Nichols' heels. He glanced back once. The pity in his gaze turned her stomach. Holding back a sob, she searched for the water cup. A little comfort in a cup might help settle her stomach.

The door cracked open again, and a tall man in a police uniform stepped through. "Marley?" he asked.

She stared at him numbly. Cops. She didn't want to talk to the cops. "Nurse Nichols said a woman..." Marley squeaked.

"Yeah, well, I have to finish the report." He stepped the rest of the way into the room, letting the door close quietly behind him. Her belly quaked again, and the all too familiar band wrapped around her chest.

"We've got some questions to answer before I get your counselor." The band snapped tighter. "Answers, Marley. Now. You're last name's not Hamilton. It's Volkov, right?" The smirk on his face told her everything.

Her chest seized, and she couldn't breathe. She heaved, unable to draw in a tiny bit of air. Pressing back into the bed, she put some distance between them. Her water hit the floor as she abandoned it for the nurse call button.

She didn't know if calling Nichols would do any good. But no way she'd stay alone in a room with a man who knew her real last name. She slammed the call button half a dozen times as the cop crossed the room.

Chapter Sixteen

Her room door slammed open, and two nurses followed by Alan spilled inside. Marley curled up at the head of the bed, her knees at her chest, her breath in tight gasps.

"What the hell is going on here?" Nichols demanded. She glared at the officer then rushed over to Marley. "You okay, honey? What's wrong?" She ran her hand along Marley's arm. Heat and reassurance soaked into her skin, and she slowly uncurled. But her breath still stayed locked in her lungs.

"Look at me, Marley. Breathe with me. In and out," the nurse cooed. Marley tried but only managed a loud gasp. "Shhhh, honey. In and out. With me."

"What's wrong?" Alan snapped, his voice fierce but concerned. He pushed past the cop who shot him a dark look. The sight of Alan, here and worried about her, the tone of his voice. The tightness in her chest eased and breath returned.

"Panic attack," Nichols said, not an ounce of contempt or accusation in her voice. She watched Marley for a breath or two, then rubbed her arm again. "That's better. Nice and slow. Go easy, honey." The nurse stood, and her whole disposition changed. Her head slowly swiveled in the direction of the officer, her mouth turning down in a deep frown.

"You," she said, accusatory and angry. "What are you doing in here alone? I'm pretty sure procedure is to wait for an advocate and a female officer." She waved a finger in his face. "You are out of line. I'm reporting your badge number."

The officer towered over her, his face a pit of snakes, but Nichols never backed down. "Ma'am," he said in a tight voice. "I have every authority…"

"The hell you do. Out." She stepped forward into his personal space, forcing him back. Alan slipped around her to Marley's bed. He sat on the edge practically pulling her into his lap. Marley resisted at first, but then she saw the fury in his expression. He was protecting her. Her white knight finally arrived. She leaned against him, loving the warmth flowing through her.

Nurse Nichols wasn't finished. She took three more steps until the officer's back hit the door. She gestured to the exit, and the man slipped out. Shaking her head her head, she faced Marley. "Officer Smith isn't usually so terse. I don't know what crawled up his butt. 'Scuse my French." A tinge of pink popped in her cheeks. "I'm sorry, honey," Nichols continued. "You okay? Do you need anything?"

Marley managed to shake her head.

Alan spoke up. "You have some experience with Smith?" he asked.

Nurse Nichols nodded. "He's been here in the ER more times than I can count. With some nasty cases." Marley's eyebrows shot up. "Oh no, honey. They seem to give him the hard ones because he usually handles them well." She bit her lip. "I'll see if he's calmed down. Threatening to report him might've been a mistake. But shoot, he knows he's not supposed to be in here." Crossing her arms, she shook her head.

Alan pressed his head against Marley's. "He wasn't...professional when the ambulance came for Marley."

Nurse Nichols peered down her nose at Alan. "Mr. Reid, he took one look at the girl and knew what happened. You were the only man there, and your name is mud lately."

Alan threw a hand up in the air. The other remained firmly around Marley's. "For tax evasion. Not sexual assault." The words struck a nerve, and Marley shivered in his arms.

Kissing her head, he rubbed her back, up and down once, and pain sizzled down her spine. She jumped away from him with a hiss. "Sorry, Mar. I forgot about your back."

What happened to her back? Marley's head slowly cleared, but everything still held fuzz around the edges. Alan's touch felt odd, but she welcomed it. If any other man came near her, she'd run for the hills.

Troy.

Her body burst into tremors and whimper escaped her lips. Alan pressed her tighter, glancing at the nurse for help. She shook her head.

"I'll call the doctor. She needs something and a less angry cop on her case." She turned to the other nurse who'd stood by the bed, silent the entire time. Marley'd forgotten she'd stayed in the room. "Go get him," Nichols said with a sharp nod. "You can stay 'til he arrives, Mr. Reid." They both knew full well his staying violated every policy—visitor, victim, family. But Marley was grateful someone would break the rules for little old her.

The doctor arrived a few minutes later and consulted with the nurse. Alan stayed, saying nothing, just holding her. For the first time since she'd woken up, her mind settled on Alan and his presence here.

How did he know to be at the hospital? Closing her eyes and drawing in his scent, she attempted to recall more of the night, without Troy. His image flashed a few times through her random thoughts, but she pushed beyond. Alan quickly soothed the tremors that followed.

A picture of Alan's porch formed in her mind. His street, his house, his front door but no Alan. She tried to twist her hair, but her wrist screamed in protest. Resigned, she replayed the scene. A jumble of images, a kind face, a cab, the red door flashed in her mind. Curling closer into him, she thought harder, holding her breath. Alan's face swam before her, saying "Calling an ambulance." She remembered telling him no, for fear he'd find out about the drug in her drink.

Her body froze like an icicle. She slumped against him, exhausted and humiliated. Her eyes stung, and his fingers brushed across her cheek. "You okay?" he asked.

"I'm sorry," she said feebly. "So sorry."

He squeezed her tighter. "You have nothing to be sorry for."

Finally, the doctor turned his attention to them and introduced himself "Richard Hartling," he said, shaking both her and Alan's hands. He focused on Alan. "I need to ask you to step out." His words were firm, commanding but not harsh. Marley liked him immediately.

"Can I go too?" she asked trying to make the situation a tiny bit less terrible.

"I'm afraid not, young lady. We need to talk." The doctor's warm voice held a sliver of steel in it. Alan set her carefully back against the pillows.

"I'll run out for some supplies," Alan said vaguely as if he didn't know what to say or how to bow out. He looked back at her, his blue eyes full of sorrow. He pressed his lips and stood, wiping his hand on his pants. "I'm going to the coffee shop." He announced his intentions as if he wanted everyone to understand he'd be close by. Maybe he said it for her, but the tone said "Nobody hurts her." Her lips turned up in a slight smile despite the crazy and the pain.

Alan headed to the door as the doctor picked up the conversation again. She watched Alan rather than listen. Something was happening here, and her skin tingled.

"Let's start with your real name, young lady."

Alan paused. His shoulders fell, but he continued out the door, shaking his head. Fresh tears rolled down her cheeks. She desperately wanted him to stay while she spilled her guts to the doctor. But Alan was already gone.

Chapter Seventeen

Alan stepped into the hall, blowing out the breath he held as he crossed the threshold. He was in deep, with a woman whose name he didn't know. He shut his eyes, envisioning snowy mountains, ski trails, warm fires—his usual meditation images. Slowly the tension evaporated from his body. Meditation therapy pulled him through the IRS crap. Apparently, it worked during personal crises as well. He opened his eyes on the busy hallway, other ER rooms buzzing with activity.

An image of her back with the gashes and scrapes rose before him. Next, her bloody head, her damaged wrist, and finally the marks and bruises on her thighs. His body flushed with heat, his shoulders hiked up to his ears. Taking a long blink, he pushed the thoughts away. He'd find out who did this and serve up some justice. He walked back to the waiting room, jaw clenched, fists at his side. He needed better meditation material.

As he rounded the corner, he ran smack into Officer Smith. Alan rubbed at the sore spot on his wrist from the cuffing earlier. He blew air out of his nostrils, not apologizing for running into the man. They eyed each other, and everyone in the waiting room could probably smell the testosterone.

"Officer Smith," he said, his words clipped. "The

doctor is in with her, and I'm going back as soon as he's done." He raised an eyebrow to see if Smith challenged him or not. Messing with a police officer was not his style, but something seemed personal and hell, the man scared Marley. Alan wouldn't stand for it.

Smith nodded, his face stone, but his eyes glared. "She'll be questioned as will you, Mr. Reid. I expect you to cooperate."

Alan nodded, his temper still flaring. He'd always claimed he had a long fuse. Apparently, he found the end. "Oh, I will, as long as you follow procedure properly. Even the nurse understood you stepped over the line." He narrowed his gaze at Smith, resisting poking him in the chest.

"There are questions about her injuries, Mr. Reid," Smith said through gritted teeth. "They're rather suspicious."

"Ya think?" The sarcasm popped out of its own volition. Clearing his throat, he dialed it back. "I hope you can get to the bottom quickly and find out what happened."

Smith leaned in, leering at Alan. "I already know."

Tired of the bullshit, Alan called Smith's cards. "What's your problem with me, Officer Smith? What have I done to piss you off?" He paused as Smith built up steam. He cut the cop off. "And don't tell me it's Marley. You were angry at me when you arrived."

Smith's gaze darted around the room. He seemed to realize everyone was watching him. He pulled back. Alan glanced around, noticing the captive audience of patients and loved ones watching their discussion.

"I know who you are, mister. I know what you've done to this town."

Alan's eyebrows popped up as the puzzle pieces fell into place. He could see Smith's hostility went beyond the incident with Marley. He knew Alan's name and problems. Time for some contrition. "Family or friends working at one of our bars?"

Smith narrowed his eyes, seeming wary. "Lots of families in my neighborhood are in deep shit because their jobs are gone, thanks to you and your greed. Good people out of work, almost on the street because you're above paying your share."

Alan nodded, his anger gone. He'd endured a long line of confrontation from various people. First cop though. Unclenching his fist and relaxing his shoulders, Alan said, "If I try and toss away the blame, it won't make a difference. Then let me say how honestly sorry I am that I put your loved ones in such a position. I truly apologize you were swept up in my business problems. I intended no harm."

Smith blinked at him. "Are you for real? You're running off with millions, living on Boswell Street, and sitting high and mighty in the bar on Birch."

Alan examined his shoes. "They let me keep the house because the mortgage is paid. And the Tavern wasn't part of the group." He waved away his words. "Officer Smith, I'm working as manager at the bar unpaid. I'm lucky enough to keep a few people while I scrape up the money to run the place." He shrugged.

Smith's brow furrowed. "You don't have the money?" He cocked his head to the side. "Seriously?"

"Not a dime," Alan said flatly, crossing his arms over his chest. "The house and the tavern are the only things I have left."

The furrows on Smith's brow disappeared. "Wait.

You didn't steal the money? Your partner really ran out on you? Some newscast said something about him. Your best friend, right?"

Alan nodded. "I haven't seen him in weeks." He shrugged. Smith's words affected him more than he expected. Tears burned at the corners of his eyes. It was tough admitting to strangers how much your friend ditching you hurt.

Smith's stance relaxed, and he held open hands out to Alan. "I'm sorry, man. I assumed." Then he laughed. "And we know what that makes me."

"No," Alan said, shaking his head. "You saw a woman injured and in danger. You came to her rescue. Thank you." He held his hand out. Smith grabbed it immediately and they shook. Alan sensed their audience approving, small head nods, hidden smiles. Relief flooded through him. "I'm going for coffee. You want some?"

"No, I'm good. Thanks for the offer, Mr. Reid."

"Alan," he corrected.

"Rick."

Alan returned Rick's nod as the scent of testosterone faded away.

****

Marley wished more than anything Alan could've stayed. Stayed to support her, ease her fears, and hear the bullshit.

Dr. Hartling glanced at her chart. His gaze turned to hers, his expression grim. "The police counselor will discuss your injuries, and how you came to receive them. Do you want to share with me also?" he asked.

Marley squirmed but understood talking would only help her. "I went to a club. My ex-boyfriend spiked my drink." Her gaze dropped to her hands. She couldn't meet Dr. Hartling's eyes.

His kind expression, a bland mask when they started talking, became darker and darker as she shared her ugly past. "Not Mr. Reid?"

"Oh God, no." The words flew out of her as finally looked up. "No. A guy named Troy Elton. I only remember bits."

"It makes sense, with the ketamine in your system. Are you aware of what the drug can do to you?" He crossed his arms, his mouth in a thin line.

"Yeah, kinda." She worried her fingers. "I've never done the hard stuff. Never did K before, ever." But did she really know? A few years ago, she'd take whatever Troy offered.

"You're a recovering addict then?" He scanned his laptop, making a click.

"No." She rubbed her forehead. "Recreational only."

Doc lowered his the computer screen. "Not recovering or not an addict." He cocked his head to the side. "We can find a rehab facility for you." He sounded disappointed like his own daughter let him down. Why did people always try and parent her? Well, not like her real parents. Thank goodness.

She glanced from the doc to the nurse. Both standing tall, worried about her, trying to help her. Ugh, project much? Marley ducked her head again. "Not a junkie, I swear. I haven't tried anything over a year, almost two."

"I see." He clicked the laptop again. "Well, Miss Volkov." He glanced up at her confirming her real name. "You have lacerations on your back, similar to road rash."

Marley broke in. "Brick wall. Troy pinned me to it."

The doc held up a hand. "You don't have to justify your injuries to me. The counselor will discuss it with you." He glanced at the screen again. "Sprained left wrist and the worst of it is the concussion. You have a hard head, Miss Volkov."

Her mouth quirked up in a half smile. "I'm Russian." She shrugged which hurt like a bitch. An elastic bandage wrapped loosely around her wrist, but the tiny movement jiggled something. "Ow. Should it hurt this much?"

"I'm afraid so," the doc said. "We haven't given you any pain meds yet. I needed you awake, conscious, and talking before I drugged you up." He smiled. "And situations such as this, it doesn't hurt to have you sober when the police talk to you."

"You take the fun out of a hospital visit." Her joke felt stale even to her. She glanced away from the doctor, trying to think of something intelligent to say, anything to say. "So, what's the prognosis?"

A faint flash of a smile crossed the doc's mouth. "Overnight for sure. Longer if you're still dizzy." He tilted his head, "Tell me honestly, Miss Volkov, do you feel safe at home?"

Marley almost laughed, but the weight of the air in the room stopped her. He meant Alan, not Becca or Jex. "Alan didn't do it. I'm not living with him or Troy. I'm actually without a home at the moment." Heat bloomed on her cheeks.

"There's a women's shelter…" the nurse began.

Marley held up a hand. "I know. We're at Iverton

General right. Women's Safe Haven then. Yeah, the name is a little misleading." Nurse Nichols's face puckered with concern. "I'll find something. Don't worry."

"Well," the doc said. "I'm not releasing you until you have a safe place to rest and recover." He pointed his stylus at her. "I mean it. If I have to find a relative or…"

"No family," she said too quickly. The doc's eyebrows shot up. "I mean, I don't have family around here. They're back…home?" She really didn't want her sociopathic parents here. Especially since she hadn't seen them for seven years.

"I see," he said, his mouth turned down sharply. "Due to the nature of your injuries, I'm putting the police counselor as your health advocate." He didn't look up as he dropped the bomb.

"What do you mean?" Marley blurted. Instinctively, she pulled the covers up to her chin, like a child.

"Miss Volkov, it is my opinion, based on your injuries, you have been sexually assaulted. You have no home to speak of. I want to ensure you're cared for when you leave my hospital."

She didn't like the sound of that one bit. The iron band on her chest reappeared. Her gaze flew back and forth from the nurse to the doctor. Nurse Nichols blank expression told her nothing. Marley's rib cage seemed inches smaller. "So, I get a social worker and have to report to her like some ex-con on parole."

"You get help," he said, his voice authoritative. Marley swallowed, saying nothing, her heart rate dramatically increasing by the minute. The doctor spun on his heel and headed for the door. "I'll see you in about four hours when you're in your new room." And he left.

Nurse Nichols came over to the bed, adjust the blankets. "He's a good man, Dr. Hartling. He lets his heart lead sometimes. And you, young lady, spoke to his tender side the second he laid eyes on you."

"Not creepy at all," Marley said, settling into the bed.

The nurse waved her hand dismissively. "No, no. He has a daughter." She glanced at her watch, a high-end step counter. "The orderlies will be taking your bed up after the counselor is done. She'll be here soon." She sat on the edge of the bed, her brown eyes deadly serious.

"We did a kit on you when you came in." She patted Marley's hand. Marley blinked at her not understanding. Nichols lowered her head, her gaze still locked on Marley's. And then she understood. She curled into a ball, hugging her legs with her good arm.

"Just in case," she continued. "No vaginal penetration, hon, but the police will still want to talk with you. The counselor, Pat Mayer, attended. She'll be in soon. Unfortunately, other young ladies had issues tonight." She stood, dusting off her scrubs as if wiping away the ugly of the evening.

"Rest while you can," she continued. "Pat's going to ask some hard questions." She left the room without another word.

Marley nodded slightly, not wanting to set off the pain in her head again. Questions were fine, even hard ones. As long as no one asked about her police record or her parents.

An image of Smith, fuming and blood-thirsty, rose in her mind. She shrank back into the pillow. If Smith knew her last name, he could trace Marlena Volkov easily. Stupid internet with its Google power. He'd know her history in an instant, probably collect an outstanding reward for information about her.

Her best bet required she sneak out of the hospital before she spoke to this Pat chick. But everything hurt, and clothing was an issue. Club clothes in the hospital were not good, especially since they'd been reduced to rags.

If she didn't talk to Pat, she wouldn't have to relive it either. Another bonus. But if she waited until they moved her, it might be a better escape. In the confusion of changing rooms, she'd insist on walking and then play a con to confuse the orderlies.

Of course, then, no pain meds either. Maybe they hadn't given her anything because of the K in her system or because they thought she was an addict. Or maybe, they were just being dicks, but pain pills right now might give her the edge to fly out the door unseen.

She pressed the nurse call button and readied a sweet voice to beg for something to help with the pain. Once she took it, gave it a few minutes to let it kick in, then zoom, she was out of here.

"Now what, Marley?" Nurse Nichols chuckled into the com.

"I need an aspirin or something." She whined.

"Nope. Not a thing until Pat's done with you. Over and out, Marley."

Pouting, she pressed again to complain louder when her door opened. Alan walked in, giving the door a little knock to alert her. She'd completely forgot about him in this scenario. Man, she must've hit her head hard to forget him.

"No drugs!" Nichols said from the com. Alan's eyes widened as he placed a coffee mug on the counter near her bed. Heat flushed Marley's face, and she turned away from him. She quickly clicked off the intercom.

"My head hurts," she said lamely.

"I'm sure it does. Hopefully, it'll be over soon, and you can sleep. I brought you a hot chocolate." His words were kind but distant. And the "No drugs" command from Nurse Nichols seemed to put him on edge.

Marley blinked at the cup on the counter. The man brought her cocoa. Her gaze rolled up to meet his. How could she dine and dash when he did things like this?

"Thanks," she said weakly, holding her hand out. Guess she was stuck here for a while.

****

"Get some rest," Alan said. He ran his fingers over her hair, wishing he could do more. Do anything to help her. "I'll wait here until the counselor comes by."

Marley yawned, her mouth opening wide. "But you brought cocoa."

Alan snickered. "An excuse to come back in. I heard something about pain meds. I thought you needed to wait."

"I hurt," she said faintly, her lids fluttering closed and snapping back open.

"Mmm," he agreed, enjoying her fight with drowsiness. Could she nap with the concussion? Neither the nurse nor doctor said to keep her awake. Of course, the doctor said little to him as he wasn't family.

Trying the boyfriend card hadn't opened doors. Hell, it'd been awkward to even use the word with the medical staff. His thousand questions could only be answered by sleeping beauty. He brushed a lock of her hair back. Patience was a virtue.

After a few minutes, the door opened to the nurse and a stocky brunette. The latter nodded curtly to him. Marley snorted in her sleep then curled onto her side. The movement brought her lids open with snap and hiss of pain.

He grasped her hand gently reassuring her as she glanced from face to face. "Got my aspirin yet?" Her voice thick with pain and sleep. He wanted nothing more than to scoop her up and take her home. She might not sleep, but she'd be safe from whoever did this.

The brunette, presumably the counselor or a female detective, took charge. She paced across the room, her hand outstretched. "I'm Pat Mayer. I'll be interviewing Marlena Volkov. Sir, you're welcome to stay, if Marlena agrees. But please don't interfere." She reinforced the point with a sharp stab of her finger. "If she wants you out, you go. No questions."

Marlena Volkov? More exotic than he'd thought. An embarrassment to add to the humiliation of not knowing her real name. They needed to talk, seriously talk.

Pat shoved her hand in his for a shake, breaking his train of thought. "We clear, Mr.?" She'd jumped so quickly into her spiel that Alan never had a chance to introduce himself.

Flashing a half-smile, he replied, "Alan Reid." Her expression fell as her gaze narrowed. God, it was exhausting. "Yes, that Alan Reid." He pulled his hand back and held up both in surrender. "Money issues, only."

Pat's eyes never left him as she addressed Marley. "Miss Volkov, is he the man who assaulted you?" She ground the words out, her mouth in a flat line.

"No. Alan didn't hurt me." Marley's words sounded stodgy, sleepy, and hardly convincing. "Troy Elton did." She pointed lamely to her wrist and to her head before reclining on the pillow, eyelids closed.

Pat's eyes sparked recognition as she turned to Alan. "Out." He opened his mouth to protest. But she marched on. "I've got this, Mr. Reid. I'm aware of her injuries, and Lana is staying with me. She's in good hands, but it's in her best interest for you to disappear."

"You can't believe I…" he began, heat rushing up his neck. Arguing with the counselor after the confrontation with Smith wasn't a good idea. But he'd never leave her alone if she needed him.

Crossing her arms over her chest, Pat said, "It doesn't matter what I think. Consider what it will look like to have your name on the documentation. Your being present when she's questioned. You have enough on your plate, Mr. Reid."

Alan gaped at her. "What do you care if…" His gaze floated up to the nurse, who pressed her lips and nodded tightly. He huffed. Marley groaned next to him, reaching for his hand.

"'s okay, Al," she slurred. "I'm good." She opened her lids. Dark green eyes met his gaze, and he knew she meant it.

He raised her hand to his lips. "All right then. I'll be on the other side of the door." He glanced at the nurse. "Call me if she needs me." Lana nodded. Gently placing Marley's hand back down, Alan stood. "I hope you can help her," he said quietly. "I hope you can help us find the man responsible."

"That's my job, Mr. Reid," Pat said, patting him on the shoulder as he passed.

As he walked down the hallway again, his mind turned the situation over and over. What a disaster. He assumed she wasn't living the convent life...Anger fired in his gut, repeating his feelings from the night they met. No woman should suffer like that—especially his Marley.

He found an empty seat in the waiting area, in the corner away from everyone. He dropped into the seat, realizing he'd left his coffee back in the ER room. Leaning his head back, he sighed, closing his eyes. Fatigue wrapped around him like a wet blanket. The energy to walk back and face the women again felt like running a marathon.

Poor Marley. Wait...Poor Marlena Volkov.

His hand automatically drew his phone from his pocket. He cracked one eye open, contemplating it. Google knew all. He stared at it for a beat, then two. Resigned, he shoved it back in his pocket.

Fuck it.

She'd tell him when she was ready or not. He didn't care. He wanted the bruises and cuts gone. He wanted her safe and cared for. He'd make those things happen. His mind wandered as he plotted and planned ways to keep her safe.

A long blink followed by a sharp head dip brought him back around. He stared groggily at the waiting room. How long had he been out?

Since Officer Smith was still there, speaking to someone with a notebook, it probably was only a catnap. He considered wandering back to Marley's room to check on her. At some point, she'd transfer to a real room. Head injuries still required an overnight stay.

He watched Smith speak with the man for a while, and realization dawned. Alan recognized the man. Robbie Koufax from the *Iverton Press*. Fuck. Smith was talking to the media. Alan had to intervene. More press coverage was the last thing he needed.

Stretching his limbs to restore blood flow, Alan dreaded the face to face. But Smith had the answers to his questions. Like how they knew Marley's real name (and Alan didn't). Reporter be damned.

Before Alan reached them, Koufax shoved his notebook in his pocket and dashed away. Alan cursed silently but still approached Smith.

"Hey," he said. "Anything new? I saw you talking to the reporter."

Smith regarded him gravely. He chewed his lip a second before speaking. "Word gets around Mr. Reid. Slow news day or something. You might see your name in lights again." He patted Alan's shoulder. Alan stepped out of the officer's reach.

"So, you sold me out? I thought we were good." Anger trickled into his words. At six am, his civility dried up.

"No, man. I tried to steer him away from that story. He made as if he'd flash your girl's name in lights and blame you for her injuries. He had some shit on you and her already."

Alan goggled. "Shit? What shit? We slept together a couple times. Not exactly a story."

Crossing his arms, Smith said, "No, not really, but when he found out her name—boom, story."

Alan's eyebrow raised, shaking a bit, as heat rose up his neck. "What's the significance of her name?"

Smith rocked back on his heels. "As a kid, she competed in beauty pageants or something, like a minor celebrity. Then she turned into a lowlife con artist. Has a police record. Good girl gone bad. You plus her equals story." Smith shrugged.

His words were a punch in the gut. Alan's blood pressure dropped, and the color drained from his face, leaving him a bit weak. He pulled in a shuttering breath, trying to hide it by not opening his mouth. His nose whistled with the effort. Pressing his lips, he struggled for something to say.

Marley had introduced herself with "I'm going to steal your wallet." And the whole thing with Becca...But a police record? He shook his head.

"Well," Alan finally managed to say. "I hope you were honest as well as kind." A flicker of an idea lit in the back of his mind as he spun on his heel, unable to meet Smith's gaze. Becca had mentioned drugs. Was that it? He beelined for Marley's room.

"They sent her upstairs, Reid," Smith called back. "About ten minutes ago. I hung around for my other case, but I kept an eye on you."

Alan turned back, giving Smith a polite nod. Asleep in the ER might have lost him his phone or wallet tonight. "Thank you, Officer," he said and headed for the nurse's station down the hall to find out the new room number.

****

A rough shove woke Alan from a dreamless

slumber. He sat up with a start, poised to jump to his feet. He glanced around the hospital room and found a sleeping Marley.

A large man in scrubs stood over him. "I don't care," he said, "what the night shift said. Visiting hours are visiting hours. Go home, man. You aren't supposed to be here."

Alan groggily stood up the rest of the way from the stiff uncomfortable chair beside Marley's bed. He glanced at the man's nametag. "Paul O'Brien, RN."

"My apologies," Alan said, gesturing at Marley. "My girlfriend."

Nurse O'Brien examined him up and down, a sour expression on his face. "No, she's not. Now move. No story for you, dude." He put a hand on Alan's arm.

Alan pulled back, but the man's grip was steel. "But she is. I'm Alan Reid." He wasn't sure why he told his name. Lately, it'd only dumped him into more trouble or made everyone treated him like a leper. His name once opened doors exclusive clubs and boardrooms. Not that he cared, especially now. It was a relief not to have to be on all the time in public.

"Yeah, I know," the nurse said. "Now go." Still holding Alan's arm, O'Brien guided him to the door. The nurses here were especially strong. Alan guessed they'd have to be with some of their patients. Iverton used to be a college campus ringed with a few bars and neighborhoods. But lately, seedier elements settled in as the town grew into a small city.

Anyway, he wasn't ready to go yet. Grabbing Paul's arm by the wrist, he twisted it enough to force the man to release him. In a calm and steady voice, he said, "I'd like to say good-bye and let her know I'm leaving for a bit." The two men locked gazes for a tense moment, and the nurse finally relented.

"Two minutes."

"Fine." Alan walked over to his sleeping beauty. She looked much younger there wrapped in white blankets, her dark hair falling around her face. Reluctantly, he nudged her arm waking her. "Marley, love."

Green eyes blinked up at him, and a warm smile crossing her face. "Hey," she said, her voice sleepy and a bit raw.

"Hey," he said. "I have to leave for a bit. But I'll be back for visiting hours later. Can I get you anything?" He tucked her hand into his, rubbing his thumb back and forth over the back of her hand.

"Nah," she said, taking long blinks. "Maybe some aspirin." She scrunched her nose.

"I'll tell the nurse," he said soothingly. He kissed the back of her hand. "I'll be back soon. I promise."

Her shoulders fell as a real smile crossed her lips. "Thanks," she said. Her eyes twinkled. "And a sandwich?"

Chapter Eighteen

The next morning, Marley twisted her hair lazily as Alan hemmed and hawed. Finally, he said, "Where are you going to stay when they release you?" He stood by her bed, arms folded, flaring his nostrils.

"You worry way too much," she said with a laugh. "Gonna get wrinkles." She tittered, settling back into her pillow. Her mind floated on a cloud, her wrist finally numb, the ache in her head quieted.

A smile cracked his lips, and he leaned a hip on the side of the bed. "What are they giving you?" he asked, pulling her hand into his.

"Good stuff." Her eyelids closed and opened, too long for a blink.

"Maybe now is a good time to convince you to press charges." That caught her attention. Her eyes flew open, her lips in a thin line.

"No, Alan. I told you. We are walking away and never looking back." She freed her hand from his to poke him in the arm. "I press charges, and when he gets out, he has a score to settle. I don't want it hanging over me."

Alan raised his chin, peering down at her over his nose. "How many times has something like this happened?" He retrieved her hand, rubbing his thumb over her knuckles. An image of Becca rose in her mind.

Old pain bubbled up from her gut. She glanced down at their hands, and a smile teetered on her lips. Despite the warm fuzzy from his presence, tears bit at her. He continued caressing her hand, and the tears spilled in a free-for-all. The bandage on her left wrist prevented her from drying her tears, but damned if she'd release his hand.

"I, uh...I've been on the street a long time, Alan." She squeezed his hand. "I know the score. I know where to hide and where to run." She tilted her head to meet his harsh stare. "I know Troy. I'm hiding and walking. End of story."

He reached out and gently wiped the tears. Pain played across his face, the tightness in his eyes, the straight line of his mouth. He shrugged. "I don't understand Marley. Explain it so I can understand where you're coming from. Because I want to break the man's legs." Alan obviously had no clue how life on the street worked.

He squeezed her hand tightly, smashing the fingers together, releasing her instantly before she protested. "I'm sorry," he said bowing his head. "I..." He met her gaze. "I need you to be safe."

She ran her fingers lightly over his hand and up his arm. "Trust me, Alan. It will keep me safer. Getting off his radar is a good thing." She patted his hand and settled back into the pillows. "Wanna get me a chocolate milkshake?" She grinned.

****

Alan shook his head. "You aren't getting out that easy. Where are you staying when they discharge you?" She raised and lowered one shoulder. His throat tightened, and he tried to clear it. He had to glance away from those green eyes. "Stay with me." He finally managed.

She gripped his hand again. "I can't." The finality to her words forced him to glance up.

"Any reason?"

"Thousands," she said, her gaze never wavering, a tight smile crossing her lips.

The ache in his chest spread, filling the entire cavity. She didn't want him. Didn't want his help. Just some clueless mark. If he'd let her take his wallet the first night, they'd have avoided the entire thing.

Remembering Becca's stupid pickpocket scheme, he found the connection. "Do you think Becca had anything to do with this?" Marley's eyes flashed wide before her mask of indifference slammed back down.

"Oh, God. No. Not her style." She fiddled with her covers, not meeting his gaze.

"But the police have your real name already." Still not looking at him, she waved her hand at his words.

Heat crawled up his neck as his temper rose. Breathing in short, forceful stints, he swallowed back his words. Anger held no place here, and he bit it back hard.

"Fine," he said through gritted teeth. "Can I pay for a hotel or help with rent?" His gut told him she had nowhere to go. "Let me help, in some way."

She tittered again. Just the drugs talking. Hopefully, she didn't think him ridiculous. "You don't owe me nothing, Alan. You saved me. Got me here. I can't ask for more." She winked at him. A wide yawn stretched her beautiful mouth. "We'll talk more later." And she drifted off to sleep.

Alan stood there a moment, more determined than

ever to help, but clueless how to do it without putting her in danger. He was torn between taking her home to protect her, and putting her over his knee for being stubborn. Rubbing his forehead, he needed to fish or cut bait. She was either in his life or out. Time to make up his mind before she decided for him.

****

A few hours later, Marley eased out of her hospital bed. Time to go, now that everyone left the room. She dressed hurriedly in the clothing Pat brought by earlier. As she peeked out of the door's window, her swirling thoughts, settled on Alan.

He'd done so much for her—getting her medical help, standing up to the cops, and bringing her hot chocolate. And now he thought he could help more by finding Troy and "bringing him to justice." So sweet.

Closing her eyes tight, she made a decision. Maybe the two of them could never be a couple, but she could help him, the way he helped her. She'd find out what happened to his money. She could do it. It was only accounting. She'd save him from the IRS the same way he attempted to save her from the street. Then they'd be square, and she could leave Iverton debt free.

A peace settled over her heart as she ducked out of her hospital room and ran smack into Officer Smith. Damn, no easy escape. She waved and continued walking, trying to brush him off. But he kept pace with her.

"A little early to be checking out." He eyed her the street clothes.

"I'll be fine," she said, batting her eyelashes. "I have a place to stay, a friend to hang with. Troy'll never find me. Don't worry about it."

"Press charges, miss. You're not the only woman who's endured an assault because of him. You'd be doing the world a favor getting him off the street." His dark eyebrows lowered making her feel like a bug under a microscope.

"Jex?" She threw the name out before she could think.

"Who's she?" he asked, a scowl on his brow. "Another girl from Steel?"

She halted, putting her hands on her hips. "Uh, okay, I'm just going to ask. Did Troy hurt Jex?"

Smith scrubbed his chin. "I haven't heard anything about a Jex. The other girl from Steel, short, blonde, thirties. You know her?"

A wave a relief washed over Marley. She felt bad for the blonde but also grateful Troy hadn't hurt a probably drugged Jex. She shook her head, determined to end the conversation. "Officer, I appreciate all you're doing for me. I really do."

"But I bet you're glad to be rid of me," he said, his voice low and conspiratorial. "I know your real name, and I've seen your rap sheet. Trust me, I can make sure it's not an issue if you charge him."

A cold dread blanketed Marley's skin. Smith probably knew her whole story on those few pages in the police file. Time to find a new haunt. Someplace without such diligent officers. Once she'd settled the books with Alan, paid him the debt, she'd hightail it for greener pastures.

Swallowing hard, she blinked and smiled widely. "Nice offer, but we both know Troy wouldn't do more than a nickel, and then he'd be after me with a vengeance." She watched the truth of it register in his eyes. "I wouldn't be safe anywhere if he got out. He'd have to go down for a long, long stretch which won't happen with a simple assault."

Smith pressed his lips, glancing away. "Fine," he said stiffly. "Tell me where you'll be so I can keep tabs for a bit."

She shook her head. He asked an impossible thing. She wouldn't be able to help Alan and then disappear if Smith watched over her shoulders. "Not necessary." She stepped away, planning as quick an escape as her aching head might allow.

He grabbed her arm, pulling her back. He leaned down. "You are aggravating," he snarled.

"And *you* are super scary when you're annoyed." She smiled, scrunching her nose.

"Fine. Find a safe place, with Alan, with your parents or Becca. Be safe." His words sincere and heartfelt. Weird for a cop but the mention of her parent forced the cold snake in her belly coil up again. *Becca? And my...*

"My parents?" she asked before she thought better. The cold making her teeth chatter.

"Yeah, I'm aware you're not a minor, but I spoke with your friend, Becca, when you first came in. She called your parents for you." He smiled sweetly, without a sliver of sarcasm or vengeance.

"Becca?" She worked hard to keep the tremor out of her voice.

"Yeah, pretty blonde, right? She stopped by the first night you stayed here. Told me she was your roommate and friend. She seemed worried about you." He shrugged. "I asked her about your next-of-kin, and she said she'd call your parents.

Marley's blood froze, and she staggered, still caught in Smith's grip. Her heart pounded at the thought of Becca knowing how to contact her parents after all these years. Not to mention the prospect of her parents showing up. Smith steadied her with his other arm.

No wonder they knew her full name. How did Becca know it, and how did she find Marley in the hospital? An ugly picture formed in her mind, and she shivered.

"You okay, Marley?" he asked, suspicion tainted the syllables. Or did she imagine it?

She bit her lip, shaking her head slightly to erase the idea of Smith being in on some kind of conspiracy. "Yeah, of course. Uh, you don't know if Becca told them where I am?" She sounded nonchalant, indifferent, but her voice trembled.

Smith's brow furrowed. "I'm sure she did. They'd be worried about you." He smiled again, and she resisted the urge to reprimand him. If he knew her past, certainly he knew Becca's as well.

Cop or no cop, enough of the bullshit. No more men slapping her around and telling her what do to. Why couldn't they all be like Alan? He never pushed her, well except when he pushed her away. But it was…business. She slammed the door on that train of thought and squared herself to deal with Smith.

"Fuck," she muttered. "She called them to mess with me." His eyebrows shot up. "Do you know how screwed I am now? And Becca is Rebecca White. Ring any bells?

Smith straightened to his considerable height, towering over her. "Regardless, Miss Volkov.

According to our records, you're a missing person. And I found you. I'm helping close a seven-year-old case. I'd think you'd be grateful."

Scowling, Marley huffed out her nose, furious. Her vision flickered red at the edges. "If I wanted those cocksuckers to find me, I would've called them." She brandished her phone, waving the contact screen for Smith to see her parent's tab. An epiphany hit her hard, and she stepped away from him.

Becca must've hacked her phone at some point. How else did she know Marley's real name, her parents, everything? The little phone was the only place she kept anything real about herself and her past. And the bitch violated it.

She pulled the phone back against her chest. "Did you look at my phone too?"

Smith eyed her, his expression serious. "Yes, I looked at your phone. When a young woman is found passed out in a stranger's yard, we investigate it. Especially when the man has been in the news lately for criminal activity. I tried to help you." The warmth disappeared from his words, and he was all cop now. "I did the right thing. I don't know or care about your mommy issues. You were bloody and broken on a suspicious guy's lawn. Don't be pissed at me for protecting you." He crossed his arms, staring daggers at her. Damn, he excelled at his job.

Marley took another step back, trying to avoid his gaze. He didn't know it, but he'd landed her in a word of trouble. If Verna and Bernard showed up in Iverton, her life here was over. And she couldn't leave yet, not with the favor she owed Alan. She bit her lip, thinking. "I gotta go," she said robotically to Smith and walked down the hall, her thoughts a thousand miles away, planning what to do if Mommy Dearest darkened her door.

She'd never go back, not now, not ever. They couldn't drag home by her hair like some kid. She was an adult, fully capable of taking care of herself. She paid her debts. She'd honor the one to Alan, and then she'd run fast and far. Running was always the solution when it came to her past.

Part Two

Ginny Frost

Chapter Nineteen

Another two weeks passed, and still nothing from Marley. She'd disappeared from the hospital without a word. Alan tried the number from her little phone several times, but the call reverted to an ambiguous voicemail account. Needless to say, she never called back. He itched to speak to her, to help her take Troy off the streets, but apparently, she'd been steadfast in her dismissal of pressing charges. The deadline to remove Becca from her life expired a while ago, and Marley disappeared without a trace.

Now sitting in his lawyer's office, Alan pushed thoughts of Marley from his head and concentrated on the situation at hand. Conversations with counsel sucked on the best days, especially when they sorted through your possible futures. Jason Demeck, a decent guy for an attorney, needed to work on his bedside manner.

Alan ran a palm over his face, pushing the despair down into his gut. Peeking through his fingers, he caught Jason's eye. "We done?" he asked.

Jason sat back, his eyes rolling. "You can't hide, Alan. And looking through your hand isn't going to make it any prettier." He skimmed his fingers over the paperwork on his desk. "How do you want to go forward?"

Alan placed his elbows on his knees. "I can't sue Conrad if he's MIA. You're lawyer to us both. Where does that leave me?"

"In a hole," Jason tented his fingers. "We can expect the IRS report soon. They may or may not have criminal charges pending. Find your partner."

Alan fell back against the chair. "You have a pack of dogs you can send after him, right? How am I supposed to find him?"

"We have resources here, Alan but it's a conflict of interest for us to hunt him down. Honestly, you'd be better off hiring a detective."

Grousing, he said, "There's no money for a PI. And aren't you the one trying to find out how the money disappeared? If we find him, fine, but the money is still missing. Find it."

Jason sighed as if they hadn't beaten the conversation to death. "It's beyond me, Alan. I can protect what you have, cover your ass on the legal aspects, keep you out of jail. But I'm not a detective, regardless of what those TV shows say about law firms. Hire a forensic accountant and a private eye. Go over the files. You know him better than anyone."

Narrowing his gaze, Alan said, "I've been searching for him. Why hasn't anyone else?" His right eye twitched. He was tired of the games, the tasks pushed around from person to person. "In the time Conrad has been gone, something should've turned up about his whereabouts."

"Alan…" Jason licked his lips, an annoying habit. "It's not criminal yet. It's a bad audit with implications of criminal activity. No one's going to search for him until it gets legal."

"And if I ask you to? Before it gets legal?"

"Looks bad. Especially since he skipped out on the audit. If the IRS comes back with criminal charges, they'll find him."

Alan stood, his temper teetering on explosion. "Then I just keep waiting and taking it up the ass." He snapped his jacket down too hard pretending to straighten the wrinkles. "It's me who has to deal with the police, the public, the papers."

"The police?" Jason sat up. "What happened with the police?"

Alan didn't tell him about Marley or her late-night hospital visit. He never shared any more information with than necessary. He waved the lawyer's comment away. "Merely an interaction, nothing more than some harsh words, and I apologized to him for closing bars and putting people out of work."

Jason pointed a finger at him. "Tell me you didn't…"

"Explain to a man with a gun? A man who saw his friends and family struggle because I seem greedy. I'm trying to offset some of my negative press by sitting in my bar, day after day, smiling, helping, being nice."

Folding his arms, Jason said, "I'd rather you were locked down at home until it's over."

"I have a business to run. A much smaller business now, but I run it." He headed toward the door. "Let me know if you can actually help me."

Jason stood as well, buttoning his suit coat, his gaze not meeting Alan's. So much for confidence. The gesture sparked Alan's resentment toward the lawyer. How long had he known Jason? How many times had he or Conrad called on the man? And now he treated

Alan like dirt. Perhaps he should consider new council. Too bad he lacked the funds.

"Alan, we've received a preliminary accounting documentation from each business and the initial reports from the audit. We'll be analyzing them closely. I can give you a copy."

More disappointment clouded Alan's mood. "And do what with them? Build a fire? Make an airplane?" He scoffed. If he could have examined the accounts himself, he would've avoided Jason entirely. But he was no accountant. "Call me when you have something."

Opening the door, he stepped into the hallway, letting it slam behind him. His vision washed red, and his eye twitched sporadically. He rubbed the lid as he marched down the hallway. *Good thing I work at a bar.* A drink was a moral imperative.

Paralegals darted past him as he trudged to the front desk. Weariness sat like a weight on his shoulders. He hadn't slept well since Marley disappeared from the hospital. Maybe it was better this way. Rationality ordered he distance himself from a grifter with a sketchy past. But his heart ached for her every minute.

He dismissed the thought of her. She was out of his life on a personal level, but he might be able to help her from afar. He eagerly awaited Officer Smith's call, which hopefully contained some more info. Maybe he'd found the bastard who'd assaulted her.

The hallway wavered in his vision. He blinked, dizzy and tired, and ran smack into a paralegal with an armful of paperwork. Files flew into the air, and the poor girl crashed to the floor. Alan groaned. How could he keep Marley safe when he couldn't even refrain from knocking women down at his lawyer's office?

"My God, I'm sorry. Here let me help you," he said quickly, hoping he sounded nicer than his actions. The young woman, her back to him, hurriedly began to gather up the scattered files.

"No, it's okay," she chimed, her accent sliding to downstate. "I've got it."

Alan knelt next to her, gathering papers. "Please, Miss, it's the least I could do." He touched her shoulder, noticing her slight frame, a slip of a girl with honey blonde hair in a tight braid.

"No worries, sir. Please, I can handle it." Her head bowed, obviously embarrassed by their crash.

His sense of chivalry demanded he assist her in some way. The papers had flown everywhere like a tornado hit. He grabbed a few dozen files and as many loose pages, everything hopelessly mixed together. Straightening his pile, he pushed it toward her, feeling like a schmuck.

Another paralegal came to their rescue. "Oh, Heather, what a mess." The chunky brunette dug in, putting files back together at a rapid pace.

"Uh, here," Alan tried again when she didn't take the pile in his hands. "I'm sorry, Heather."

Finally, her green eyes met his. Marley. Alan's mouth dried up completely as he swallowed. He surveyed her up and down. A professional smart suit, tame makeup, and posh hair but still his Marley. In his lawyer's office. "Excuse me, sir."

"I don't think so," he said. Malice dripped from his words as heat flared under his collar.

****

Marley's heart raced, but she kept her composure,

and stared up at Alan with dead eyes. The mantra *Keep Calm* repeated in her head over and over as she slowly stood.

"I'm sorry I ran into you, sir," she said, her southern New York accent in place. "If you'll excuse me, I need to reorganize these files." With a tiny smile, she stepped away from Alan, but he grabbed her arm. Stopping short, she shot him a dark look.

Running into him had been a calculated risk. It was his lawyer's office and the only place to get her hands on his accounting files. Alan's appointment time with Demeck had changed, but Kristie, an employee here and an old acquaintance of Marley's, warned her.

Kristie's life used to be similar to Marley's until she pulled herself out and attended night school to be a paralegal. Thanks to Kristie, Marley slipped in here easily.

The woman owed Marley favors from way back. Usually, Marley never called them in or held them over people. But her plan required access to Demeck's files, so she dusted off Kristie's name. Getting the job had been cake. A few fake docs, diplomas, IDs, and boom, Heather.

The firm jumped across the table to hire her with her fake credentials and positive references, ones she obtained by pulling in other favors. She realized studying his numbers live and in person was the best way to help Alan. Now, established with his legal counsel, she could dive into the files, and find out how his rat of a partner screwed him over. If there were a game here, she'd find it. She was a pro.

Alan leaned down over her, his mouth next to her ear. "Care to explain what you're doing here?" he asked in a sharp whisper.

Oh well. She'd hoped to surprise him with the damning file or some other proof. She'd spill about her covert mission now if needed. He might not interfere if he knew the whole truth or he'd blow her cover. She had to decide quickly as a crowd of office workers gathered around them.

"I'd be happy to show you the room, Mr. Reid." She smiled warmly, blinking up at him. Discreetly, she tugged her arm back and strolled down the hall. The crowd muttered behind them. Alan stood stock still, his face red with anger. Raising an eyebrow, she cocked her head toward an open office door. He grumbled, and she drew a single finger across her neck, signaling him to shut the hell up before he blew it.

Marley's con artist skills made her an expert at crowd control with eyes in the back of her head. When the weight of their stares toned down, she and Alan walked into the empty office as if she owned the place. She plopped the files on the desk and shut the door behind him.

"What the f..." he began, but she placed a finger on his lips, flashing the black look again.

"Shut up," she said flatly. "You'll blow it for me."

He pushed away from her, gently. She loved how, even when she pissed him off royally, he still behaved like a gentleman. "Blow it? You're sneaking into my lawyer's office, doing God knows what."

She cut him off again, no patience to allow him to figure it out for himself. "I'm trying to help you here." He scoffed, throwing his arms in the air. Pushing his buttons was fun. Mr. Calm and Under Control until she came around. She bit her lip to hide the grin.

He sat down hard on the edge of the desk. "How can you"—He thrust his hand at her—"possibly help me?" He slammed his hand into his chest hard. Marley was impressed he didn't knock himself over.

"I'm going to find out what happened to your company. Where the money went and who took it." She crossed her arms over his chest. Declaring her resolution from the hospital aloud felt amazing.

He threw his head back and laughed from deep in his belly until tears formed in his eyes. He tried to speak a couple times but broke back into laughter each time. Marley arched an eyebrow, more amused than annoyed but still.

She put her hands on her hips. "I know a snow job when I see one, Alan. And you got screwed. I'm not convinced your IRS dudes or your lawyers are going to find what went wrong."

He wiped at his eyes. "Oh, and you can? Please stop playing dress up and go home. You should be resting after your…incident."

Her nostrils flared at his comment. Who did he think she was? Some helpless chick who sat home and waited for the cavalry? She knew from experience they never came.

Ever.

Best way to win a fight, go alone and disarm your opponent immediately. "I'm fine, Alan. I told you."

"Oh really?" he said, his tone no longer jovial. "You're over the attempted rape?" The word hit her like a slap, and she winced. Wasn't he supposed to be the white knight here? Maybe she'd figured him wrong. Anger bubbled inside, and she scowled at him.

"Alan, I've lived on the streets a long time. I can

deal with what happened to me. I'm not some candy ass from uptown who freaks when some stranger touches her."

Alan flew from his seat on the desk, standing over her, one finger raised in the air. Marley watched him wide-eyed, unsure of his intentions. Maybe she'd pushed too far. His face blazed red, and the tendons on his neck stood out. But smacking girls around so not his style. She stood her ground but prepped to fly at a moment's notice. "No one should touch you." He commanded.

Another burble of laughter escaped her lips. "You were never forced to choose between shelter and food. Troy crossed a line, but shit like that happens in my world."

Alan turned away, stomping back by the desk. "I don't like it." His tone low and growly. And rather sexy. Flashes of his kitchen table danced in her head.

Marley licked her lips. "You don't have to like it." She shoved away her lustful thoughts of taking Alan on the handy empty desk. "Neither do I, but I'm not going to spend a minute extra thinking about it."

"What about hunting him down? Making him pay?"

She sighed. "It'll never happen. He'll find another victim, slip her drugs, and take advantage of her. But the cops won't do a thing unless she's important. He'll coast through the system on ice skates and come out clean on the other side."

"Wait," he said, straightening. "Slip drugs to? He gave you something? I thought you took…" Alan shut his lips tight. His gaze shifted away.

She understood his distance, even after he played

her hero in the hospital. He thought her some kinda addict. Who fed him the lie? Smith? Or did Becca poison him from the start?

Troy's attack slapped home what happened when someone betrayed your trust. Never trust anyone on the street. She wasn't an addict—not now, not ever—but apparently, Alan thought otherwise.

Pursing her lips, she tapped her foot. "Yeah, he did. End of story." She raised her chin. "Back to business here. Leave the office and pretend you don't know me. Or fake you were hitting on me. I can't snoop if they think we know each other. Us being in here so long might mess things up as it is."

"And we are right back to you snooping in my private affairs. Jesus, Marley, you've confessed to con games, grifting, and drug use." She started to protest. "Okay, not voluntary drug-use, but still I don't want you anywhere near here."

Straightening her spine, she stared daggers at him. "Listen carefully. You've been played. Not by me. Or Becca. I'd know. Someone has messed with you and maybe your partner. I can find it. It's not my usual game, but I can see the con plain as day. Give me time, and I'll find the goods then hand the information over to you."

Alan shook his head. "You think I'm going to let you run wild with my finances. Play loose and fast with my business, my life?" He folded his arms. "No, just no."

Marley looked at the ceiling then back at him. "You believed me about the wallet." Alan glanced away. She pressed forward, working to catch his gaze again. "You stayed at the hospital with me, confronted the cop. Why'd you do it, Alan? If I'm some crook, why did you stand by me?"

He whipped his head around catching her off guard, and she stumbled back a half step. "Why'd you end up on my doorstep after Troy attacked you?" he shot back.

She laughed. "Because I felt safe at your place. Answer my question. Why protect me?"

He started to turn away again, but she grabbed his arm. He tucked his chin to his chest, his eyes blinking rapidly. "I wanted you to be safe, to be protected."

"But after the wallet thing?" She pressed, not sure what he might say. But his answer dictated if she continued the quest or not.

He grasped her hand, gently, turning to face her. His expression fading to kindness and something else. "Because I wanted you."

****

Alan straightened, adjusting his jacket. The words slipped without a thought. Not the best place or time to profess his feelings. Dammit. Talk about tossing your cards on the table. Tensing his jaw, he scowled. *Redirect the conversation, you idiot.*

He stepped closed to her to intimidate, not entice. "Right here, right now, I…" Marley misread his gesture, leaning into him, her hands on his chest. *Dammit.* He took her hands gently in his and lowered them. "Your being here is a problem," he said through gritted teeth.

She stepped back, understanding dawning on her face. "You have to trust me, Alan. I've got your back. I'm going to find your player and clear your name." She tilted her chin up, defiance in her expression.

He smiled. The words *Clear your name* hit him hard in the chest. A woman who endured years of cruelty and abuse, recently been assaulted and was homeless, and she wanted to save him.

"Marley," he whispered. "You don't have to do this. Let's go talk and figure it out."

She whipped her head from side to side. "Nope. I'm in. Now go away before someone thinks we are up to something." Grabbing up the files again, she turned to go, but he couldn't let her leave, let her do this crazy thing.

"I'm going to walk out of here and into my lawyer's office. I'm going to tell him who you are, and why you're here. Then we are both leaving the office. Understood?" He dropped the words slowly into her ear. He wasn't fucking around.

She met his gaze, a cool calm expression on her face. "Do you really believe you can intimidate me, Alan? I've worked hundreds of games. I can find your rat and set you free. I wouldn't do this for anyone. And anyone would pay me a mint too." She narrowed her gaze. "I'm good. I can do it. Trust me."

Heat rose up his neck. He stuck a finger under his collar, allowing some air to touch his skin. His thoughts held a fine coat of red. Gritting his teeth, he wagged a finger in her face. "You need to understand," he said, the tension palpable in the air, "I'm in a hole so deep, I can't see any daylight. Please don't finish burying me."

Her gaze flicked from his pointing finger to his eyes. "You have nothing to lose, Alan. I can see it in your face." She touched his hand. "Give me a week. Then, I'm history."

His brain whirled. "A week?" She nodded. "I let

you snoop here for a week, and you think you'll find things the IRS or my lawyer didn't." She nodded again. He snorted. "How?"

She wrapped her hand around his outstretched finger and kissed the tip of it. A thrill of pure lust surged through his entire body. She looked him dead in the eye with those gorgeous green orbs. "No one hired a forensic accountant," she said plainly.

"And that's in your skill set?"

She kissed his finger again, sucking slightly with a little tongue. Half his brain shorted out. "Yes, it is." She winked, jostled the files, and slid out the door.

He fell against the desk, his hip hitting smartly. "This is how they do it," he said aloud. "This is how they get under your collar, in your pants, and in your wallet." He sighed. Her words still burned in his mind. They didn't hire a forensic accountant. And the business had used temps, like Lizette.

The IRS poured over his accounts, but what were they focusing on? On the taxes, on the evasion, not on the sources, bad investments, and secret accounts. If there were any. Marley might be able to crack the system and find what everyone else missed. Or she could be planting evidence to clear him.

Alan loosened his tie. The heat disappeared, but the worry returned. He suppressed the urge to run to Jason and rat her out. Most of him wanted her to try. The weeks of suspicion, the meetings with IRS agents and lawyers tired him to the bone. Maybe Marley could find Conrad and end this. Maybe she'd find a different culprit.

She was right about the money being gone, most of the business too. He had nothing else to lose. And based on his gut feeling, someone would do jail time over the IRS report. He was already down the river. Might as well swim and enjoy the view.

And maybe somehow at the end, Marley might wait for him. In an insane world where a man like him could fall for a girl like her, anything was possible.

Chapter Twenty

That afternoon, Marley smiled at Jason Demeck as she passed him in the hall. He put out a hand to stop her and launched into a speech about taxes, cases, and her being part of the team. Her gaze fell vacant, and she blinked too often until he stopped talking.

"Well, Miss Stockwell," he said. "I guess that's enough for now. See Kristie and finish settling in." As his gaze drifted over her body, he quirked an eyebrow, one side of his mouth turning up. A slimy sensation poured over her. "I think you'll fit in nicely here."

Marley repressed a shudder. She cocked her head to the side, hiding her disgust. "Thank you, sir." Spinning on her heel, she headed back to her desk. The douchebag had the audacity to run his hand over her ass as she walked away. A kneejerk reaction spun her back around, ready to rip him to shreds. At the last second, she held her tongue, giving him a vague, vacant smile. Revenge always tasted sweeter cold. And she knew a thousand ways to repay him for such a dick move. Some of them rather painful.

Grinding her teeth, she tromped back to her desk, hiding behind the cubicle wall until Mr. Hands disappeared. Obtaining Alan's file would be cake. Security here was surprisingly lax. Hell, they hired her with little or no background check. You'd think a lawyer would be more paranoid.

Anyway, playtime with the file might be difficult. The thing required serious study. She believed someone must've pulled the Salami Slicing Trick and got too greedy. A good con man knew how to keep the income steady over time. From what Alan said, his grifter took too big a bite. His partner's disappearance looked seriously suspicious. Alan trusted the guy implicitly, the fool.

The figures told the tale. She knew it. The lawyer knew it. Alan seemed to believe the numbers hid the real villain. A sweet, giving guy, ripe for the picking. No wonder his head was underwater. But he'd helped her; she'd help him.

Taking a breath, she stuck her head out of the cubicle. No Demeck, no one in fact. After a quick smooth to her skirt, she wandered down the short hallway to Records, which always left its door open. The cute young thing behind the desk would melt in her hands like butter.

"Hi, Greg." She batted her eyelashes. "Can ya help me?" Cocking her head, she winked.

"Ugh, it's Grey, Miss…ugh. You're new, right?" He blinked at her rapidly, as if he were batting his eyelashes too. "Do you have something in your eye?" Oh good, he's as dumb as a post. No need to seduce him.

"Nah, Grant. I need the Reid/Bennett paperwork. Thanks." She turned her back, fiddling with her necklace as if she'd been waiting for hours.

"Mr. Demeck put the file to bed for the day. He returned it to me, after Mr. Reid left. So, yeah. You don't need it."

She spun, gasping a huge breath. "Greer, you know the importance of their case. Mr. Demeck asked me to bring it straight to him." Huffing, she put a hand on her hip.

"But he just gave it to me."

"And he then asked me for it back." She leaned over his desk, flashing her cleavage. "Do you wanna be the one to explain to him why he can't have the file?"

Grey's brow furrowed, and his mouth opened and closed a few times. "But he just gave it to me to file."

"And now he wants it back. Geez, Grady." She hunched closer, whispering, "Do I have to spell it out for you?"

He blinked, several times, his brow as wrinkled as ever. "Uh, no?" He bit his lip, his gaze roving over his desk. They landed on a large green file folder. He touched it gingerly, then straightened his spine. "Uh, here. Bring it back when he's done. I'll file it properly."

He held the folder out for her. When Marley grabbed her side, Grey didn't let go. They tugged back and forth several times. Marley mentally rolled her eyes. Swiping money from a retiree was a hell of a lot easier. Not that she did those things anymore.

"Grey," she hissed, "Mr. Demeck will be angry." Whether it was her tone, her threat, or finally getting his name right, he released of the file with a pout.

"Okay, Miss...what's your name anyway?" He tilted his head like some cocker spaniel.

"Thanks, G. I'll return it in a sec." She whirled and strutted back down the hall, swinging her ass hard in case Grey noticed she was female. Of course, he might not be into women. She swatted her forehead with the large file, her skills rusty with age. But apologies could wait for later.

The thought stopped her short. She pressed her lips, sipping a breath, remembering it was a game, a con. No apologizing for trying to seduce the man, regardless of his sexual orientation. Alan's niceness was rubbing off. She shook her shoulders as if bucking off the mantel and walked on.

Back in the safety of her cubicle, she quickly switched Alan's files into a blue folder. Green indicated an ongoing case. Blue held finished cases. No one would question her copying a finished case. Paperwork abounded here. Everything in triplicate and mailed out to various clients. If anyone asked, she was copying files for the IRS and the State. The office didn't know the meaning of paperless.

Mission complete, she slid the originals back in the green folder and headed back to her pal. "You were right, Grey," she said sheepishly, holding out the file. "He didn't need these now. Sorry." Tossing her hair, she giggled stupidly.

Grey, the lug, blinked at her again. "Uh, okay. Sure." He took the folder, scrutinizing it closely. "You didn't lose anything, did you? You kept it for a bit." He thumbed through the pages.

"Nah." She waved a dismissive hand. "I copied some stuff from another file. Sorry I didn't bring it back right away."

Narrowing his gaze, he asked, "Did you copy this?"

She gaped at him, feigning anger and disgust. Then for more effect, she purposely let her vocabulary degrade. "Just 'cause my hair's blonde, don't mean I'm stupid, Grey. I know what to copy and what files they want. You don't gotta accuse me of doing the wrong thing."

His hands flew up. "No, no. I…the case is open and Mr. Demeck doesn't want extra copies around. The IRS might want something we're 'still searching for.' If you know what I mean."

"Well, I don't. And I didn't copy the file. Wanna go to Mr. Demeck and discuss it further?" She glared at him, hands on hips, lips pressed. Marley discovered through her conning, men reacted the same to both tears and anger from a woman—run, fast.

"Uh, I…no. No, I asked because it's a hot file and…"

"And I returned it. Geez, Grey. Leave the new girl alone." She stomped her foot like a toddler, crossing her arms over her chest.

"Can I help with something?" Demeck stuck his head in the door. Marley grinned to herself. Here's where Mr. Wandering Hands could validate her.

"Mr. Demeck." She wiped a non-existent tear from her eye. "Grey here thinks I'm doing the job wrong. I'm trying to be efficient. And…" Sniffing, she pouted, leaving the sentence hanging.

"Grey," Demeck said, his tone jovial but firm. "Heather is doing her best." He tipped her head at Marley, indicating her boobs rather than her person. "Let's give her some time to settle in here."

Grey frowned but didn't protest too much. "She had an active file. I wanted to ensure…"

Demeck slid the rest of the way into the room and put an arm around Marley. "I'm sure it's fine. Right, Heather?" She shrugged, and he pulled her in tighter. She grimaced but ensured only Grey saw it. His eyes widened, and he swallowed hard.

"It's fine, sir," he said flatly then glanced at Marley. His whole expression changed. Sympathy and worry covered his face. "Do you agree, Heather?" He lowered his chin a bit. Grey the White Knight.

Marley wiggled out of Demeck's grip. "We're fine. Thanks, Mr. Demeck. Thanks, Grey. Sorry for the misunderstanding." She hurried past to her desk to the ladies' room before anyone could follow her. Best to hide for a bit.

Sitting in a stall, holding her breath, she cursed herself for such sloppy work. She hadn't run a read game in months. Rusty wasn't the word for it. She needed to pull it together before she landed Alan in more trouble. Tonight, she'd pour over those records and find out what the hell happened to his business.

****

Sitting in his car outside the law firm, Alan's mind reeled. Marley in Demeck's office? Mind-bending, but he put faith in her to find the information no one else could. Why not? Nothing else to lose.

His cell buzzed. The hopes of a text from Conrad still crashing into him each time the phone went off. Fumbling with the device, he checked the screen.

I'm stopping by the Tavern later, Reid. We need to talk.

Officer Smith's text forced Alan to sit up. Did he find Troy? Alan's heart rate tripled. Putting the bastard away would make him feel better about Marley being out on the streets of Iverton. His city wasn't a shiny beacon of safety but not rampant with crime either.

The drug scene had exploded here as in many other small cities in upstate. Alan knew about it only on the periphery because of his businesses. He texted back he'd be back at the tavern in a few minutes. Starting his car, he peeled out from the curb back to Birch Street.

Shortly after Alan arrived at the Oakwood, Smith rolled through the door. The two sat at an empty booth in the back of the tavern. Smith didn't beat around the bush.

Diving right in, he said, "Mr. Reid, we really can't do much without Marley pressing charges. I've ID'd Troy. We know his hangouts. He's a low-grade drug dealer, mostly party drugs, but I can't pull him in without cause. I can't arrest him without a warrant." Smith folded his arms over his chest. "Vice has him in their short list, but…" He held his arms out to the side.

Alan sighed and slumped in the chair. Rubbing his forehead, he considered his options. How could he help Marley and keep her safe on the streets? Since she refused to stay with him, turned down money for a hotel, perhaps he and Smith could keep that asshole, Troy, behind bars for a while.

Not to mention the fact she was researching what happened to his business, to his partner on her own time. Working at the law office instead of finding a real job or going to school. Someone at Hobard and Demeck would realize she lacked credentials, and then they'd both be up shit's creek. He needed to fix this, yesterday.

Peering at Smith, he asked, "If I convinced Marley to press charges?"

Smith nodded shortly. "Assault might put him away for a small stretch. But if we can get him charged with attempted rape, might be better. Not the nickel and dime stuff associated with a drug charge."

Alan shook his head. "She won't do it. She wants

to walk away and never look back." He ran his sweaty palms down his pants as he stood. "I'll try."

Smith stood too. "Be safe, Reid. I don't want to visit you in the hospital." He nodded, grabbing his cap. "I'll let you know if the situation changes."

Alan headed for the door, his mind spinning. He had to take care of the creep, somehow. But first, he had to see what his girl was up to.

Chapter Twenty-One

A pang of fear bubbled in Marley's stomach as she waited for the elevator. The stupid file barely fit in her bag. With her recent luck, she expected Grey to pop around the corner and join her. She dug down into her skill set. Swiping a file was nothing. Merely another pocket to pick and she'd picked hundreds.

A calm rolled over her as unused skills shook out and she tried to seem as bored as possible. The door slid open without incident, and Marley hit the button.

"Hold the door." *Fuck.*

"Sure," she called back, jamming her finger into the close door button. "Ack, sorry," she said as the doors pressed closer. A briefcase wedged between the panels, and the doors rolled back open. "Oh, good. You made it." She grinned up at Mr. Demeck.

"Thanks for holding the door, Heather." He didn't seem to notice she'd done no such thing. With his cell phone to his ear, he chatted away.

Marley half listened, in case they mentioned her guy. Demeck maintained a huge client list. So probably not, but a little spying never hurt.

She fiddled with her bag as the doors reopened, allowing Demeck to exit first. Taking slow steps, searching for keys or lipstick or a bus pass, she crossed the lobby to the door.

"Hey, Heather," a man called. Internally, she groaned. Another obstacle. Grey wandered over to her. He smiled, a genuine one, not the blank stupid look he'd given her earlier. "We"—He waved to other coworkers clustered at the revolving door—"are headed over to Beacon St. Bar. Wanna come for happy hour?"

Happy Hour with office coworkers. What were they thinking? Happy Hour people were ripe for pickpockets and pickups. How could these marks not know?

"Uh, well, since you're new, we thought…"

Staring up at him, she returned to the conversation. "What? I'm sorry," she soothed.

"You, uh, wrinkled your nose. I'm sorry if I offended you. Maybe you don't drink or aren't into bars or something. We wanted you to feel included." He glanced down, scuffing his shoe. "Especially after the file thing today. I get a little too intense sometimes."

She cocked her head. Drinks with coworkers who were being nice? What a concept. She'd never done such a thing in her life. Ever. Bars were for picking up marks. Marks like Alan. Shutting her eyes, she shook her head, banishing the thought. Not a mark but a friend, former lover, nice guy.

"So, no then…" Grey broke into her thoughts.

"Oh, sorry," she said hiding that he startled her. "I have a lot on my mind. The job is new and a little confusing. And my nerves…" She glanced over at the crowd waiting for Grey, wondering what it was like to live that life. "Thanks for the invite, but I gotta hit my sister's place and walk her dog." The lie spilled out of her effortlessly.

"Oh, okay. What kinda dog?"

Dammit. Prolonging the conversation was the last thing she wanted. The weight of the stolen files increased with every word. She shifted the bag. "A little guy, high energy." She searched her databanks. "Jack Russell or a terrier or some mutt." Flipping her hand dismissively, she finished, "And he pees everywhere if I'm late."

"Oh, brother." Grey smiled, and damn if he wasn't kinda cute. With dimples on both cheeks, he resembled a cherub. "What a mess. Maybe next time then."

"Oh." Marley thought she'd throw him a bone. "Put your wallet in your front pocket. You never know at those bars. "

"Huh, okay." He waved as he walked back to the group, who filed out the door, laughing and smiling.

Marley watched them go with a sliver of regret. Decent folk but what would she talk to them about? Her whole life boiled down to cons, lies, and more messes than she could handle. It didn't matter. She'd be gone by the next happy hour anyway.

She glanced at her phone. If she hurried, she could catch the Number Two bus.

****

She slid back in her seat, bag clasped tight on her lap, letting her thoughts wander. Absently, she tugged at the elastic at the end over her braid, freeing her now blonde hair. Her to-do list still contained several huge items. File stolen, check. Now to analyze the accounting. Complicated but in a logical way. Nothing really different than what she'd done for Becca. She'd have the file done in two days max. Then redeem Alan. And finally disappear from Iverton and all its…

An image of Grey's smile flashed in her mind,

followed by a rather vivid memory of Alan naked on top of her. Her legs pressed tightly together as she focused on something else. Alan remained off limits. She owed him for the hospital, the save from Troy. She'd pay her debt and not darken his door again.

When the bus stopped near the Iverton Motor Lodge, she shuffled off, the bag still clutched against her chest.

****

Alan saw her exit the bus and hurriedly grabbed a parking spot on the street. The neighborhood seemed a little sketchy, but he thought his car would be safe for a few hours. She stood on the sidewalk for a beat, glancing around, a huge bag over her shoulder. He waited.

She darted up the block, moving fast for a woman in heels. Alan exited the car, set the locks, and followed her. She used her speed rather than stealth to hide her destination. Perhaps she realized he followed her. After another block, she turned into the back parking lot of a seedy cinderblock motel, making a beeline for one of the orange doors.

"This is your safe place to stay?" Alan shook his head and closed in on her. No longer caring if she saw him, he loped over to her. Marley spotted him right away, her eyes wide.

"What are you doing here?" She pulled the bag against her tighter. "Are you following me?" She sounded as if she wanted to kick his ass. Well, too bad.

"I thought perhaps we could discuss everything. Like adults. I mean you did infiltrate my lawyer's office." He leaned against one the motel doors, trying to seem casual, hiding how much he needed answers.

"Go away, Alan. I know what I'm doing." She fished a key out of her bag and opened one of the orange doors. "I'll inform you when I've found something."

Bristling, he leaned over her. "I don't need any more trouble than I'm already in. A longer vacation in federal prison helps no one." He hissed the words between gritted teeth. Finding the answers should have been top priority, but her new blonde hair distracted him. She looked the epitome of sexy assistant in her short-skirted suit and heels. Thoughts of taking her in the suit on the motel bed rushed his brain.

"By the time I'm done, you won't see a day of prison." Lifting her chin, she unlocked the door. After sliding inside the room, she attempted to close the door in his face. Alan managed to stick his foot in the frame before the heavy door slammed shut.

"Enough, Marley." He shoved the door open and entered the shabby room. She spun, her mouth screwed up in a frown. The door crashed closed behind him. "I'm done with the games."

"I'm doing this for you. Shut up and be grateful." She tossed the bag on the bed and bent to unbuckle her shoes.

A thrill ran up his spine. Marley bent forward, her new blonde hair framing her face and ample cleavage peeping out from her blouse. He swallowed as every drop of blood drained to his cock. He knew better. With her record and her reputation, nothing good would come of another tryst. But the tiny skirt just brushing the tops of her thighs said differently.

"Keep the heels on." He growled the words, not caring. He'd have her now. On the crappy motel bed, in the suit with that blonde hair.

Marley popped her head up but didn't stand. A sly smile dawned on her lips. "I'm not sure I heard you correctly." Her silken voice channeled straight to his cock.

"Yeah, you did." He stepped closer to her, his groin in line with her luscious mouth. "You heard me exactly. Keep the shoes on." Running a hand over the blonde hair, he couldn't hold back a groan. An image of wrapping those locks around his fist as he took her from behind. The fading bruises on her thighs gave him pause, but Marley urged him on.

Licking her lips, she purred, "And the suit?" Her breath caressed his crotch, and he resisted the urge to shove her head in closer. Her right hand stoked his thigh and another thunderbolt hit his spine.

"Take it off."

She glanced up at him, her face inches from his zipper. "Now?"

"Now." He grasped her arm and eased her upright. Snapping the button on her suit jacket, he wriggled the cloth over her shoulders, revealing a lacey camisole which left nothing to the imagination. His gaze raked her up and down, his body screaming to take her now. "This is how you dress for work." His voice held a strained note, his desire threatening to shut off his ability to talk completely.

She shrugged one shoulder, causing a delicate strap to slip down. He growled again pulling her against him, showing her how her outfit affected him. He kissed her hard, his hand thrust in her hair.

He ran his fingers down to her ass, squeezing it. "You better have panties on." He nipped at her ear as his hand plunged under her skirt. They were there, a tiny scrap of fabric. He tugged, and they snapped right off. He raised them up to show her. "Really?"

She pulled away from him, crawling onto the bed. On all fours, her hair a tangled mess, she gazed back at him with a burning heat. "Maybe I need some lessons."

All control disappeared. Alan lunged forward. He flung her skirt up over her hips, dropping his pants at the same time. He took a moment to appreciate the sight before him—Her bare ass, her heel-clad feet, her everything—He bit his lip.

Marley swung her head around to look at him. "Alan," she urged.

Grabbing a condom from his wallet, he quickly put it on and slid inside her, riding her hard into the bed. Marley screamed with pleasure at each thrust. She wiggled against him, her heels digging into his legs.

He held her hips, wishing he could grab her hair, but there wasn't opportunity. Marley thrashed and pressed meeting him stroke for stroke.

Her groans became more intense more desperate. "Alan…" she begged, and he knew what she needed. But the police report loomed in his mind.

"Are you okay, Marley?" he whispered.

"Yes, God, yes. Please." His fingers found her clit and he worked a careful pace. He slowed to an easy rhythm, letting his fingers take her higher.

With a firm stroke and a flick, she exploded against him, screaming his name over and over. He came in a torrent, her spasms sending him over the edge. Groaning, he collapsed against her on the bed.

Marley twisted and curled against his chest, her breath coming in gasps. She found his tie and twirled it around her fingers, pulling him down for a sloppy kiss. "Well," she said softly. "That was something." She giggled.

He sighed, pushing her hair away from her face. "The blonde hair…" he said, running a finger down her cheek.

"And me resisting you." She snuggled against his chest.

"Maybe." A thousand reprimands and question ran through his brain, but he needed a moment to hold her close, keep her safe, have her be his.

****

Marley closed her eyes and drank in the scent of him, sandalwood and all man. Her brain flashed the same old story—mark, someone she owed a debt to, cut and run. Every fiber of her being yearned to stay with him. Well, maybe not in this shithole but stay. She gave herself three breaths before pushing away.

"Can't keep your hands off me, huh?" Though her words sounded flippant and cold, she didn't mean a syllable. Distance should be the best policy with him, though her heart and body craved him. She stood, smoothing down her skirt.

Alan propped up on his elbow. It was comical to see him on the bed, fully dressed except the top of his pants hanging open. He smiled sheepishly, and another chunk fell off her iceberg heart. "I probably shouldn't have. After what you've been through." He reached out a hand to her, and she couldn't resist.

He pulled her down on the bed next to him. "You okay?" he asked, running a thumb over the back of her hand. "I didn't mean to make it awkward, I only wanted…" His gaze dropped to their entangled hands.

"To get laid," she quipped, unable to pull her hand free. Maybe she should toss him out, lie saying he crossed the line. Biting her lip, she couldn't force the falsehood out.

"I wanted you." His blue eyes met her, and another avalanche of snow ran down her chest.

Her shoulders sank. "Alan, we talked about it. We can't do this to each other."

"Then why are you employed with my lawyer if you're set on abandoning me?"

A smile stole out. "The same reason you're in my hotel room."

He released her hand and shifting to sitting on the bed. "I should go."

No. Don't leave.

"Yeah, probably a good idea." She scooched back a few inches, not wanting any more skin to skin contact.

He stood, his back to her, straightening his pants. A giggle burst from her lips and he glanced over his shoulder at her.

"Oh, come on. It's kinda funny," she said. And damn sexy. But he has to go.

Once he redressed into his usual suave, business self, he asked, "So can I have those files you took from Demeck?"

Her gaze darted to her bag near the door, then back to meet Alan's. He'd seen her glance and smirked at her. "You brag you're an amazing grifter, been conning for years, but that was a tell." He reached down and grabbed the bag.

She didn't bother to chastise herself. Part of her knew she wanted him to find the files but not take them. She wanted him to stay and solve the puzzle with her.

After rolling her shoulders, she held out her hand for the bag. "I'll show you how good I am."

His gaze flashed over to the bed for a good second then back to her. "Now there's a tell, Reid. Let me change and we'll find out how your partner screwed you."

Alan glanced down at the bag. He hefted it as if checking the weight. The bag contained his whole life. "If it's the same to you, I'd like to find evidence proving both myself and Conrad innocent."

He'd stay. They'd work together as a team, and he'd stay. She squelched a grin and said, "Challenge accepted."

Chapter Twenty-Two

Marley rubbed her eyes. Paper records sucked out loud, and the crappy hotel chair didn't help. She regretted not sweet-talking Grey into giving her a thumb drive of the file. But it was a dead end. Computer files were easily altered. She knew full well. Some of her best work included tweaking numbers on various mark's accounts.

Alan stopped pacing, stood behind her, and rubbed her shoulders. His strong hands felt amazing on her sore neck. She wished they hadn't gotten dressed again. Doing tax work would be much easier naked.

She glanced up at him, a small smile playing on her lips. "Are you thinking what I'm thinking?" she cooed. His hands dropped as he sighed.

Sliding into the seat next to her, he said, "I'll lie and say I'm thinking about food." His gaze darted to the V in her shirt and back up again. "I still feel pretty guilty about…" He waved at the bed. "You've been through a great deal." His cheeks pinked. Adorable.

Reaching across the table, she put her hand on his. "You've really lived a soft life, huh?"

His eyebrows shot up, and he pulled his hand back an inch. "What do you mean?"

Licking her lips, she met his gaze, giving him a long, analyzing look. "I'm okay, Alan. Troy is a douche, and I'm fine. "

"But he assaulted you, hurt you. And then I…" he trailed off, his gaze not meeting hers.

"If I didn't want to, Alan, I would've punched you in the throat."

His gaze whipped back to her face, his mouth open in an O. She giggled.

"I can take care of myself, mister. I've been doing it a long time." Rubbing her fingers over his thumb, she waited for him to take off his knight's armor. Part of her hoped he wouldn't.

Shaking his head, he cleared his throat so he could speak. "I don't want to hurt you. I hate that he touched you at all. I…"

She squeezed his hand, halting his words. "You've done enough, Sir Galahad. Let's focus on the numbers." The last thing she wanted to do. Cuddling on the bed, making small talk, wild riotous sex—the things she really wanted. But white knights don't take the peasant girl for anything more than a ride. She sighed, ruffling the paperwork. The tension in the air beat on her like a wall of heat.

"How about some food then?" He pulled his hand away and shot of darkness floated through her. How would she ever get over him? He kept showing up and being perfect. Taxes then out. Save him from his asshole partner and then fly off to somewhere warm. She watched him pull out his cell and call someone while these thoughts ran through her head. Tears stung the corners of her eyes, and she blinked it away quickly.

"Ten minutes," he laughed. "It's always ten minutes."

"What?" She snapped back to reality, erasing the

mushy thoughts.

"Chinese food. Doesn't matter where I am in the city, it's always ten minutes. I hope you don't mind I ordered for you. I went on automatic, ordering my usual."

Standing from the table, she stretched, arching her back. "Usual Chinese order. Oh, honey…" She dropped her arms and pouted at him. "Does someone not eat right?"

He smirked. "Someone works crazy hours at bars. Some of which have terrible food."

"And Chinese is better?" she teased him, unable to resist. The nervous energy inside her needed an outlet somewhere and mocking him helped. Of course, she hoped he'd swoop her up in his arms and kiss her passionately, rip her new panties off.

She ducked her head, not able to meet his gaze with the lustful thoughts rushing through her. A cold shower might do the trick to cool the heat. But then again, a shower for two held entertaining possibilities. *Dammit*. She headed for the bathroom anyway. A splash of water on her face would have to suffice.

"You okay?" Alan called to her. A wave of relief washed over her when he didn't follow her. Banging doggie style on the bed had been a serious breach of her promise. Banging in the shower would negate the oath completely.

"Yeah, give me a minute."

"Uh, sure."

Did he sense the heat too? He didn't show it. But that was Alan—all cool and suave one second, holding her down on the bed the next. She let the tap run to clear the pipes.

A knock sounded on the door, startling her.

Alan called back again. "Well, they're quick. I hope you're hungry."

****

A weird tension filled the air. Marley stuck her head out of the bathroom and scanned the room to locate where the vibe emanated from. Alan headed for the door, fishing out his wallet from his suit coat. The dark feeling persisted.

Cocking her head to the side, she watched him, considering asking him not to answer. Not a great neighborhood therefore, the possibilities behind the door were endless.

It seemed to take him hours cross the room, as if time switched to slow motion. As he reached for the door, something clicked inside her. She found her voice. "Don't answer it." She sounded thin and tinny, like a child.

Alan glanced over his shoulder at her, his brow furrowed. "I'll check. But it's probably the food." He shook his head dismissively. "You worry too much."

"Says the guy who puts all his time and effort worrying about me." She crossed the room to stand behind him. "I have a weird feeling."

"Do you get these feelings often?"

She slapped at his arm. "Check the peephole."

He did, making an exaggerated display of peeking through the fisheye. It wasn't like him. Alan never played around. She swallowed harder as the tension in the air became thicker. "It's some older couple. Probably lost."

He reached for the handle before Marley could stop him. Opening the door a crack, Alan greeted the couple.

"Something I can help you with?" he said in his business voice. She didn't hear their response, but the black sensation deepened in Marley's gut. She wedged under Alan's arm trying to see the couple.

She gasped, grabbing his arm in a vice grip. A single syllable dropped from her lips. "No."

Alan opened the door slightly wider and turned to Marley. "Your parents?" he asked, his brow deeply furrowed, his mouth a slit.

How had they found her? Hell, Alan didn't even know she was staying here. Becca. It must've been her. Becca and her ring of spies around the entire town. "Shut the door." The words came out as a shriek, but Verna and Bernard Volkov pushed past Alan and enveloped her.

Chapter Twenty-Three

"Oh, my baby. I finally found you. My sweetie," Verna cooed, her arms tight around Marley.

"Marlena, I've waited for this day forever." Bernard dabbed at his eyes, his arm around both Marley and Verna.

Marley stared at Alan. He'd let them in. Why hadn't she told him about her parents? And now, they were here, and she was totally fucked.

"Uh, come in?" Alan's words a question rather than an invitation. He closed the door, his eyes darting back and forth between Verna and Bernard.

Marley shook her head slightly to signal no, but Alan missed it. Then she opened her mouth to protest, Verna cut her off.

"Oh, honey." Her arms still gripping Marley tight, Verna tried to crab walk deeper into the room. The old bat knew how to position things, how to work a crowd, how to manipulate people.

Marley pulled at her mother's arms. "Let go of me, you bitch," she growled.

"Sweetie," her mother cooed, swinging her around to face away from Alan. "Keep your voice down, dear." Her tone sweet but her words dripped pure venom.

Bernard's voice sounded behind her, booming to fill the space, showing everyone his importance. "You must be Alan. It's a pleasure to meet you. I've heard so much about you."

Marley managed to break her mother's hold. She rushed over to Alan, darting behind him away from her father's reach.

Alan's head swiveled back and forth, a confused expression on his face. Bernard trapped Alan into the handshake, his other arm on the shoulder, boxing Alan in. Dammit, the two were ensconced in the room already. She'd have to work hard to remove them.

"Uh, hi." Alan pulled his hand away with some resistance. "A pleasure to meet you." He glanced over his shoulder, and she moved into his line of sight.

Staring at him hard, she mouthed, "Make them go."

****

"I didn't know your parents lived in the area." Alan stepped back, keeping between Marley and the door. Safe from whoever these people were. She clearly didn't want them here, and he'd been a fool to let them in the room. He glanced from one to the other.

The woman, smartly dressed in a pantsuit, had expensive shoes and hair. The man mirrored Alan's own look, well-tailored suit with a silk tie. They appeared harmless, sophisticated, but Marley didn't trust them. They needed to go.

"Not the best place for a reunion," Alan said, sliding toward the door. "Perhaps…"

The man cut him off. "Alan. I don't want to drag you into our little family business here." He crossed his arms over his chest, his legs apart. Every bit of his body language telling Alan he was staying. "But she's been gone for a long time. We miss her terribly, and now we finally have a chance to see our daughter again."

"Oh yes." The woman swept in, draping herself across the man's shoulders. "Our little girl. My God, we've finally found you. I can't believe it." If those tears were anything but crocodile's, Alan would eat his shoes.

He held up both his hands to halt the drivel. "Marley, do you know these people?"

"Yes," she squeaked, one hand gripping his arm tight.

"Do you want them here?" Alan kept his tone firm, strong but not hostile. Smith might come to the rescue if he texted, but he'd rather keep it low key.

"No," she said more firmly, but her hands still trembled, and her words weren't quite steady. Her palpable fear formed a halo around her. A scared Marley threw him into caveman mode.

"You can't…"

"But my darling…" The parents spoke over top of each other, spewing overly sweet sentiments.

"Enough," Alan said using his "Bar's closed" voice. The two shut up immediately. "Marley wants you to leave. You need to go."

The man puffed up. "See here. She's our child." He kept a bit of pleading in his voice. "We aren't going to abandon her after we've finally found her." He reached out an arm toward Marley, but Alan blocked him. The man was not touching her.

"I'm not sure what the deal is, but Marley says go, so go." He put a finality in his voice. His temper checked for now, but he didn't know how long he could refrain from cold-cocking the guy.

"How dare you!" The woman stepped in front of her husband, forcing Alan to retreat back. "You have our daughter here in a seedy motel, doing who knows what. And you have the audacity to throw us from the premises. I have a mind to call the police." She huffed, sticking her nose high in the air.

Marley's trembling fingers dug into Alan's arm. He glanced down at her white knuckles as a few thoughts ran through his head. *Okay, a runaway but why such fear now?* What did she run from? Troy never scared her this badly.

He leaned back and whispered to Marley, "How old are you?" The question hadn't really occurred to him before. Especially since the hospital never asked for parental consent. But something about the man's tone made it sound as if she were a child.

"Twenty-three."

Anger replaced confusion.

It'd been years since Alan seriously played bouncer at his bars, but his muscles remembered every move. He stepped forward swiftly, not giving them time to protest. Bullying the woman to the side, he grasped the man's arm by the elbow. A rapid spin and shove forward put them at the door. Alan quickly opened it, forcing the man out the threshold and into the parking lot. Behind him, the woman squawked loudly.

Alan released the man before he protested too much. The woman followed her husband closely, sputtering and threatening. Alan stepped back blocking the door, his arms crossed. "If you want to talk with Marley, we can do it at my bar downtown."

The man sneered at Alan, his true colors finally shone through. "I know about you, Reid, about the criminal activity and the money laundering. You're not some superhero saving her. You can't 'protect' her forever."

"Are you seriously threatening your own child in the middle of a parking lot?" Alan kept his tone even but not necessarily quiet. This part of town had ears which was both good and bad.

"Marlena!" her father called. "Get in the car." He pointed to an older Lexus. "You're coming home with us. The childishness is finished."

Marley's hand grasped Alan's shoulder. He didn't move, continuing to be a roadblock for these wackos. "I left for a reason. I'll never go back, and you can't make me. I'm not some little kid anymore."

Besides their demanding nature, what forced Marley to leave their house? They obviously had money and some higher education, based on their speech. Perhaps these people were the ones who originally taught her the confidence games, and the whole situation was just another ploy.

"Oh, really?" the woman snapped. Her sweet disposition disappearing in a greasy cloud. "Well, little girl"—She dug into her oversized designer purse—"This paper says you're still under our guardianship due to your incompetent mental capacity." She sneered, waving an envelope.

Alan licked his lips, trusting in Marley. If they were as bad as she'd said, the paper meant nothing. "We're done here," he said shortly. Gently, he took Marley's arm and escorted her back inside. Shutting the door soundly behind him, he slid the lock home with a snap.

Hammering knocks pounded the door as soon as he shut it. He didn't flinch. He didn't move, even when the shouting began. Both parents ranted at the closed door.

He stood with his back to it, hands crossed in front of him, his head down. And waited.

Marley paced the room. He watched her legs pass back and forth in front of him. If he glanced up, he knew he'd see her twisting her hair, a frantic look in her eye. Swallowing hard, he fought the urge to comfort her.

Wait for it.

Other voices joined the fray outside causing Alan to finally lift his head. A small smile slipped across his face. Marley's pacing stopped, and she stared wide-eyed at him. Holding up a finger, he stopped her from speaking.

Ugly words flew back and forth outside, a jumble of sound. The voices still angry faded slowly back followed by a car starting. Alan paused for a few more seconds as the voices ceased, replaced with tires screeching on asphalt.

Blowing out a sigh, he opened his arms wide to welcome her. She huddled into him, shaking. "Sounds like they're gone," he said softly, stroking her hair. She sobbed into his chest for an eternity. Rocking her slowly, he murmured quiet assurances.

When she finished, he pushed her back to gaze into her eyes. "Time to go," he said, using every ounce of authority in him. He wasn't dicking around. Marley needed a safe place and now. He pulled her toward the door.

She blinked tears back. "But my things...The paperwork." She tugged at her arm. "I can't."

Anger roared through him. She couldn't be this thick, this naïve. What happened to her street smarts? "You do realize you were almost a kidnap victim here?"

She shook her head. "I'd never go with them. Ever."

Taking a breath, he grasped her arms. She was tiny, fierce, but small. "Marley, love." He choked on the words. "You might not've had a choice." The reality of the situation shaking him as he said the words. His throat turned to desert and his eyes burned. Tucking her against him, he hugged her fiercely. "I need to get you somewhere safe."

"Give me five," she said, sliding out of his arms.

An unconscious growl reverberated in his throat. "Marley, you know better than most. We have to go before the police arrive."

She glanced up at him as she gathered the files together and shoved them in her bag. "My things…"

"I'll buy you new stuff."

Seemingly recovered from the scare, she scoffed. "You want to leave your personal financial files in a cheap hotel room?" She raised an eyebrow and would've been adorable if she hadn't been annoyingly right.

Together they grabbed up the paperwork, checking under furniture and bedding. Once they were clear, he rushed her out the door and into his car, with just the clothes on her back and her bag full of tax papers.

"Where are we going?" she asked timidly as she buckled up. He hated the tone in her voice. Despite her size, Marley was not some diminutive, scared female. She was a fighter. Glancing over at her, it seemed as if the fight left her.

"My place," he said. She didn't argue.

****

Marley stared at her feet as Alan navigated through town. Her parents probably knew where he lived. Once the cops arrived at the hotel and found the room empty, her parents would no doubt direct them to Alan's place.

I'm so screwed.

The image of the paper in Verna's hand rose before her. She struggled not to cry. That damn paper and the idiot judge who'd issued it. He'd totally been in Bernard's pocket and dismissed Marley's complaints with a flick of his wrist. How could a girl not want to live with her parents in the lap of luxury? Why did Marley keep running away? Simple. Her parents were vultures, and she the carrion they dug into daily. And she wanted to be as far from them as possible.

Stupid Troy and that nosy cop, Smith. She paused, the truth dawning on her—Becca. She'd totally find her folks and sic them on Marley. They'd never believe a pretty girl like Becca'd have any ulterior motives.

Her thoughts broke off as Alan's voice sounded in the quiet car. "Hey, Rick. Can I bother you to meet me at my place? My neighbors will probably call you anyway." He glanced at Marley and hit the speaker button.

"Now what, Reid?" Officer Smith's tinny voice issued from the phone. "I can't keep policing your house. Get your act together, man." A hint of joviality colored in his voice, but not much. When did Smith and Alan become buddy-buddy? Might be good or bad. Marley continued to stare at the files, her ears perked.

"I might have some trespassers. I'm heading there now. ETA ten minutes. Oh, and they may've already called the police on me for kidnapping their daughter. Maybe you could intercede and keep it quiet."

"Marley's parents?" Smith's tone changed, the joviality gone. "They contacted us after they missed her in the hospital. Showed us some old judge's outdated order."

She leaned back against the seat, as relief melted her body into the seat.

"Well, they found her and threatened her. I'm taking her to my house. Wouldn't hurt to have you there too."

Smith sighed through the phone. "I'll see what I can do." He didn't sound remotely happy.

Alan clicked off the phone and glanced over at her. "Want to tell me now or later?"

She groaned, curling up in her seat. "Long story," she finally said after a few beats. Turning away from him, she watched the traffic pass outside her window, Alan's place ten minutes away. They'd probably be waiting at his door, but if the court order was invalid, she had little to fear. Too bad her brain was frozen in terror.

Her body contracted, and tears spilled down her cheeks.

Chapter Twenty-Four

Alan parked the car a few blocks from his house. Marley lay, curled in a ball in the passenger seat. Leaning back, he allowed his body to relax, taking a few slow breaths to settle his racing heart and clear his head. A thousand questions circled his brain, and the young lady next to him knew the answers. He didn't think she'd give any information easily. And haste and anger would do more damage than good.

"Marley," he said, keeping his tone even. "I hope my place will be okay." He didn't want to say *safe* to give her the impression other places weren't secure. But wherever they ended up, they'd be together.

Alan waited. She remained silent.

"Or I'll find us a nice hotel, far from here." He stared straight ahead, resisting the urge to pull her into his lap and hold her until she regained her brave, bold self again.

She raised her head slightly and shook it.

"No to my place or the hotel?" Anger stacked in his chest. Anger because the fearless woman sitting next to him couldn't even speak. "Talk to me, Marley."

Sighing, she unfolded in her seat. With a groan, she turned her head toward him. He winced at the sight of her, puffy eyes, blotchy cheeks. She blinked rapidly, her chin tilting down, her gaze on the floor.

"Tell me how I can help." It took everything in him not to whine. His heart ached in a way he'd never experienced before. Not even when Conrad abandoned him to deal with their mess alone. He reached for her. She took his hand weakly, her head still bowed.

"Your house is fine," she said, her voice hoarse with crying. "I want to sit in the dark and forget the whole thing."

Alan glanced down the street toward his house. The lack of flashing red and blue lights indicated Smith hadn't arrived. He didn't want to swing into the driveway before the officer did.

"Forgetting is not an option. Can you tell me anything before we have to confront these people again? They certainly saw me at the motel, and my face is anything but anonymous in Iverton. They might already be at the house. Smith is our backup, but I'd do better with some more information."

Pulling her hand back, she wiped at her cheeks. "So, what? You want me to sit here and give you my entire backstory while we wait for him to show?" She rolled her eyes. "I'm not much of a storyteller."

He sighed, throwing his hands up. "Give me a basic understanding then."

"Fine. I ran away at sixteen. My parents put me on the circuit, entering me in every meat show available. They used me to promote their business, their social status, and that bullshit." She pulled her legs up, wrapping her arms around them. "I was never a person to them, only a commodity. So, I left."

She dropped the words like stone, no emotion in her voice other than a tiny tinge of sarcasm. Staring straight ahead, she hardly blinked as if the speech were rehearsed. Alan waited, but she didn't continue.

Marley lived through hell more than once. She'd blown off Troy's attack like swatting a mosquito. Alan studied her blank expression, her faraway look. The defense mechanisms kicked in again—minimize the story, manage the damage to her heart. Finally, he said, "And what's the real story?"

Her head snapped up, anger burned in her eyes. "Fuck you." She opened the door and leaped from the car. Shit, she was telling the truth. *Great move, imbecile.* After removing the keys, Alan launched himself out of the car after her

"Marley, please. I…I didn't know." She continued to stalk down the sidewalk away from his place, still dressed in the remains of her business attire. He ran to her, stopping in front of her. "I'm sorry. I made a stupid assumption." She tried to push past him, but he grasped her arm.

"Let go of me." Her words shrieked, full of fear and loathing. He immediately released her, raising his hands in submission. Planting her feet, she glared at him, as if she dared him to come at her. A wave of relief flowed over him. He liked angry Marley much better than sad, defeated Marley.

He pressed his hands together, never losing eye contact. "Again, I'm sorry. But please, get in the car."

She huffed, spun on her heel, and stalked back to the vehicle. He slid into the driver's seat as she slammed her door. Slouching down, she folded her arms and crossed her legs. Good, hostility worked.

His mind raced back to her dead words. The circuit. Meat show. What circuit? Drugs? Prostitution? Her parents didn't appear to deal in human traffic, but who knew these days? All roads led back to her con games. They must've planted the seeds for Becca to sew.

Resisting the urge to touch her, comforting her, he asked, "Explain 'the circuit'." His words even and emotionless.

She shrank further into the seat. "God, I can't believe I'm telling you." She ran a hand over her face. "Beauty pageants," she muffled the words into her hand.

"I'm sorry, what?" He must've heard her wrong.

"Ugh." She threw her arms up. "Beauty pageants. Miss Sunshine, Miss Fall Harvest. Any stupid meat market contest in a five-hundred-mile radius. My mother'd dress me up and throw me out on stage for the vultures to pick over."

A chuckle rose in his throat imagining a little Marley with curls and a frilly skirt tap dancing for judges. Not what he expected.

"What was your talent?" he asked, a sliver of laughter dusting his words. He pressed his lips together, needing a tension break. Marley slapped his arm.

"You're a pig like the rest of them." But her eyes glowed. "At first, singing, but I sucked out loud. Then Mother settled on gymnastics when I stopped growing at five feet nothing." She smirked, healing the ache in Alan's heart. "Made costumes easier too. Not too much material to worry about."

He raised an eyebrow. "Worry? Why?" More images of Marley, now in leotards danced through his mind. He really shouldn't be thinking that right now, what with the police and her parents seconds away. Still, the thoughts lingered. Maybe once everything settled, he'd ask to see her routine.

"Do you know anything about the lower end of the pageant circuit?" Alan shook his head. "Well, it's as cut-throat as it comes. Girls steal props, costumes, do sexual favors for judges, cheat, lie. All that shit. I don't know if the ladies are more professional in the more serious contests, but the little hokey ones I did attracted some odd folk. Including my parents." She re-crossed her arms over her chest, rubbing at her biceps as if she felt a chill.

"Want me to turn the car back on for some heat?" he asked, positive the cold had nothing to do with her shivering.

"No. I'm fine." Her gaze ran over him then wandered out the windshield. "It sounds stupid..."

"Obviously the whole thing bothered you."

She fidgeted in her seat. "I took off because I didn't want to be someone's trophy."

He studied her, arms crossed, eyes staring distantly, an air of bitter anger hanging over her. There was much more than she claimed. He wanted the truth but not at the price of hurting her more. "You hated it and left."

Whipping her head around, she glared at him. "Seriously? Understatement." Her fists clenched and unclenched in a rhythmic motion. "You can't even...Maybe Conrad hated it and left."

Her words punched his chest like a sledgehammer. He closed his eyes, letting the pain roll over him. She had every right to dismiss his pain if she thought he was writing off hers. He wasn't. *But how do you ask a young woman you've just met to spill her guts to you?* "Marley," he said swallowing hard. "I know exactly how it feels when someone you care about—when family—betrays you." His gaze met hers, and he let her see a glimpse behind the wall.

Her eyes filled with tears. She blinked, causing two fat drops to skate down her cheeks. Sniffing, she said, "They used me. They exploited me to forge connections, to be famous. They treated me like an object, a means to an end. My mother hated I never won anything big. By the time I hit fifteen, it became more than dress me up and show me off. She offered me to judges." She swallowed hard. "More than once."

A cold spike of anger burned through Alan's veins. Her mother sold Marley for a plastic crown. He wanted to smash something, preferably her mother's face. Grabbing the steering wheel, he stared out the windshield, talking slow short breaths. He'd been angry when he'd found out about Troy's assault in the alley. Now fury boiled in his gut. Good thing Smith was on his way. He might strangle the woman on sight.

They sat a long while, but eventually, Marley touched his arm. "Let go of the wheel, Alan. Your knuckles are white."

It took some effort to release his hands. When he did, Marley took his hands and rubbed them, bringing the sensation back.

"I never told anyone before," she said, not meeting his eyes. "It still sounds crazy to me. Parents are supposed to love you, not use you as their personal Barbie doll."

Alan tucked a hand under her chin lifting her head. "No one gets to use you. Not your so-called friends, not your boyfriend, not your parents. Marley, I promise you, if I have my way, no one will ever use you again."

****

Marley glanced at Alan, the impact of his words hitting her hard. The sentiment sounded heavenly dropping from his lips. No more use. No more abuse. She allowed herself a full ten seconds to soak it in and believe. But she knew people used each other all the time, in little ways, in big ways. It's how the world worked. You couldn't really trust anyone but yourself. When the ten seconds ended, she swept the silly words into the dustbin where they belonged.

"Anyway…" She cut back to the original topic, keeping her emotions tightly under wraps. She'd learned the hard way not to open her heart about her family. She'd been taken by more than one person who'd offered to help her. Alan might not be in the same category as Troy or Becca, but he wasn't perfect. The IRS investigation loomed over his head.

"I ran away when she forced some old dude on me. She and Dad chased, I ran farther." She shrugged, swallowing down the lump in her throat. She was done trying. Especially now, when a confrontation with the bastards themselves seemed imminent.

"And you've been running ever since?" His tone warm and caring, but he didn't mean it. Just manipulating the situation to get her in the sack again, keep her locked down at his place. No…yes…

A niggling voice buzzed at the back of her head, reminding her he'd invited her to his home once before. A louder voice shouted about his dismissal of her the first time she visited. His privacy and image of more concern than her. She scrunched her eyes shut tight, quieting the voices.

"Yeah, whatever." She waved his words away,

turning from him to watch out the window. Blue lights spun off in the distance. Smith finally.

Alan shifted in his seat, but she didn't turn back to him. Eye contact right now might burst the damn. "The paperwork your mother flashed, what was it?" She hated his voice dripped with sweetness and concern. *Please. Stop the act, Alan.* No one was that nice. Especially when they found out the girl they were screwing was a homeless degenerate who might be mentally ill.

"I know a little about it," she finally answered. "Got it thrown in my face one time when I 'visited' the police station." She put "visited" in air-quotes. Might as well confess her felonies too. "I skipped out of there pretty quick."

Alan drew in a long breath. "Any validity to their claim?"

"What?" she snapped, anger replacing melancholy, thank God. "You want to know if I'm nuts too?"

"Not my point," he said calmly, though his hand tapped the steering wheel a few times. "Is the court order valid? When we drive up to my house, can they take you?"

She shook her head. "No, I don't think so. I never did any tests or went to a shrink. Besides, didn't Smith say it was old?" Alan nodded. "I first heard about it three years ago. I figured they must've bribed some judge because I was over eighteen. They held no claim over me anymore."

He scratched his chin. "Without some sort of trial, they couldn't have done anything."

"Bribes work," she said with a dismissive snort. Her parents were totally capable of it. They bought everything and everyone. Money solved every problem. Marley had thrown off that mantle and chosen to live a simple life. Though lately, being transient without a real job was boring. Probably Alan's influence. Crossing her arms, she slumped in the seat, way too tired.

"All right," he said, placing one hand on the key. "We go forward. Smith and I stay between you and your parents." Marley slowly rose in her seat. He sounded confident, heroic. He might just rescue her and keep her away from the monsters. He started the car and drove slowly toward the cruiser parked by his driveway.

Chapter Twenty-Five

As predicted, the old Lexus sat in the driveway of Alan's house. Marley's stomach dropped to her toes. A patrol car with flashing lights parked askew behind it, partially blocking it in. Three figures stood in the driveway, silhouetted by the patrol car's headlights. Smith's tall figure stood like a statue. The other two jangled animatedly obviously explaining their presence to the cop. Marley took a deep breath as Alan stopped the car by the curb.

For a quick getaway, she thought. Glancing at him, she threw a small smile his way. If anyone could get her through this, it was Alan. He was more than she deserved. Her stomach flip-flopped at the idea of his genuineness.

She reached for the door handle, but her hand refused to move. Alan grasped her arm gently. She met his gaze.

"Let me go first," he said matter-of-factly. He exited the car, straightening his jacket as he stood. The car door slammed shut, causing the people in the driveway to jump. Alan strode toward them full of purpose. Totally sexy. Marley bit her lip, suppressing the rising heat. Slowly, she opened her own car door, slipped out, and closed it without a sound. She crouched by the side of the car to hear them without being seen.

Alan's neighbor rushed out as he stepped onto the driveway. The same woman who witnessed Marley in the doorway. The woman stopped at the edge of the property, wringing her hands. Marley walked slowly toward the group, the hostile voices of her parents finally reaching her.

"We have the law on our side, sir. So, step out of our way," her mother chided Officer Smith, who merely raised an eyebrow. He stood like a stone wall between her parents and Alan, who finally spoke up.

"Officer, these people seem to be trespassing on my property…" he began. He held his phone loosely in his right hand. The screen flashed, then darkened. Maybe he was recording the encounter.

Behind him, his neighbor cut in. "They've been here for a bit, Alan. They drove up like they owned the place and started pounding on the door. I called the police for you." Marley pressed her lips, trying to hide her smile. The woman was starting to grow on her. "You're welcome."

Alan glanced behind him at the neighbor, a smirk on his lips. "Thank you, Mrs. Marconi."

Her parents turned in unison to Alan. Two sets of eyes sparkled with hate. Marley ducked behind the car, not wanting them to spot her yet. She'd lock herself in the car if necessary. Smith wouldn't let them hurt her. Neither would Alan.

"There he is, Officer." Her mother thrust an accusing finger toward Alan.

"He's the man who kidnapped our baby. Arrest him." Her father puffed up his chest like some giant blowfish. Pathetic.

Marley crept closer to hear the conversation better.

"Huh," Alan said, scratching his chin. "Kidnapping is it, now? Weren't you trying to do that at the motel?" His finger swung back and forth between the two. Her father bristled, her mother glubbed like a fish out of water. Alan faced Smith. "These are the two who barged into Marley's motel room, and then tried to force her into their car." Marley giggled at Alan stretching the truth, but only a little. She paced closer, almost at the end of the drive now.

"Marley!" her mother called, sounding desperate and relieved at the same time. "There you are, baby. We're here for you. Finally here. We can take you away from the bad man."

Alan scoffed side-stepping to block their view. "I'm the bad man, huh?" He shook his head. He said something Marley couldn't hear, but her father's face turned a deeper shade of red.

"You stole her," her mother screeched, always with the flair for the dramatic. "You took her and used her for your own pleasure. Filled her full of drugs and passed her around to your criminal friends." She started sobbing, burying her face in Bernard's chest.

The words hit Marley like a punch to the gut. She pressed her hands to her mouth, a sob and laugh spilled from her lips. Anger, fear, and loathing slashed through her until her head spun. She stepped forward and stumbled. Wiry arms caught her. Little Mrs. Marconi's arm wrapped around her shoulders. Another spike of fear smashed into her, and she tugged away from the woman.

"There, there, dear," she cooed. "I won't let the nasty lady put her hands on you. You stay right here with me." Marley blinked at her, not believing the words. The woman smiled, a hint of rose dusting her cheeks. "I'm terribly hard on Mr. Reid, but he's a good man. I've made sure to keep him on the right path. He's like my own son, he is." Marley's flight response faded, and she sagged in Mrs. Marconi's arms. The fight continued in front of her.

"See!" Her mother shrieked again. Marley didn't have the strength to cover her ears. "My baby's about to drop. Lord knows what he's done to her." Her mother leaped forward. Smith deftly caught her, blocking her from charging down the driveway. Alan slid left, making a second line of defense.

"Listen, Officer..." Her father pulled out his salesman pitch, speaking out the side of his mouth but too loudly to be a conspiratorial whisper. "Let us take our daughter, and we'll be out of your hair." Her father's gaze rolled up to Smith's bald pate, and he cleared his throat. "What I mean is...if money's an issue." He winked at Smith who merely rolled his shoulders.

The officer held his arm out to stop both of them from moving forward. "What you mean, sir, is you want me to place Marley in your custody." Smith glanced back at her, his brown eyes both warm and steady. Relief flooded through her. A good guy, for a cop.

"She's our daughter." Her father flapped his hands toward Marley.

"This is ridiculous." Alan stepped forward, even with Smith. "You don't get to show up and collect her."

Her mother sniffled, blinking back crocodile tears. "She's our daughter. Of course, we can collect her."

"Marley," Alan called back to her. She stood straighter. He smiled over his shoulder. "Double-checking, but you are over eighteen, right?" His smile widened.

More tension drained. "Yes, Alan. I told you before. I'm twenty-three."

"Huh," Alan said scratching his chin again. He cocked his head at Smith. "Correct me if I'm wrong, Officer Smith, but Marley is a legal adult." Smith nodded. "So if her mommy and daddy showed up out of the blue, demanding she come with them, they haven't a leg to stand on." Smith nodded again.

"You," her mother sneered. "You are an idiot. I have paperwork right here saying Marley is to be remanded to our guardianship. She isn't a legal adult. She's our daughter and ward because of her mental deficiency." She flapped a ragged paper at him, probably the same one from the motel.

"And the last time she was evaluated? Last time she stood before a judge?" Alan raised an eyebrow.

Her father stepped forward, his chest butting against Smith's still outstretched hand. "I know your type, Reid. Fill her head full of meaningless legalese. We have the paperwork. Officer, do your duty."

Alan held up a finger. "Hold that thought." He raised his cell to his ear. "Did you hear everything? Yep. Yes, very much over twenty-one. Ah, I see." The more Alan spoke into the phone, the more her parents scowled and growled, trying to get Smith's attention.

Smith glared down at her father. "The man's on the phone. Try and be polite."

"Who the hell is he talking to?" her father snapped.

Alan pressed a hand over the phone. "My lawyer,"

he said in a stage whisper. And knowing Alan, he probably winked. He raised the phone to his ear again. "So, you're saying"—He glanced back at Marley, his eyes bright on his serious face—"Without a current court order, they can't claim guardianship. Marley would have to be evaluated by order of a judge to be remanded to their guardianship. I see. Set it up, will you?"

Marley staggered in Mrs. Marconi's arms. Court? Judge? Trial? Testing? What the hell was Alan playing at? "Oh, God," she whispered and slowly slipped to her knees. They'd get her back and with a court order. She'd be right back in prison again.

Alan ended his call, pocketing his phone. "So," he said, dusting his hands together. "You want her. You'll have to fight for her. Get a lawyer because we'll see you in court." He jabbed a finger at them as he said the last words. He spun on his heel, moving toward her. His eyes widened when he saw her on the ground and he rushed forward. He didn't see her father lunge at him, but Smith caught him up easily, lifting the man into the air. Such a pathetic sight: her father's legs swinging back and forth. It gave her a glimmer of happiness.

Alan swooped her up, enveloping her in his arms. Almost crushing the life out of her, he whispered in her ear. "They'll never hurt you again. I swear I will do everything to keep them away."

"But court." She gasped, when he finally allowed her a bit of air. "I don't want tests and no judges. They'll lock me up for sure."

Alan shook his head. "If anyone can pass a psych test, it's you. You excel at manipulating people." She frowned at him. "I mean that in a good way," he teased, kissing her forehead.

Her parents still shouted behind them, but Alan ignored it. "Want to stay here tonight or somewhere else?" She peeked around his shoulder, watching Smith try to herd her parents back into their car.

"Somewhere else. Definitely." She took in a deep breath, worried they'd follow her everywhere, threat of lawyers or no.

"Fantastic," Alan said. "There's a great little motel downtown." Marley elbowed him hard in the ribs. "Ooof. Okay, not there." He held out his hand for his neighbor. "Mrs. Marconi, as always, you've done a bang-up job. I can't thank you enough." He shook her hand

"I always keep an eye, Mr. Reid," she said, a toothy grin splashed on her face.

"You certainly do. I might be away a night or two." He glanced back over to her parents, now finally getting into the car. "Watch the place for me?"

"Absolutely," she said and backed off the driveway allowing the two cars to exit.

Alan led Marley to his car. They stood on the sidewalk waiting for the others to drive off. Smith waved as he went, but her parents waved with only one finger. Alan gathered her up in his arms again. "How does Turning Stone sound?" he asked.

"Oh, Alan." She curled into his chest. "Thank you." Her heart cried in pain knowing life with Alan was a pipe dream now that Verna and Bernard had arrived.

Chapter Twenty-Six

Marley, slouched in the passenger seat, chewed her thumbnail. Alan drove effortlessly down the Thruway toward the casino. She fidgeted, hating the interstate, hating how someone else always had to drive her because she couldn't do it. She glanced over at his calm face as he overtook an eighteen-wheeler. He didn't blink, her nails dug grooves in the seat. She'd never taken driving lessons or owned a legal license. One of those small details you don't consider when running away at sixteen.

His gaze shifted over to her as he drove. "You all right?" he asked, putting a hand on her drawn-up knees.

Instinctively, she slapped his hand away. "Eyes on the road," she barked, a sliver of fear in her words.

Furrowing his brow, he frowned. "My driving or your state of mind."

She swatted his arm. "Concentrate on the road," she said, hating the fear spilling in her words. Two things scared her—her parents and the interstate. God, what a baby. "I'll feel better when we get there."

"Does it really bother you?" He didn't sound mean, but his words insulted her anyway. One more horrible thing Alan witnessed. One more time she was a scared little girl curled up in his front seat.

"I hate car travel. Now shut up and drive." She

239

snapped, desperately wanting the conversation to end before she confessed one more character flaw tonight.

"Shutting up," he replied with a wan smile. He tapped the radio and classical piano poured from the speakers.

"Ugh," she said aloud, quickly covering her mouth. The man tried to help, and she snapped at him and made fun of his music. She side-eyed him, surprised to see his smile morphed into a grin.

"Not the most exciting, but a good choice after tonight's events. I need something soothing and benign."

"Don't fall asleep at the wheel."

"I'll do my best."

How did he do that? How did he answer so calmly when she bitched and griped and made fun of him? He totally rolled with it. If anyone had a reason to blast someone, to lash out, it was Alan.

"You're not pissed I'm a heap of trouble?" she asked, her voice full of caution. She wanted the answer but didn't at the same time.

He glanced at her, and her blood pressure spiked again. Turning his gaze back to the road, he said, "It was a crappy day. I know crappy days. I wished I'd had someone around to be nice to me when my world fell apart."

A silence fell between them. She pulled in a breath, unsure what to say, angry, sad, and grateful. The emotions boiled in her stomach until it ached. Showing him her real feelings still resembled walking naked through downtown. "My world didn't fall apart. Pu-lease." She crossed her arms and her legs, turning away from him. But even her best moves couldn't hide how he'd hit the nail on the head.

****

Alan let the conversation die. A quick glance at Marley verified she hurt and needed to hide. He closed his lips in a line to repress a small smile. His super-tough girl had a human side after all. He couldn't wait to get her to the hotel in fair Verona and get his questions cleared up. He'd call Demeck back and set up a meeting with a judge. Then he and Marley would look over the tax files and discover where the money went. Finally, they'd find Conrad.

His thoughts stopped cold, and his breath skipped. He would never believe his best friend left with the money. But he was out there somewhere. The only things to keep Conrad away this long were death or injury. Hope fluttered in his heart that Conrad had only broken a leg.

"You okay?" Marley's voice roused him from the dark thoughts. "You're kinda pale. 'Cause I'm being a pain, right?" She twisted her mouth, as if trying not to bite her lip. She had some tells. Then again, he did too.

Cocking his head to the side, he pondered disclosing his true thoughts about his current situation. Opening up to someone he hardly knew...But he trusted her implicitly despite her profession and tendency to lie. Could he spill his guts and still meet her gaze? He stared at the road, thinking hard, unsure how to answer her simple question.

A jangled ring broke through his thoughts, saving him from spilling his guts. "Ah, my lawyer," he said, hitting the speakerphone. "Hey Jason, tell me some good news."

"Speaker, Alan?" Demeck's voice crackled over

the line.

"Driving," Alan responded, both hands on the wheel as per Marley's request. "Marley's right here. What's the next step?" He glanced over at her. Her white face glared back at him. *Oh dear*.

"From the info you gave me before…"

Marley slapped his arm, mouthing "Before?" Alan cocked his head at her, trying to be apologetic. He felt compelled to find out something about her background after the whole hospital mess. He didn't pry too far, a name and criminal record check by Demeck. Now it seemed a dick move but then…

"I can set us up with Judge Harrison in the next month. Preliminary hearing only. And you might want to use Lester for this. The judge will most likely order psychological testing and set another court appearance. Everyone needs to be present therefore my office will contact the parents. I need to see their writ. Any chance you can get me a copy to pass on to Lester?"

"Not a problem. The officer involved must have addresses and phone numbers. I can pass those along." He glanced at her when she struck him for a third time. Red apples flushed on her cheeks, causing her skin to pale more than ever. Her gaze held a dangerous glint. "Uh, I'll call you in the morning."

"Good 'nough," Demeck replied, and the phone call ended.

"Pull over," Marley gritted the words between her teeth.

"We're in the middle of the Thruway." He held a hand out toward the dark road before them.

"Then get off the next exit." Her voice cold, flat, and serious. Nothing like he'd ever heard from her.

Maybe now she'd turned the game. That tone told him he was the long con (though not very long in the scheme of things). Soon she'd disappear from his life. The thought cut like a knife to the chest. He didn't want her to go. He just lost his best friend. He couldn't lose Marley too.

Chapter Twenty-Seven

Marley's shaking fingers danced over the door handle as Alan pulled into a service area off the Thruway. Her heart raced a ridiculous rhythm as her brain skittered images and demands for her to run. Her parents, another judge, more debt to Alan. No, anything but that. Just the idea of Bernard and Verna getting their hands on her again caused her stomach to twist.

As soon as he shifted the car into park, she bolted from the car, bag over her shoulder. Lacing her shaking fingers together, she refused to glance back at him. Her vision narrowed. Weaving through the cars, she dashed helter-skelter for the rest area building. Somehow Alan beat her to the doors. Panting, she screeched to a halt, inches from his chest. A sob burst from her lips, and she pressed them tight to stop anymore sounds from betraying her.

Through gritted teeth, he whispered, "What the fuck, Marley?"

She stepped back lightly, running a shaking hand under her dribbling nose. "I gotta pee," she stuttered, waving her hand at the door to hide the tremors.

"No," he said quietly, his gaze darting from her to the other travelers entering the building. The strain in his face said he didn't want to cause waves, but if she needed to escape, she'd make a scene. "You ran away from me." He stared at her hard, and she avoided his eyes. Those icy blues always cut right through her, right from the first time she met him. Cut through her and made her spill her guts, forced her to behave like an adult.

She lowered her head, letting her bangs shield her from his gaze. "Let me by, Alan." Her voice lost its strength, but at least she didn't whine the directive. "I have to pee."

"What's this about? You were fine until I got on the phone." His words drifted off. "I'm not going to let those people put their hands on you. I want to protect you. You see that, don't you?"

Still hiding behind her hair, she shifted, jutting out a hip. "Please. I don't need protection." She threw quotie fingers around the word protection. "Get out of the way, Alan." If he'd shut up, she could vacate. Hit the road and never look back. Why didn't she take off immediately when Smith told her about contacting her parents? Adrenaline pumped through her. If he didn't move soon, she'd bolt for the parking lot, steal a car or something. Her nerve screamed, her muscled jumped. Another second more seemed too much. "Move!"

His brow furrowed, but he slid to the side and opened the door. Still trying to be the gentleman. Her shoulders dropped. He was a prince, through and through. And she chose to ditch him. Again.

He caught her arm as she stepped through the doorway. Not hard but enough to capture her attention. "We need to talk about it, Marley. I don't know what to do here."

"To start with, get your nose out of my business." The words poured out of her, full of spite, but she didn't mean it. She wanted both of them to disappear together. To hide out in some exotic location, with a huge bed for the next six weeks until her parents found another meal ticket. But it would never happen. Alan wouldn't run away with her, never leave his problems here in Iverton and start over. He wasn't that person.

"Out of your business?" He sounded snooty, like some upper-middle-class asshole who doesn't understand why his Mercedes won't start. "You've been in my business since you sat next to me in my bar. What the hell has changed in the last five minutes?"

People glanced at them as they passed in and out of the rest station. A few men scrutinized Alan, glancing to his hand on her arm then to his face with a frown. She could scream, struggle, throw out a "help me" statement. But she didn't want him in trouble, just gone.

"You're like the rest of them, Alan." She ripped her arm from his grip with more force than needed. But drama drove home her point. "You're no different from Becca or my parents. Trying to control me, trying to shove me in the direction you want. Trying to turn me into something I'm not." She stepped back, straightening her spine, glaring at him. "Just because I'm short doesn't mean I'm a child. You don't own me. You don't get to control my life. I choose where I go, what I do."

His expression collapsed in a tangle of confusion, his brows knitted together. His voice dropped to a whisper. "Marley, I only wanted…"

She snorted knowing what came next. "The best for me, right? So did they. And Becca too. Wanted the best I could give them. Offered up money, a home, a warm bed, but only if I continued to perform. I'm not your project. You only need me to get your ass out of the hole Conrad left you in."

She started through the door, halting when he spoke again, the tension in his voice palpable. "Is that what you think? I only want you to..." He paused and when he began again, his voice was quiet. "Go. Go to the Ladies'. I'll wait here."

Tossing the stupid blonde hair (another concession), she marched through the door, refusing to glance back at him. The bathroom appeared miles away as she walked across the wide space, determined to retain some dignity.

He'd wait. Why? To take her to the courthouse? To the hotel to count cards? (Why go to a casino?) Or for more sex? *Why else would a man like him want a woman like me?* Her accounting ability and prowess in bed were all she had to offer. The fact he got to play hero and "save her" merely a bonus. He didn't want her for herself. *He knows nothing about me, if he thought he'd drag me to court to confront my parents.* The judge would side with them, the psychologists would report her a criminal and life would be over.

Time to go.

Chapter Twenty-Eight

"Then what happened?" Eric asked, drying a mug with a bar rag.

Alan wrinkled his nose. In this day and age, did the boy really need to dry glasses with a towel? After taking a long slow sip of Jack Daniels, he finished the story. "I sat down at a table inside the rest area and waited."

"And?" Eric hovered around Alan, waiting for an interesting tidbit. But in the end, there was nothing to tell but another sad chapter of Alan's story. Lost the business, lost the best friend, and now lost the girl.

"I waited. I waited for hours." He sipped his drink. "She never came back. Took off from the restrooms at some point. I asked someone to check after a bit."

Eric put the glass down on the bar. "So that's it?"

Alan shrugged, numb from head to toe. "Yes. It's done." Driving back down the Thruway to Iverton, he'd raged, screamed at the passing cars, cursed himself for letting her go. But what choice did he have? She was not his property or his project, but her own woman. He had no right to stop her from living her life.

Why didn't he tell her everything? Poured his heart out like some sap from a cheesy movie. But he wasn't that man. He'd shown her his love by putting himself on the line for her, but she dismissed it. His fault for not stepping up, not sharing, not telling her how she put color back into his world, gave him hope for a real future, showed him starting over could be a good thing. He'd have done anything for her, except share.

"So," Eric asked, his hands on the bar, hunching over, "no way to contact her?"

Alan shook his head. "She's in the wind. Won't answer her phone. I won't use the police to find her."

"Yeah, that'd be pretty shitty." Eric scrubbed his chin. "Didn't you say something about a trial?"

Placing the empty glass back on the bar, Alan nodded. "Yes, I hoped she'd come back. I set up the guardianship procedure with the lawyer. But without her, her parents will probably get a new thirty-day emergency guardianship. And we'll start over. Now they're closing in on her and are in touch with people who personally know Marley. She's in the system again." And Becca, the bitch who'd started it …

"Do you think they'll find her?"

"Eventually, everyone turns up." The two men exchanged a knowing look. Still no Conrad, and now Marley disappeared. At least his protégé Terese still lived in town. Not everyone had vanished from his life.

"Why the hell are they chasing her?" Eric asked, folding his arms over his chest. "It doesn't make sense.

"They have some weird notion"—Alan continued, waggling his glass at Eric—"Marley can still be a meal ticket, a source of income, like before." He shrugged again as Eric filled his glass. "Especially now that she can run con games and dupe innocent people out of tons of money."

"But would she?" A ghost of a smile crossed Eric's lips. He must've known Marley's games from the start.

Alan smiled back, holding up his glass to his employee.

"No. Not today. Not in the future. Not ever. Not my girl." He downed the amber liquid, loving the burning sensation in his throat. Whiskey helped him feel something, and Eric never let him get drunk enough to make a fool of himself, again.

"Well," the bartender said. "Here's to happy endings."

****

Same seat. Same drink. Marley watched Alan from the door of the Tavern. He and Eric were engrossed in conversation, neither smiling. Her spirits slumped. They probably weren't talking about her. It'd been two weeks since she ran out on him. Hope that he still cared fluttered in her heart.

Chewing her lip, she debated. Alan at the bar again. A sure sign to finish it. She'd just walk over, hand him the file folder, show him where the embezzlement occurred, and walk away, fast. It was that simple. It was that hard.

Glancing over at him, hunched there, once again, she cursed the place. Every time she came into the tavern something compelled her to do the right thing, to be a better person. Probably because of its gentleman owner and his huge heart. Swallowing, she set her shoulders and crossed the room.

Eric saw her first. His dark eyebrows shot up almost to his hairline. He slowly put down the glass and cleared his throat loudly. Alan paused, drink midway to his mouth. He squinted at Eric whose gaze darted from Alan to her and back again. Alan shook his head, pressed his lips, and lowered his glass.

It took forever for him to glance up at her. A cold

sweat broke out on her palms. Her foot began to tap on its own, sounding far too loud in the busy bar. Tap, tap, tap. When her lip started to tremble, she snapped herself into place and waited to meet his gaze. The blue glacier returned, cold and stony, hard as ice. His eyes narrowed as they met hers. Then he turned back to his drink, never saying a word.

An icicle dagger plunged into her stomach and a gasp escaped her lips. Her hand pressed her belly, trying to hold in the pain. Dammit, she'd hoped for a screaming match or a hug or something. The cold shoulder hurt more than she ever imagined. But what did she expect? She dumped him hard as he tried to help her, save her from her worst nightmare, and ride off into a better life. She walked. He had every right to be angry and cold. She deserved nothing more.

Chapter Twenty-Nine

Alan's stomach turned with a fiery, greasy queasiness. He clenched his jaw until his teeth hurt, holding back the bile bubbling in his throat. He'd tried to wait her out but, in the end, he'd searched for her. Text and calls met with no response. The days passed, and he'd heard nothing. Both his lawyer and Officer Smith—Rick—had no luck. The trial date for her guardianship hearing approached quickly. But no Marley. She'd left him. No bones about it.

A black veil slowly covered over him in the weeks since she'd jumped ship. The nagging darkness, the ugly thoughts much richer than when Conrad bailed. He no longer slept. Night after night, he lay in bed, staring at the ceiling, his limbs hollow. Then in the morning, getting out of bed became an impossible task. Today, he'd needed to physically pull each leg down on the floor before standing. Something had to give. People left. The story of his whole life.

His mother walked out on his family, his father died young, and then Conrad, the only real friend he'd ever connected with, gone without a word. Marley. He'd been stupid to get attached to such a wild, free spirit. She'd made damn sure to tell him she didn't need him. She'd said it over and over, but his heart never listened. He thought for once, he'd get a woman to stay.

For once she wouldn't want a more star-spangled life. For once she wouldn't look at Conrad and forget Alan existed.

Of course, it wasn't the case with Marley, but she'd left him too. And after everything he'd done for her, the risks he'd taken with the police, the integrity of his business, his reputation. Dating a con artist was a bad idea from the start, but he'd fallen head over feet and no one left to blame but himself.

Well, except her.

One quick glance at her hardened his heart. The heat spiraled out from his stomach to his chest, his legs. Fire radiated through him, burning him until he was a charred, dead husk inside. Seeing her put the last nail in the coffin.

"Hey." Her soft voice spoke behind him. Alan resisted cringing at the sound. His heart raced despite the emptiness that consumed him. He waited, hoping she'd just go.

Eric stood by, his chin elevated, his lips a flat line. He said nothing but his gaze met Alan's. For once, Alan didn't know how to respond. Throw her out? Let her talk? It was his bar—his legacy and he always knew what to do. But not now. His lips parted, and he paused, waiting for the words to come. Instead, he sipped the whiskey hoping it contained a solution.

"What do you want?" Eric asked. The contempt in his voice like a bucket of freezing water over Alan's empty soul. He jerked, slamming the glass down harder than he meant to. Amber liquid sloshed from the glass and over his hand. The cold bit his skin, and he reveled in finally feeling something.

"Leave us," he said flatly. Eric's eyebrows shot up,

but he walked back down the bar. Not before he gave Marley a dark look. The man was entitled to his opinions. As long as he kept them to himself. Alan swirled his drink slowly, waiting.

Marley slid into the stool next to him, reminiscent of the moment they met. He worked hard not to scoff, not bothering to offer her a drink.

Anger buzzed in his gut. *Come on, young lady, and sit down. Like nothing happened.* Like she didn't walk out of him when he killed himself trying to help her. He sipped his drink, but the warmth of the whiskey didn't cut it anymore. He put the glass down.

"Well?" he asked, still not facing at her. He heard her shift in her seat, and something thunked on the bar top.

"Your files. I thought I should return them." Her voice quiet, subdued. Not the usual boisterous Marley, not the charming con artist. Not the overconfident woman he thought he loved.

"Did you now?" He glanced over at the Manila folder stuffed full of paper. They'd never had a chance to do more than glance at it before the shit hit the fan. A sour feeling rolled through his stomach. He'd forgotten about the duplicate financial files. A stupid move. Some con artist ran off with his personal information, and he'd blanked. The pain overwhelmed his logic and reason, leaving him open to deceit and ruin. Anger stacked in his chest, brick by brick until he wanted to burst and fling the papers away. The money, the documents meant nothing. He wanted Marley, but she rejected him. He stared hard at the folder, willing it to solve his problems.

"Uh, it was the least I could do," she said with a

slight tremor in her voice. She touched the folder then snatched her hand back like it scorched his fingers. "You'll need it."

He glanced at her quickly, not wanting eye contact, not wanting to let the anger burst from him or open himself to the pain again. She twisted on the stool, like the first night, her bottom lip trapped in her teeth. Good, let her sweat. He certainly had over the past weeks. He raised his glass again, stopping midway to his mouth. "You could've mailed it."

He immediately regretted saying it. If she sent it, she wouldn't be here. And honestly, he really did want her here, wanted her to explain and apologize and tell him she'd never leave. But it was fairy tale crap. He gulped his whiskey, hissing as it burned down his throat.

"Yeah, I guess." She paused. Her legs twisted back and forth with the motion of the stool. Then she stopped. "But," her voice now full of steel, more solidly than a second ago. "I thought I should to tell you personally what I found in the files."

Oh, good. She did paperwork and wanted to share. Her mathematical talent came in handy while she ripped his heart out and left it at a cold rest area in Central New York. Hu-rray.

"Shoot." He continued to stare at the far wall. Even if she found anything, it didn't matter. Demeck told him a few days ago that without Conrad, Alan was sunk.

Marley fumbled next to him, opening the folder, shuffling papers. "Fine. We'll play it all business." Her voice sounded rough. Clearing her throat, she continued, "Now you're gonna have to actually look at the papers, Alan." He shot her a side-eyed glance, as his mouth twitched into a frown. "You want me to save your business or not?" Her voice cracked on the last word, but the rest exuded steel and confidence.

"Fine." Alan drained the last of the whiskey from his glass and shifted on his stool. Sitting here, intimately angled toward her and the open file on the bar shoved an arrow straight through his chest. Ten minutes. Ten minutes and she'll be gone. The thought lightened the load on his chest, but at the same time, his heart shriveled even smaller. He wouldn't look into those green eyes. It might stop his heart entirely.

****

Marley straightened her shoulders as she skimmed over the papers. She knew it would be hard, but honestly, it felt like shoving a fork in her eye. Alan didn't look at her, not directly, but Eric on the other hand…his gaze blazed into her like a blast furnace. A cold drop of sweat trickled down her back—the same sick shaky feeling she'd had when Becca gave her first solo con. She swallowed hard and plunged in.

Handing Alan her list of funny accounting entries, she pointed to a flagged item on a spreadsheet. "The IRS probably tagged your company here." The entry from six months ago showed a large transfer of funds to a private account. "There are three of these transactions in a week's time. But"—She shuffled through the stack of papers grabbing another item with the same color sticky flag—"your quarterly tax report doesn't reflect the transfer. And there's no billing to correspond with the money. It's just gone."

Alan studied the two papers, chewing his lip as he thought. "Conrad talked about picking up some new properties. He'd been scouting a couple of smaller cafés and coffee shops. But he never mentioned a purchase. We always visit the places together at least once before we buy." His brows furrowed, and Marley pushed on.

She tapped the pages in his hand, loving this. Using her skills to actually help someone, even if he hated her right now. So thrilled to solve the puzzle that she didn't care. "That's what the IRS is focused on. But I'm not sure how much those guys will really analyze this puppy." One of his eyebrows quirked up but he still didn't meet her gaze. "There's much more than these three oddball entries."

"Go on."

Glancing at his face, she searched for a reaction. Damn Alan and his stoicism. Not even an eyebrow twitch. She pulled the next set of flagged pages. "This shows someone used Conrad's login to transfer those funds to an off-shore account, probably the Cayman Islands. Becca always used Grand Cayman." A quick eye twitch told her he heard her, but he offered no further information. "It looks bad for him if he did actually transfer the money. But seriously, even the most stupid criminal wouldn't transfer such a huge sum using his own login."

"Then it seems as if I did it?" he asked, pulling the spreadsheet pages closer. He ran a finger down the line of numbers, his gaze scanning between the sums and the account numbers. Tapping one of the questionable transactions, he said, "I don't recognize the account number on this one." Before Marley asked, he added, "I don't have our account numbers memorized, but we have a strict policy to use local banks. Keeps the money in town, something we both believe in."

Placing the next pile on top of the spreadsheet,

Marley said, "So here are Conrad's access code entries for any money transfers. Tons of tiny ones. Nothing huge except for the three." She added another sheet. "Here are yours. More of them but still reasonable amounts for supplies, payroll, and other regular expenses."

"I look bad then," he asked now focused on his own entries. "Conrad never bought the properties. I usually worked with the Realtors. He charmed the prospects then passed them over to me to seal the deal."

Marley cocked her head. "You managed the day-to-day plus property purchases?"

Alan shrugged. "Conrad wined and dined them. I persuaded them to sign on the line to whatever deal he came up with. We occasionally used a part-time accountant. Someone to help us deal with the excessive paperwork. Usually a temp. Though Lizette stayed with us for a while. But she left long ago." He sighed, pushing the papers away.

"Wait, what part-time accountant?" He never mentioned someone else having a hand in their finances. Alan hinted he and Conrad handled the whole thing with only a few other employees in the actual business office.

"Didn't I tell you? She asked for emergency medical leave. I can't remember the exact date. Something about a sick mother in Tacoma. Like I said, it happened long before the mess. I haven't heard from her since then, but the IRS knows about her and is handling it."

"They didn't pull her back to question her? It's a criminal investigation, right?" Didn't he understand how incredibly fishy the whole thing sounded?

Especially with the last piece of evidence.

"I guess," Alan said. He held a thousand-yard stare. "The IRS hasn't told me anything about her. I'll call her."

Marley's hand shot out, grasping his before he picked up his cell. "Wait. How long did she work for you?"

"Lizette? A few days a week over the last few years. Mostly evening hours because she worked some other part-time job. She's..." Alan smiled. "Well, an interesting woman. Conrad hired her. I trusted him." He tapped a finger on his lips as his eyes grew wide. "You think…"

"How savvy is she? Those tiny transactions are bots, moving money around and out."

"Bots?" Alan's eyebrows furrowed.

"Automatic programs. They're practically invisible. One placed in your accounting software could automatically transfer money around to accounts in Switzerland, the Caymans, and Asia. And if it used small enough amounts, you'd never know."

"Lizette put a bot in my computer?" He sounded shocked and confused.

"From what you told me, Conrad was a good friend and a smart businessman. If he actually embezzled, he'd have hidden it better. Your accountant probably had a hand in it. Probably her whole fist."

"God, really? She was…" Alan flailed for words then drew an hourglass in the air, his eyes rolling.

"Oh my God, you pig," she smirked. "Hired someone to take care of your money because of her nice rack? Did you drop pencils on the floor forcing her to bend over and pick them up?" Playfully, she elbowed his side. The contact snapped him out of his dreamlike state. Their gaze met and Marley's breath caught in her throat.

No ice remained in his gaze. Red-rimmed sadness stared back at her and regret shook her so deeply, she couldn't breathe. They both glanced away quickly, awkwardly. Marley's hand slipped to her chest as she gulped a breath. All her stupid decisions led to pain and guilt, for everyone. Taking a trembling breath, she pressed forward.

"Seriously, the bountiful beauty handled your money because..." She let her words drift off, trying to keep the situation light.

"She claimed to be a CPA." He paused. "Attractive women can't be good accountants?" The warmth in his tone forced her to glance at him again. A familiar spark lit in his eyes. Heat rose on her cheeks as she turned away. In her universe, beautiful girls weren't allowed to do math much less pass a CPA exam.

"I'm just saying," she hedged.

"I know what you're saying. But we checked references. Neither of us wanted to end up in this boat." He sighed, fanning the pages on the bar.

"But here you are."

"Here we are," he repeated. "Why do you suspect the accountant? The IRS must've investigated her by now. It's always the accountant, right?" He looked at her expectantly, with those sad eyes. She couldn't hold his gaze. Thankfully he'd opened the door to show him more of her discoveries.

"Here," she said, handing him another set of spreadsheets. "These go back over two years. I have another set going back four, but I found our money shot."

He raised an eyebrow. "Interesting term. What the hell do you mean?" He still sounded playful, but a tension lay beneath his voice. Time to show her cards.

The tip of her finger glided between several entries on the list. "Twice during the quarter, a deposit went to a numbered bank account." She pointed to the sheet in front of him. "The same account as the large amounts. If you go through each of these quarters, there were dozens of small transactions—a few dollars, tens, or hundreds of dollars—sent. Not a huge deal for a company your size, but there weren't any expenses matching the amounts. Probably a remotely controlled transaction. Send a code to the system and boom, the program transfers money."

Alan's eyebrows raised. "Over years?" he asked. "Amounting to?"

Marley showed him her notes, handwritten pages covered in mathematical equations, lists of numbers and personal comments. "Until the big ones, approximately ten grand. Over time you might not have noticed much, but it added up." She skimmed the spreadsheet again. "All monies transferred using what looked like Conrad's login. The big and the small. I think it's a dummy account."

"Well then. The finger points directly at Conrad. How does our accountant factor into it? She's the culprit? But we offered a good salary and her other job...I don't..."

Marley rushed over him, excited to show the *pièce de résistance*. "First of all, she would've found these weird withdrawals/payments, whatever you want to call them and either questioned them or supplied the proper expense for the money. Secondly—" She flipped to the last page of the stack of spreadsheets. "The first time you have one of these weird expenses, the money was transferred using another login. Maybe the accountant?"

"Lizette? Probably. Let me see." Excitement filled his words. His hand shook as he picked up the sheet to examine it closely. "Here?" he asked, his voice filled with hope.

"Yep." She grinned, proud of herself for finding it for Alan. Now his friend was exonerated. They'd put their business back on its feet again and Alan would be happy.

"It's only for $300," he said, hope fading. "Is it enough?"

"Yes. Your lawyer is good. I researched him and listened in on him whenever possible. He can take the entry and create a case out of it. She tested the waters on the first one. To see if you questioned it. To see if she could get away with it. When she did, she became more cautious. She stole Conrad's login and set the bot loose in your system."

"Then why take the huge chunks if she was happily robbing us blind when we were completely oblivious?" He put the page down on the bar on top of the rest.

Marley shrugged. "Something happened and she needed capital fast. The con collapsed or Conrad smelled a rat. Could've been anything. But the one little slip might save you both. The IRS will have to question her and then the house of cards will fall down."

"Huh," Alan said. Not jumping for joy or hugging her until she split. She tipped her head. His mouth hung open. Perhaps he never believed in a light at the end of his crazy tunnel. "Just like that?"

She grinned. "Just like that." Serenity filled her chest. She'd done it. She'd solved Alan's problems, as she'd promised she'd do. Used her powers for good for once. Tears threatened, and she blinked them away.

Alan turned to her, looking at her face to face for the first time. "Well. Okay." He smacked his lips twice. Marley cocked her head, urging him to finish the thought. "Then where's Conrad?"

Chapter Thirty

Alan released a slow breath. His mind whirled, processing the information Marley had thrown at him. Lizette. It made sense, much more than Conrad being the culprit. But where was he? How could he still be off the grid? Running his hand over his face, Alan steeled himself. Never mind Marley presented a good solution to him in a rapid fire of numbers, but she did it in person. Seeing her, hearing her voice pained his heart, but she was finally here. Hope seeped back into the cracks of his armor.

He waved a hand over the paperwork sprawled in front of him. "It's conclusive?" Marley nodded, her mouth spread in a wide smile, her eyes shining. "Why didn't Demeck find this?" If Marley found the information in a matter of weeks, how come Demeck didn't find it after double the time?

"I scanned back pretty far. Usually audits only do one fiscal year. I went back six. The first weird transaction happened more than three years ago. But only one entry and a small one at that. Easily missed even by a lawyer. A forensic accountant would've found it easily."

Alan sighed. "My mistake in not hiring one of those then," he said, despair filling him again. The mess might have been avoided if he'd done the right thing immediately. And again, where was his business partner? Another thought occurred to him. "You scanned six years of accounting?"

Marley nodded, her smile still firmly in place. "I checked to be sure there weren't any other weird transactions similar to one. Best to be thorough when the IRS is involved." She shrugged it off. As if she hadn't saved him from bankruptcy, maybe from jail.

His throat dried at the idea of jail time, locked away with no one minding the store. "I can't..." The words stuck in his throat. "I can't thank you enough." Tears burned in his eyes. She'd saved him, came through for him in the end when she held no obligation. Maybe she still felt something.

Blinking rapidly, he straightened the paperwork, organizing it, and placing it back in the folder. The busywork allowed him the time to control his emotions.

"Thank you, Marley," he said again.

Shrugging, she said, "I promised so..." She twisted on her stool, her legs swinging. "I wanted to help."

He patted the full folder. "This does." They both sat in a calm silence for a few beats. Staring down at his empty glass, he wondered where she'd been since the rest area. He needed to know but hated to push her after all she'd done. "So, now what?"

Marley smiled, her lips pressed tightly together. "I guess..." She licked her lips, her eyes peeked at him behind thick bangs. "I guess that's it."

"Marley," he said, strain in his words. "Please..."

"I gotta go anyway," she said, her voice thick as if she teetered on the edge of tears herself.

He grasped her hand before she stood to leave. "You don't have to go anywhere," he whispered. She pulled back, and he gripped her tighter, not willing to let her go again.

"I can't Alan," she said, her voice a somber, pained. "I have something I have to do."

"You helped me, let me help you."

Her gaze met his. Tear brimmed on her long lashes. "I have to do it myself. Alan, I don't need anything more from you."

He shifted closer to her. "Don't you?" he asked. She blinked hard, turning her head away. Twin tears rolled down her cheeks. "Where are you living? What are you doing for money?"

Tugging her hand, she refused to look at him. "I'm fine," she said with no conviction. "I've got it."

"You have nothing, Marley. No money, no shelter, but you have me. Please let me help you."

Her gaze flashed up at him, red hot despite the tears. "I don't need help. I've been fine on my own for a long time. I'm not going back. Let go of me."

He released her hand, and she hopped from her seat. His heart ached to see her like this, a wounded animal lashing out at anyone who offered aid. She stood, panting, her eyes scanning the room. Alan sighed, resigned. He couldn't fix this, couldn't fix her. His shoulders dropped as his heart broke again.

"Well, Marley. I've worked out a deal with my lawyer to schedule a preliminary guardianship hearing. It's scheduled for two weeks from Thursday at the courthouse, one p.m. Everything is set to go. You have to testify." He said each word carefully as if juggling a dozen eggs. He wanted her free from her past, and a trial the best way to do it. Hopefully, Marley saw it too.

"Alan…" She shuffled a few steps backward. "I

don't…I have something else that day."

"They might ask you to see a psychiatrist for testing but…"

She stiffened, her bottom lip trembling as she crossed her arms over her chest. "I can't," she whispered. "I can't take the risk…I can't go back there." She lengthened the distance between them with a dozen tiny steps.

He stood, both his hands stretching out. "No sane judge would let those people have guardianship over you. You're not some scared little girl anymore, Marley. You are a vibrant, vital woman. The judge will see that."

"No," she squeaked, another step backward. "You don't understand…"

Alan's heart squeezed. He'd love to seek revenge on those two horrible people who called themselves her parents, but freeing Marley from their grip would be justice enough.

She stood taller. "No one will believe me. They'll see my record and either toss me in jail or condemn me to live with them. I'd rather be on the run than go back."

"You won't go back. I can practically guarantee it."

He walked toward her slowly. If she'd only let him hold her, caress her face, maybe she'd see the truth. Her touch had done wonders for him. Her eyes widened with each step he took. "Marley, I'll be right there with you the whole way."

And she laughed, a hysterical cackle. Throwing her arms open wide, she glared at him. "Alan, I wasn't born yesterday. I go to court, I'm done for. Stop trying to be the white knight. There ain't no such thing." She whirled on her heel and sprinted from the tavern.

The tiny remnants of Alan's heart crumbled to dust. "I wish you believed," he said to the slamming door.

Chapter Thirty-One

As she sat in the diner's booth, Marley placed her fear in a box. Damn it, Becca wouldn't intimidate her. After Marley said her piece, she could close this chapter of her life. Her bargain basement clothes were pitiful compared to Becca's designer labels, but Marley wasn't in it for money anymore. And a dress and shoes purchased honestly from a church's charity store held more value than a stolen designer bag.

A cold tension filled the air as Becca stalked down the row of booths to where Marley sat. "Entrapment is a thing," Becca said as she flung her bag into the seat across from Marley who didn't twitch. The woman held no power over her anymore. After seeing her parents in person again, Marley feared little else.

"You think I'm wearing a wire or something? Please Becca, I just wanna talk." She folded her hands on the table, happy they only trembled slightly. She might not fear Becca, but her fingers itched to reach over the table and strangle the woman.

Becca glanced around the restaurant. "Where's your man? Hiding in the back booth with a tape recorder?" She slouched in the seat, apparently getting comfortable. "Did he tell you what he tried to pull? Amateur." Signaling the waitress, she leaned in over Marley. "What's the plan? He's got reserves, right?

You got him on the hook, I know it."

Marley straightened her shoulders, ready to plow into dangerous territory. No sense in beating around the bush now. "How did you find Verna and Bernard?" She cocked her head waiting for the woman to spin a tale.

"Who?" Her bleached eyebrows furrowed. "Do I know them?" She held her cup up for the waitress to fill. Nothing like a prop to make the con seem more casual.

"I'm not here to play, Becca. I'm done. I told you. You pushed me, and I pushed back for the first time. You must've been pissed." Marley leaned back in her seat, letting her coffee cool without a second glance. Becca said nothing, sipped her own cup, and stared over the top.

Marley continued. "I didn't deliver on Alan. In fact, he came at you when you framed me. You probably hated that too. So"—she leaned in—"you're the only person who could've sicced my parents on me."

"Oh, they're your parents. God, how awful. You never reconciled with them after the abuse, did you? How are they?" Her tone slithered with sarcasm and triumph. Marley let it roll off. The words didn't even pinch.

"I have no clue." Marley kept her tone flat. "I haven't actually spoken to them much. And I won't. They're out of my life. Like you."

Becca scoffed. "Oh honey, I'll never be out of your life. Do what you want. You're my little puppet for life. I didn't teach you everything I know. I have ways to come at you that you have no idea about." She raised her cup to her lips again.

"Like this?" Marley tossed the printout of her spreadsheet on the table. Doubt flickered in her companion's gaze. "See," Marley tapped the papers. "You were the front man, the face. I hid behind the numbers. I bet every single person on these pages remembers your pretty, pretty mug." She watched waiting to see if Becca believed her. A drop of sweat trickled down Marley's back, but she stayed calm, solid. She had the bitch right where she wanted her. No more games. No more hiding. She was done. And so was Becca.

Swallowing hard, Becca waved a hand over the sheets, dismissing them. "Your boy tried the same thing. It won't work. Iverton's police force is a joke and a half. Nothing will stick. You know it as well as I do."

Marley sighed. "Well, I guess I shouldn't have emailed all those people then. Maybe not mentioned you and your games or how much they'd been bilked out of."

A scowl darkened Becca's face. "You didn't."

"Of course, I did. And I contacted Robbie Koufax from the *Iverton Press*. He's an amazing reporter. We talked about so much." She smiled lightly, letting it sink in.

"Seriously, Volkov? You'll go down for everything on that sheet if I do." She tapped the pages but the fire died in her eyes.

Marley tapped her chin. "You're right. Huh, good thing my friend Rick here—" She waved over to the front of the diner where Officer Smith sat on a stool. With his uniform absent, he just looked a guy from the neighborhood grabbing some late-night pie and coffee. He winked at Marley and turned back to his food.

"Good thing Rick introduced me to the assistant DA here in Iverton. I've been talking to her and to Robbie and the bunko squad and…" Marley waved a hand in the air. "Oh, and my lawyer." A public defender but Becca didn't need to know.

Becca's mask of polite refinement dropped and the real demon behind appeared. "Don't you dare, bitch. I'll take you down with me. I swear I'll bury you. I found your parents. I got Troy after you. What makes you think I won't escalate more?"

Becca's words bounced off her. She shrugged, standing up from the table. Rick sauntered down to their booth and stationed himself behind Marley. Becca didn't scare or intimidate her whatsoever but having a six-foot-plus cop standing behind her didn't hurt.

"Go ahead and try. You don't scare me anymore." She calmly reached over and snagged the spreadsheet. "I think I'll keep this just in case." She smiled warmly, spun on her heel, and headed for the door. A feeling of lightness and relief washed over her as she tossed a five at the cashier.

As she hit the door, Rick's deep voice sounded filling up the diner. "You wanna put the cuffs on here or outside. Either way, you're coming with me, young lady."

It was over. Almost. The court date with her parents loomed in her mind. She could leave Iverton now that the Becca chapter was closed. The DA promised to help her relocate safely. The only loose end—Alan—and he was another story.

****

Marley slowly pulled the door of the courthouse open. Probably the stupidest move she'd ever made.

Peeking inside, she glanced at the enormous entrance. What was she thinking? No judge would give a twenty-three-year-old con artist a pass. He'd take one look at her Women's Center donated clothing, ten-dollar haircut and lock her up for the fashion *faux pas*. She pulled the knobby suit jacket tighter around herself.

"Excuse me," a snide voice sounded behind her, and Marley froze, ready to bolt down the steps if necessary. "You're blocking the door."

Her shoulders dropped back down as she cursed herself for being a mouse. She swung out of the way and allowed the woman to pass into the building. She watched her toddle off on incredibly high heels, briefcase swinging when the thought hit her. Her parents might be anywhere. Better to go inside before they tried another kidnapping. She scuttled through the door.

Her thrift store flats clopped on the marble floors as she searched for some indication of the courtroom Alan mentioned. A large desk for either information or security stood off center in the enormous room. She headed toward it, running her fingers through her hair, putting on her best con face.

"Hi there," she said sweetly to the man behind the desk, not quite in a uniform but official looking. "I'm not sure where to go."

He grinned back at her, dull and sweet. An old voice in the back of her head told her how she could charm the dupe into dinner and drinks without much effort. She cut the voice off, finished with that world. Finished the day she met Alan. The day Smith clapped the cuffs on Becca. She had skills she might use in an emergency but not today.

She told him her real name, and he directed her to a courtroom down the hall to the left. She smiled blandly, trying hard not to flirt. "Thanks." She walked with as much poise as she could muster in the rotten shoes. Once she rounded the corner, her confidence drained away. A dozen doors lined both sides of the hall. Her brain couldn't recall the room number and numbers were her forte. If she couldn't remember one number, she was doomed. Might as well get the straight jacket now.

Tears burned in her eyes. Why did she come here? Swallowing hard, she lifted her chin. She was here because of the expression on Alan's face. All that hope in one man. The same one who'd never given up on his best friend. She'd still scoured the papers for news about their case. Only the local paper reported the IRS's expansion of the investigation due to new evidence. She wished she could've handed Lizette to Alan personally.

The article contained one picture of him, a new one. Sadness still held an aura about him, but the fucking hopeful gleam in his gaze did her in. Here she was, ready to lay down her freedom because of some cute guy. She sighed, slumping against the wall. Still time to run, but she tired of running.

Straightening, she focused, recalling what the man at the desk said, trying to figure out the number. Her eyes rolled to the ceiling as she walked slowly down the hall, hoping to remember before she hit the T intersection. And of course, since she wasn't paying attention, she ran smack dab into a small group of people in the middle of the hallway.

"There you are," a familiar voice said.

Marley's heart stopped. Her eyes floated down to

meet blue crystal. Mouth open, her apology stuck in her throat. Alan stood in the center of the hallway, dressed in a smart suit making him look damn sexy. His eyes sparkled with joy, his mouth stretched in a wide grin. "Alan…" The word rushed out in a gush of breath.

"I knew you'd come."

He was here. Here for her, with nothing to gain. She tried to suck in a breath, but nothing filled her lungs.

He reached out his arm as if to wrap it around her shoulders. He stopped short letting it fall. Marley still couldn't breathe. "Um," he said unsure. She stood there like a badly dressed, gaping idiot. How did she expect him to react? "Marley meet Emanuel Lester, your representative today."

"Hello, Ms. Volkov. I'm pleased to finally meet you." A tall, dark-skinned man in another great suit put his hand out. Marley slapped her dead fish of a hand in his, giving him a lame duck shake.

She glanced between the lawyer and Alan. "I can't pay you," she blurted out. The two men chuckled.

Alan ran a hand down her arm. "Everything's been taken care of. Not to worry."

She blinked at him, a sickness swelling in her stomach. She didn't want a sugar daddy. She wanted a partner. Maybe, she'd read Alan wrong the whole time. But he didn't want her. He was protecting his investment. Her lip quivered. "No, Alan. I can't." She shook her head.

Alan stepped closer, and she waited for the "You can pay me back in bed." or "You owe me." Instead, he chuckled again. "Marley, you saved my business with your superior accounting skills. It's the least I could do."

His answer soothed but didn't set her mind at ease. She wanted the pledge of undying love and caring. But it was a fantasy. He was standing up for her, helping her, but he didn't love her.

"Okay," she said, trying to tramp down the pain. "I guess it's fair."

"Excellent," Emanuel said. He turned toward a pair of closed oak doors. "Shall we?" He held his hand out for Marley to pass through but she hesitated.

Alan put a hand on her shoulder, giving her a light squeeze. "We'll be there in a minute." Emanuel nodded and entered the room.

"Hey," Alan said, his voice sweet, smooth as silk. "I'm glad you're here."

She glanced up at him through her bangs. "You didn't believe I'd come?" she asked, knowing the answer full well.

"I hoped," he said. And the dagger in her heart twisted tighter.

"Alan, why?" she asked.

He stepped in front of her, pressing a finger to her lips. "Because I believe in you. You are the most amazing woman I've ever met. I saw the exposé in the paper and Becca's arrest. I knew it was you. You're a fighter. I wanted you to fight." He cupped her face.

She waved a hand toward the courtroom. "For what?" she asked, letting the sarcasm pour into her words. "Tests and humiliation?"

He moved closer, leaving only millimeters between them. Marley's heart jackrabbited as she gasped for breath. Heat coiled through her body. Not an all-consuming flame, but a slow steady heat.

"No, Marley," he said softly. "For this." He kissed her slowly, gently but with a passion that rocked her on her feet. "I want you to fight for us. To fight together for the things we want. I want to be a team. You and I against the world."

"Alan, I...I..." And it hit her like a steamroller. She wanted it too. Every time the two of them came together over the past month, they'd been a team—in bed, at the hospital, with the taxes, with her parents. No one had ever made her feel equal to them, much less as if she soared above him. She wanted this. She wanted him. Together they could take on the world and win.

She raised her gaze to his, looking him full in the eyes. "Alan," she said, her voice steady and confident. "No one has ever been there for me like you have. Not one person in my whole life. The fact that you're here today, standing up for me with nothing to gain, makes me feel..." Her words cut off as the tears she'd fought to hold back ran down her cheeks.

"Marley, I'll always be here for you. I know I joked about owing you for saving the business, but honestly, I'd have come no matter what happened with the IRS."

Marley waved his words away. She knew all that without him saying a word. Just being at the courthouse today said a thousand things. He was here. For her. To help her. To stand by her. She raised a hand to her mouth to stifle a sob.

"Alan..." She gazed into those icy blue eyes again. "I love you. I want to be with you. No matter what happens today. No matter what happens with the IRS. I want us to be together, to be a team."

Actually saying the words released the chains that

had held her her whole life. Loving Alan was freedom. She didn't have to run anymore.

Alan leaned forward, his forehead pressed to hers. "Wow, I…" He swallowed hard. "You do?" His voice almost sounded teary. "Well, I do, too, Mar. I love you and want us together." He reached down and threaded his fingers through hers. "I'll always be there for you. Always."

She squeezed his fingers back, her heart bursting with joy. Alan loved her. Alan wanted her. She blinked, realizing where they were and what was about the happen. The judge, the trial, her parents. Somewhere during the conversation, her fear had evaporated. She was ready to face her parents. "Let's go kick some ass."

"That's my girl."

They turned and walked into the courtroom.

Together.

Epilogue

Alan glanced over at Marley's sleeping form next to him. Absently, he reached over and touched her new dark blonde hair. With a sleepy groan, she twisted toward him, cuddling into his side, her face the definition of serenity. A smile slipped over Alan's lips as thoughts of a future with Marley swooped through his mind.

"Penny for your thoughts," she said sleepily, her eyes still closed.

"Emanuel said he'd call today…and today is almost over…" He paused, glancing over at his phone.

With a smirk, Marley sat up and wrapped her arms around him. "You're more worried than I am. I'm telling you, Reid, the judge's expression said everything. He had to work hard to keep the disgust off his face. He almost managed it." She laughed, placing kisses down his bare shoulder.

"How can you be so sure? I mean, after everything…" He grabbed the cell phone willing it to ring.

Marley wrapped her arms around him, her bare breasts pressing into his back. "I'm here with you. Nothing could go wrong."

Alan slapped his forehead, "Why would you say that out loud?" As he finished his sentence, the phone rang. "Yes?" He answered quickly before even checking the caller ID. Emanuel at last. He hit the speakerphone.

"We are good to go, Alan. The last of the paperwork is filed," Emanuel began. Alan's phone beeped with another call coming in. Alan ignored it.

Nothing was more important than Emanuel's information.

Lester continued, "I'm forwarding you the official ruling. I hoped the judge would dress down her parents in court, but we got what we wanted. Marley is a free woman. And the restraining order against the Volkovs was granted."

Marley let out a cheer. "Awesome. I've got Rick Smith on speed dial if they try anything."

"You're in good hands, Marley. I wish you the best." Alan could hear the smile in Lester's voice. The man loved to win. The phone beeped again. He glanced at the caller ID of the incoming call. Forwarded from the office? Huh.

"You'll let us know if we need to sign anything or…" Alan let the word drift away. Now was time for celebrating, not dotting I's or crossing t's. He grinned.

"I'll be in touch," Emanuel said with a laugh. "Congratulations, Marley."

"Thanks, Em. You're the best." She leaned over Alan's shoulder to speak into the phone, putting her in a perfect position.

He clicked the call off, turning his head to kiss the beautiful woman by his side. That was the last of it. No more worries. The restraining order and the friendly neighborhood police officer would keep the villains far from his girl. Everything was perfect.

The phone chirped again, interrupting their passionate kiss. Oh, right. The call to the Entertainment Group line. He'd closed down the office a few days ago. No sense in sitting in an empty room waiting for the IRS, the police or Conrad to call. All the incoming calls now forwarded to his cell, thanks to Marley.

After clicking on the voicemail icon, he jumped through hoops to retrieve the message. After a few seconds, a distant voice sounded in his ear. "Hey, me again. I'm getting on a flight now to New York. I'll call you as soon as we arrive. Give me about eighteen hours or so. See ya." There was a pause and then the voice continued, "Oh, Interpol..." The call reverted to garbled static and then cut off.

Conrad.

A word about the author...

Ginny Frost writes contemporary romance with a sexy, funny kick. In her downtime, she plays clerk at the local library—the perfect job to feed her reading addiction.

She lives in upstate NY with her very own kindhearted ogre, their two smart and sassy daughters, and an evil cat named Flash.

You can find her online at:
www.ginnyfrost.com
www.facebook.com/ginnyfrostauthor
and Twitter @ginnyfrost14
http://ginnyfrost.com/